THE INNOCENT

Hildy didn't hear her little brother until he had snuggled up beside her on the attic floor. "Christian," she said, sitting up. "Thank goodness. Was Julian angry?"

Christian nodded, the tears sliding silently down his cheeks.

Hildy pulled him close and rocked him. "Momma would have helped if she could have," she whispered. She knew that inside her brother were scars that would never heal, and she hated her father for it. She would never be able to understand his cruelty, nor forgive him for it.

"How was your fishing trip with Mr. Kaiser?" she asked.

His dark eyes were filled with tears. "I didn't get to bring my fish home. How come you and Momma were out there?"

"We went on a picnic. And when Momma sent Julian back to get her sweater, she grabbed me by the hand and we went running through the dunes and down to the beach." In a hushed tone that couldn't hide how upset she was, she said, "Christian, I think we were running away again."

He sat up. "Again? But why? Why do we keep running away?"

FORBIDDEN GARDEN

FORBIDDEN GARDEN

Diane Guest

A Bernard Geis Associates Book

BANTAM BOOKS
TORONTO · NEW YORK · LONDON · SYDNEY · AUCKLAND

FORBIDDEN GARDEN
A Bantam Book / January 1987

ISBN 0-553-26273-4

Published simultaneously in the United States and Canada

Bantam Books are published by Bantam Books, Inc. Its trademark, consisting of the words "Bantam Books" and the portrayal of a rooster, is Registered in U.S. Patent and Trademark Office and in other countries. Marca Registrada. Bantam Books, Inc., 666 Fifth Avenue, New York, New York 10103.

PRINTED IN THE UNITED STATES OF AMERICA

O   0 9 8 7 6 5 4 3 2 1

FORBIDDEN GARDEN

1

The lack of sound was what made him lift his head to look at the sea around him. Where earlier the sky had been flat and gray, like the glass in a light bulb, now a line of clouds had gathered along the horizon, thick and black. Still, the ocean was quiet. The swells rolled under him noiselessly, but sometime during the past hour, while he sat thinking about his ruined marriage, the wind had gone, leaving the sails slack, the boat without any forward motion.

Kaiser had checked the weather reports before he left Noank and the Connecticut shore. Overcast but calm, with a chance of an isolated squall. Kaiser hadn't been concerned. He had been through bad weather on *Seabird* before. He knew that there wasn't much the forty-five-foot sloop couldn't handle if her skipper kept his wits about him.

He stood up, alert now, and stopped to listen. A shadow of sound made him look to the northeast. It was then that he saw it coming: a solid wall of rain, turning the smoothness of the water to foam. He knew from experience that the wind would not be far behind. He had hoped to avoid bad weather, but with the way his luck had been running lately, how could he have expected anything else?

He reached up and touched the faint scar on the side of his face, something he did sometimes when he was trying to concentrate. His lean, handsome face was still tanned, the result of his last trip to Khartoum. It made the scar more pronounced; it made Kaiser look tougher than he really was.

The sense of personal failure that had kept him deep in thought faded before the approaching storm, and he forced himself to concentrate. He quickly put on his foul-weather gear and secured the boat, making sure that everything movable was tied down. He reefed the mainsail and settled in behind the wheel. "Stand by, Kaiser," he said to himself. "Here it comes." In the same instant a sheet of wind-driven rain hit him, making it almost impossible to see. But he didn't care. It gave him something to think about besides his wife—his ex-wife as of this morning.

The boat shuddered for a moment as if confused, then with a single lurch adjusted to the new rhythm as Kaiser headed her into the wind.

He had no further chance to consider the wreckage of his marriage. His one concern was to get through the squall unscathed. The salt spray stung his face, and the day that had dawned so benevolent and warm for early October had turned chillingly cold. The wind, blowing with threatening force now, compelled him to turn the boat off course, and the waves that only moments earlier had rolled silently under the hull came crashing down across the bow.

He turned the boat on a diagonal course into the wind and took a deep breath. He wasn't worried, at least not yet. He had been through squalls like this before. Still, experience had taught him never to trust the sea, so he forced himself to concentrate on the feel of the wind to let him know what the waves might do. The storm was full upon him now, and he cursed himself for not having taken the mainsail down.

Almost as if it had heard, Kaiser saw the mainsail blow out before a sudden gust. "Goddamn it!" he muttered. He didn't dare leave the wheel, but through the wind-driven spray he could see the ripped sail flapping and jerking, making sharp, crackling sounds like shots from a rifle. He gritted his teeth and switched on the engine, holding the boat at an angle across the tops of the waves. There was nothing to be done now but hope that the maniac sail wouldn't do too much damage.

He wasn't sure how long he battled to keep the boat from foundering, but it seemed like half a lifetime. Each time he thought the wind was dying down, a fresh gust hit him, engulfing him in an ocean of rain and sea spray. Fitting end, he thought grimly. Survive a divorce only to drown at sea. He wondered if Toby would grieve. Probably not. After all, she had plans of her own. But with Henry Crandall? The feeling of incredulity that had been with him ever since she told him about her affair hit him again. Simple Henry Crandall, who had always reminded him of a homemade cookie, with arms too long for his jackets and trousers too short for his legs. Toby Kaiser's lover.

A new gust brought him up sharply, and he jerked back hard on the wheel. "You are going to kill yourself if you don't pay attention," he said out loud, and was relieved to find that he could hear his words above the howl. That meant that the wind, though still strong, was erratic now, coming in fits, leaving time in between to breathe, to hear himself speak, and to think.

"Henry Crandall," he said, and his voice cracked in disbelief. "Beautiful, witty Toby Kaiser in love with Henry Crandall, walrus extraordinaire." A huge wave hit the boat broadside, forcing him once more to think about the here and now. Time enough to puzzle it out later, he decided. Right now he had to determine how much damage had been done and how far off course he had been driven. He made himself relax, loosen his hands on the wheel. The angry sea around him had turned blue-black, but the wind had shifted and was blowing steady from the west. He strained to catch sight of the land he knew should be there somewhere off the bow, but he could see nothing. He swore under his breath as he checked the compass. By all calculations he should be just east of the channel. He hoped so.

He was tired, his muscles ached, he was numb with cold, and all he wanted was a hot cup of coffee and some dry clothes. He stood up and edged along the side of the boat, trying in the last rays of light to assess the damage done by the torn mainsail. "Poor girl," he said softly. He could see now that the forestay had pulled loose. "Looks like you'll need some fixing up when we get into harbor." He was relieved to find that he had lapsed into his old habit of talking aloud to himself. That meant he was relaxing. When he sailed alone he solved more problems, carried on more debates, settled more arguments than he could count. Even five years ago, when Jamie died, it had been the talking that had saved his sanity. He had gone out alone in *Seabird* and aloud relived every moment he'd ever spent with his three-year-old son, finally crying where no one else could hear his pain.

Kaiser had been hit hard by the death of his only child, but somehow the way Jamie had died made it even harder. Congenital heart failure, the doctors had said. The child had died quietly in his sleep, and the very quietness of his passing had left Kaiser defenseless, without time to prepare. There had been no wild screeching of brakes, no careless driver to blame, no frantic rush for help, no sleepless vigil by a hospital crib. There had been no witness to Jamie's passing. Not his father, not his mother. Just a silent slipping away of a tiny person in the black of night.

Where had Toby been all that time? Kaiser wondered suddenly. He was shocked now to realize that he didn't know. They had lost their only child, grieved, and buried him, but they'd done it side by side, never together. And now, thinking about it, he realized that while he had talked about everything that ever mattered to him, he'd never talked to himself about his marriage. Or about his wife. He wondered why.

He thought back to the afternoon she told him that she wanted a divorce. He could see the scene as clearly as if it were projected on a screen somewhere in the back of his head. He had been in the middle of a debate with himself over a short piece he was working on for *The New York Times* about the departure of Baby Doc Duvalier. It had been a "gimme," one of those columns that was supposed to write itself. It was easy, but he found himself struggling over it. You never know when to quit, Kaiser told himself, but he knew it was one of the reasons he was among the best journalists in his field. He never accepted a one-sided opinion as fact, nor did he ever intend to write one.

This was to be his last column for a while. He had finally decided to take a leave to write a book: an eyewitness account of the 1968 Soviet invasion of Czechoslovakia. It had been in his mind ever since he left Prague in 1973, but he'd never done anything about it. Then he'd decided it was time to write it all down before he forgot—as it seemed everyone else had—that it had ever happened. He promised his publisher he would have the rough draft together in less than six months, and he'd meant it.

He recalled turning his attention back to his column when Toby burst into his office unannounced. She stood in front of his desk, breathless, as if she'd just run a long way. He was startled to see her, because Toby never went anywhere unannounced. She looked lovely, as always, though a bit flushed, and he was about to tell her so when she silenced him with a gesture. Assuming something horrible had happened, he was halfway to his feet, then realized with a shock that she had been drinking. Toby never drank. Not even when Jamie died.

"Kaiser," she said with a faint slur, "I want a divorce."

He'd looked at her with surprise, seeing her condition,

not hearing her words. "My God, Toby," he said, coming around the desk, "are you in the sauce?"

"Don't worry about that." She waved him away with her hand, then turned and sat down hard on the edge of a chair. "Kaiser, listen to me. I've always been lousy at this sort of thing, so listen. Now. I want a divorce." Suddenly she was dead sober.

This time Kaiser heard her. "A divorce," he said. It had not been a question.

"I'm not in love with you anymore," she said, hurrying. "I'm in love with someone else."

He looked hard at her. It was Toby sitting there. His wife. Familiar. Predictable. And yet it was a stranger who had just spoken.

"Mind if I ask who?" Kaiser asked calmly.

"Henry Crandall."

Kaiser remembered sitting down as if in slow motion. He was numb, he knew that much. And disbelieving. Maybe even stunned. But what else? Where was the rage, the hurt, the righteous indignation he ought to have felt? Where was the despair? Why wasn't he on his knees, begging her? He had been happy with Toby, so why was he taking it so calmly?

She had answered for him. "Kaiser, you don't love me. You love the idea of marriage, but not me. Someone else will come along and you'll pick up right where we left off."

"Jesus, Toby, am I that much of a cold bastard?"

She'd appeared genuinely offended. "You? A bastard? My God, Kaiser, you're the furthest thing from it. You're charming, you're handsome, and in spite of it all, you're still the sweetest man I ever knew. You have more friends than you know what to do with. And women . . . well, women simply adore you." She stopped then, trying to find the words that would explain to him what had happened. "I'm selfish, Kaiser. I don't want to be married to someone whose interest is the whole goddamned world. I want someone for whom *I* am the whole goddamned world."

"And that someone is Henry Crandall?" he'd asked as calmly as he could.

"If you laugh, Kaiser, I'll kill you."

"I'm not laughing, Toby. Believe me, I'm not laughing."

"Henry may be a joke to you, but he can't open his eyes without thinking about me. I need that, Kaiser. I love him for that."

"But I need you," he said, and it sickened him, because he was an honest man and he realized that what he'd just said was a lie. He didn't need Toby.

"You may need someone, Kaiser," Toby replied quietly. "But I'm sorry to say, my darling, it isn't me."

The sea had grown suddenly quiet around him, the wind steady but gentle now, as if trying to make up for its earlier mischief. He exhaled. It shouldn't be long before he would be in the channel. He switched over to automatic pilot and hauled in the remains of the shredded mainsail. He could now see the familiar channel markers leading to Nantucket harbor, and even though he was only borrowing his brother's house for a while to hide and lick his wounds, oddly enough he felt as if he were coming home.

It was dark when Kaiser reached the house, and it had started to rain again, a fine, chilling drizzle that he could afford to ignore since he was already drenched to the skin. Mrs. Minstrell, John's long-time housekeeper, was waiting just inside the door, and she welcomed him as if he were her long lost son. Kaiser thought of her as one of those people who had the rare ability to make others feel like dear old friends, even if she'd never laid eyes on them before, and he was glad to see she hadn't changed. At least someone still loves me, he thought.

Mrs. Minstrell was a huge woman in her late fifties, with a face so pleasant it was impossible not to smile back into the mirrors of the eyeglasses she wore balanced on the end of her nose. She had pure white hair, already done up for the night in old-fashioned pink rubber curlers. Kaiser smiled to himself. She always reminded him of a comfortable, overstuffed chair.

Mrs. Minstrell and her husband Fred had been John's caretakers for the past fifteen years, living in the house year-round and caring for it with all the ceremony one would reserve for an only child. John often said that the best thing he'd ever done was to marry Julia. The second best thing was to hire the Minstrells.

"Well, Patrick," Mrs. Minstrell said—she was one of the few people who ever called him by his first name—"it's about time you got here. I was frantic. Your brother said to expect you sometime this afternoon, but here it is almost nine o'clock. And just look at you. You're soaked to the skin." She didn't wait for him to speak as she moved quickly across the foyer to the stairway. "Come along. As soon as you change into some dry things you can eat."

Kaiser followed without protest, acutely aware now of his discomfort, anxious to be rid of the wet, heavy clothes. Besides, he was starving, and he knew from past experience that Mrs. Minstrell probably had something fantastic waiting for him in the kitchen.

"I've opened the east bedroom for you, as usual," she said, moving up the stairs with surprising grace for such a large woman. "You'll get plenty of morning sun."

"You remembered," he said, and was suddenly conscious of the water sloshing out of his sneakers and onto the highly polished floor. He stopped, but she called to him over her shoulder, "Pay no attention. A little water never hurt anything." She sailed majestically down the hall, opening the door at the far end. "Just come down to the kitchen when you're ready, dear," she said. Kaiser had the feeling that she was suppressing an urge to pat him on top of the head.

He smiled. "You're a goddess, Mrs. Minstrell. I'll be down in a minute."

"Spinach lasagna," she said as she left the room.

Spinach lasagna, Kaiser thought, and was filled with a wonderful sense of well-being. "You were right, Toby," he said. "I *don't* need you. All I need right now is Mrs. Minstrell and her spinach lasagna."

Within minutes he stood naked, his wet clothes abandoned in the bathtub. He wrapped a towel around his middle and went into the bedroom, not quite sure whether he could resist the need to eat long enough to take a shower. A faint stabbing in the hard muscle of his stomach made the decision for him, and he crossed to the bed, where he had left his duffel bags.

He dressed quickly and was about to leave the room when he became conscious of a sound and listened, first out of simple curiosity, then out of genuine concern. Someone was crying.

He hurried to the window and opened it wide. Dim lights from the house next door were visible through the fog, and it was from there that the sound came—a sobbing, not loud or hysterical, but soft and as constant as the sound of breathing. As he stood looking out into the mist, it seemed to him that the sobs were as full of misery as any he had ever heard.

He stood still, trying to decide whether it was a woman or a child, then decided it made no difference. Whoever it was, their tears seemed unstoppable, like blood flowing from a wound that would never heal.

Kaiser didn't linger over coffee. He was exhausted and all he wanted was sleep. But once in bed he lay wide awake, listening to the silence, trying to imagine what tragedy could have occurred next door to cause such despair. He sneered at himself in the dark, the journalist scoffing at the novelist. After all, how much could anyone possibly detect from a simple sound? Probably a maid smashed a couple of dishes and was afraid she'd be found out.

He put it out of his mind and began to think about Toby. His beautiful, talented ex-wife, his partner and companion for eleven years, now a stranger. Not to mention the fact that for two of the eleven she had been sleeping with Henry Crandall. Not only sleeping with the simple jackass but apparently falling in love with him, all the while Kaiser was busy using his superior talent to analyze other people.

Kaiser was a brilliant journalist. In all humility, he knew that. The Pulitzer Prize had been only one of a long series of professional accomplishments. His natural instincts, his keen sense of fair play, his ability to lay bare the bone, had all combined to make him one of the best in his field. He swore softly. How in hell, then, had he made such a mess of his marriage? Where were his powers of analysis while Toby was falling in love with someone else? And worse, why had he been so untouched when she told him she wanted a divorce? It had been a shock, true, but the worst revelation had come when he realized that he really didn't care, when he had to admit that he felt little sense of loss. He frowned in the dark. He thought that he and Toby had had a good relationship. They'd shared an interest in politics, were compatible lovers, liked so many of the same things. But had they ever really done anything together? Or had they simply moved along side by side, never honestly touching? Things had been different once, he knew—for that blink of a moment when they'd had Jamie.

Kaiser pushed the thought away. His son had been dead for more than five years, but it still hurt to think about him. Maybe that was part of his problem. Lately he'd come to realize that he had been going through life looking straight ahead, translating thought into action without pause, never glancing over his shoulder to see where he'd been. That was when he had decided to stop and write his book, to take some time for quiet remembering. That was when Toby had dropped her bomb.

"Ass," he said softly. "Kaiser, you must be some kind of ass." He let out a long breath. He decided it was going to take him a while to get used to being a failure. Maybe a few days here on the island in virtual isolation would be just what he needed. He made a mental note to do something nice for the Minstrells.

Life on the island followed a certain pattern, and in spite of the fact that Mrs. Minstrell had greeted him with genuine affection, he knew his appearance had caused a disruption in the household. On Nantucket the summer residents came in June. They brought money and prosperity to the island, and for that prosperity the natives paid a price: from June until September, the island belonged to the tourists. But with the first cold winds of October, the natives took their island back, settling in for a long, quiet winter.

Kaiser knew his visit wasn't a catastrophe for the Minstrells, but a disruption. It occurred to him to ask Toby to pick up something for them in New York, then he remembered that Toby was no longer a part of his life. "Oh, well," he said to himself, "I'll just do it myself." Then, almost as if a light had been flicked off, he fell into a deep, blank sleep.

2

Kaiser woke late, with a sense of anticipation so strong that he wondered for a minute if he had an important appointment to keep. He sat straight up in bed, then collapsed back against the pillows when he realized he had no reason even to get out of bed.

Nonetheless, his natural restlessness, together with a sudden curiosity to find out who was living next door, caused him to swing out of bed and into a pair of sweatpants. Normally he didn't jog for exercise. He didn't need to. He'd always been active, and physically was in great shape, but this morning every muscle in his body ached. He decided he needed to do something to loosen up.

There was no sound of life in the house as he slipped down the stairs and out the front door. The terrain was almost flat, and running easily, he moved up the cobbled street and out onto a dirt roadway which curved along the north shore of the island. The foul weather had blown off to the east, leaving the air cool and crisp, but the sun was warm, and by the time he got to the old water tower, he could feel his muscles beginning to loosen up. Running without effort, he veered off onto the path that wound down toward the ocean.

The beach was deserted. Even so, had it not been for the

sudden rising of a flock of terns, Kaiser might never have
seen the child—a speck on the horizon. The little boy,
intent on something swimming in a shallow tidal pool,
didn't look up as Kaiser approached. He had hair the color
of the sand, and Kaiser guessed that he couldn't have been
more than five. Jamie, Kaiser thought. He still couldn't see
a child without remembering. He wondered what so young
a boy was doing out here all alone. And inappropriately
dressed at that. All he had on was a short-sleeved T-shirt
and a pair of thin cotton shorts.

The child didn't see Kaiser until he knelt beside him.
"Looks like he lost a leg," Kaiser said, looking at the crab
the boy was studying.

Usually children liked Kaiser—he was honest in his
affection for them, and they knew instinctively that he was a
friend. He had a rare ability to cast off his adulthood
without seeming silly or patronizing. For this reason,
among others, Kaiser was unprepared when the child
snapped his head up violently and turned a pair of horrified
eyes on him. "Please don't tell," he whispered. "Please."
And without another word, he was off across the sand, half
running, half falling in his haste to be gone.

Frowning, Kaiser leaned back on his heels and watched
until the little boy had disappeared beyond the dunes,
unable to imagine why the mere sight of him had terrified
the child.

After a while he stood up, brushed the sand from his
knees, and began to jog back the way he'd come. He felt as
if he could run forever, but as he approached the paved
section of the road he slowed to a walk, taking the time to
get a good look at the houses along the bluff. There were
several of them in a row, his brother's house being the last.
All were rambling, gray-shingled structures that Kaiser
guessed to have been constructed around the turn of the
century. They all had been built away from the road, set off

from it and each other by high walls topped with hedges which seemed, oddly, to be growing out of the brick.

John had owned the house for about fifteen years, having found out about it from a friend of a friend, to his good fortune. Normally, houses along the bluff passed from father to son without interruption, but in John's case there had been no one left in the family.

With his wife and two sons, John spent every summer on the island, flying in from Boston on Friday, weather permitting, and back to the city on Monday morning. A painless forty-minute trip except when the island was fogged in. Then John was forced to take the Nantucket ferry to Hyannis, a four-hour trip to Boston by boat and car.

Kaiser had never been able to understand his brother's willingness to put up with such inconveniences just to spend the summer on the island, particularly this one, where the fog rolled in and out on a whim, making any kind of predictable travel plans impossible. In fact it was not unusual for John to leave his house in town, with the sun shining brightly, only to arrive at the airport, a scant three miles away, scarcely able to see because of the fog.

Kaiser smiled to himself. His brother seemed to take it all in stride. It came with the territory. Maybe that was why the people he knew who lived on this island were such a laid-back group. They had to be.

He opened the gate and went up the walk to the front entrance, pausing only momentarily to glance at the house next door. It was not far from John's, the two properties separated only by a high brick wall, and yet there was a curious sense of remoteness about the place out of all proportion to its actual location. Beyond the banks of shrubbery there was no sign of life, and from where he stood, he could see nothing but the second- and third-floor windows blindly reflecting the westward movement of the sun. He opened the door and was almost run down by Mrs. Minstrell, who was on her way out. Over one arm she carried a sensible black satchel purse, and over the other a straw basket. "I'm off to do my marketing, Patrick," she said. "Anything special you want?"

He shook his head. "I'll leave it all up to you, Mrs. Minstrell. I trust you implicitly. Besides, I promised John I'd be no trouble."

She smiled, and again Kaiser had the feeling that she was about to pat him on top of the head. "Nonsense," she said. "I love to fuss. You know that."

She turned to leave, but Kaiser stopped her. "Who's using the Ferrare house?" He pointed next door.

"The Ferrares," she said with uncharacteristic sharpness. "Bad business."

"Julian Ferrare?" Kaiser was surprised. "Himself? I thought he kept the house only as a convenience for friends who wanted to use it. From what John told me, the Ferrares never use it themselves."

"They never did. Not until this last summer. A wretched business if I do say so. But you'll have to wait until I get back if you want to know any more. If I don't get to the market before ten, there'll be nothing left worth buying." She turned and walked down the front steps, calling over her shoulder, "If you can't contain your curiosity, Fred is out in back, mulching the rhododendrons. He can tell you as much as I can about the poor devil."

Poor devil? Kaiser wondered what she meant as he walked down the hall to the kitchen. Julian Ferrare a poor devil? That was an odd twist. He poured himself a cup of coffee and walked to the back door. "Fred?" he called, but Mr. Minstrell did not answer.

Kaiser sat down on the back steps in the sun and sipped his coffee, puzzling over Mrs. Minstrell's choice of words. Everybody who knew anything about classical music knew the name Julian Ferrare. He was said to be the most brilliant concert pianist since Paderewski. Kaiser had seen him play once in concert in Vienna a few years earlier, and he could well understand why Ferrare was reputed to be one of the finest technicians in the world. But it had not been his technical skill that had impressed Kaiser. Rather it had been the feeling of tremendous power the man transmitted through his music; that, and an almost hypnotic stage presence. Together they caused him to be received with frenzied enthusiasm wherever he performed.

Kaiser had heard him called a lot of things—genius, brilliant, supreme egotist, arrogant, charming, even, according to Toby, irresistible—but he had never heard anyone call him a poor devil. He called again to Fred, with the same result.

Kaiser stretched his legs and relaxed, surveying the garden. It was a private place, bordered on one side by the house and the patio where he sat, on two sides by the high walls and hedges, and finally by the bluff that ran along the back side and fell almost perpendicular to the sea below. At the foot of the bluff a narrow strip of sand separated the land from the water, a bathing beach of sorts, accessible only by a steep wooden stairway that inched its way down the side of the cliff. John had it built so his children would have safe access to the water, but Kaiser had never seen them use it. They always seemed to prefer sliding and scraping their way down through the scrub brush to the sandy strip below.

He got up and walked to the far edge of the garden. High above he could see a dark, shifting wedge of wild geese moving south across the sky. Below, the ocean stretched gray and restless. From where he stood, the view was spectacular. He and Toby had spent many a quiet summer evening watching the sun sink into the sea. Kaiser smiled wryly, remembering that Toby had declined to come this past summer, pleading too much work. "Too much work," he said under his breath, "screwing fat Henry."

The house next door had been empty then, except for a skeleton staff; in fact, as Mrs. Minstrell had confirmed, it had never been used by the Ferrares themselves, only by a few occasional guests. Until this summer.

His curiosity rekindled, he went back inside and up the two flights of stairs to the third floor, surprised to find that it was warm there in spite of the fact that the heat had been turned off. Kaiser opened the door to the last bedroom on the east side, where he knew the windows looked down on the Ferrare garden.

"Oh, to what depths of depravity you have sunk, Kaiser, old man," he said. "Spying on the neighbors." But he had no intention of turning away. From his vantage point he could see almost all of the garden and part of the terrace. Except for an old wheelbarrow that stood along the far side of the lawn, the garden seemed to be empty, but as he extended his line of vision he could see that some wicker chairs and a table were lined up along the hedge, apparently positioned there to shield their occupants from the cold autumn wind. The Ferrares were obviously still using their garden, unlike John, who stored his lawn furniture at the first hint of cold weather.

Kaiser was about to turn away when a sudden movement in the garden below caught his eye. The little boy whom he'd frightened so badly earlier in the morning came into view, carrying a small cardboard box. He still wore shorts, but now Kaiser was relieved to see that he had put on a windbreaker. He set the box down on the edge of the terrace and began, one by one, to take out miniature figurines and place them in a line along the brick.

The boy set each piece down with careful precision until he had emptied the box, then stood up and looked back toward the house, as if expecting a signal of some sort. The wind had picked up, and Kaiser saw the child shiver, then take a few halting steps back toward the person who had appeared behind him on the terrace.

It was a woman, dressed in a black cloak more reminiscent of the nineteenth century than the twentieth. Her hair was pulled in a tight knot at the back of her head, but Kaiser could see that it was almost the same pale color as the boy's, though perhaps a shade darker.

She stepped off the edge of the terrace, having stopped only momentarily to touch the child softly on the cheek. Her face was turned away from Kaiser, intent, it seemed, on some movement far out to sea. She stood staring for some minutes, then swaying slightly, she turned and almost fell into one of the wicker chairs that stood along the hedge. She tried to put her hands up to her face, but they fell lifeless to her lap. Eyes closed, she tipped her head back against the chair. It was then that Kaiser had his first clear view of her face. He sucked in his breath. Even at this distance, without being able to distinguish individual features, he could see that her looks went far beyond conventional prettiness. She was an extraordinary-looking creature who could have been twenty or fifty. It didn't matter. She was beautiful.

She sat motionless, head back as if in a trance or a deep sleep. She seemed so vulnerable, so helpless, that Kaiser turned away, stricken by a sudden feeling of guilt to be watching her without her knowing. By the time he persuaded himself to look back, the child had come up and had placed a timid hand on her knee.

She opened her eyes and looked at the little boy. She seemed confused, as if she had no idea who he was or where he had come from. Then, shaking her head to clear it, she pulled him onto her lap and began to rock him. Kaiser opened the window a crack. The sound of her faint humming reached him; there seemed to be no joy in it, only sadness.

He wondered if she'd been the one he had heard crying the night before. And if so, why was someone so lovely in such a state of obvious melancholy? He stood and watched her with the child for several minutes, not knowing why he was so affected by what he saw. But when another woman came out of the house and beckoned the two inside, the second woman struck him as an intruder who had no business being there.

Kaiser spent the afternoon going through some of the old journals he'd kept years ago, while on assignment in Prague. He was looking for specific references he had made to one of Alexander Dubcek's speeches, but he couldn't concentrate. Ever since the morning he had the odd feeling of being witness to some kind of human catastrophe, though he could not justify it by anything he'd seen in the Ferrare garden.

Exasperated, he finally put his work aside and went to look for Mrs. Minstrell, but she was nowhere to be found. He wandered from room to room, finally decided that he was merely wasting time, then went back to the study and worked until dinner.

"Funny thing," Kaiser mused, as Mrs. Minstrell cleared away the dinner plates, "but I don't believe that in all the years John has owned this house, he's ever met the great man. Or his wife." He looked up at Mrs. Minstrell.

"He met them this summer," she said.

"Which one is his wife? The gorgeous blonde?"

"Wherever did you see her?"

"In the garden."

"Our garden?" Mrs. Minstrell was incredulous.

Kaiser shook his head. "Their garden. I was upstairs. Spying out the window."

Mrs. Minstrell chuckled. "I've done it myself on occasion."

"So the blonde is Mrs. Ferrare?"

Mrs. Minstrell nodded. "That's her all right."

"And the boy?"

"That's Christian. Their son. Poor little beggar."

"Sit down and tell me about them," Kaiser said.

"I have to get my kitchen cleaned up, Patrick," she said, "but if you want to have your coffee and dessert out there, I'll be happy for the company."

Kaiser followed her to the back of the house, where Fred had laid a fire before heading out to his weekly Rotary Club meeting. Kaiser backed up to the hearth, and Mrs. Minstrell poured him a cup of coffee. "The Ferrares never used the house themselves," she said, "not as long as I can remember—that is, not until last summer. Julian Ferrâre's grandmother used to come every season, but she was the only one. My own mother worked for her for a time, and she never saw either Julian or his sister. He came once himself, right after his grandmother died. But that was thirty years ago or more. Never since. And certainly not since I've been housekeeper here."

"So when did they arrive, and who exactly is living there?"

"They came at the beginning of the summer. The four of them. Julian, the wife, and the two children. He was away on tour in July and August, but she stayed there all the time."

"What's her name?"

"Francesca. Francesca Ferrare, the lady of the manor." Her inflection suggested that Mrs. Minstrell had little use for the woman Kaiser found so intriguing. "And now there's Julian's sister, Elise. She hasn't been there long. Only a few months. Since the beginning of September. Odd person. Timid, eccentric, but pleasant enough, I suppose. You never know what she's thinking though. Devoted to him, I understand, and Lord knows he needs it, poor devil, what with his wife in such a state."

There it was again. Poor devil. "What's the matter with his wife?"

Mrs. Minstrell shook her head. "People in town say she's

crazy," she said, drying her hands and picking up her knitting. "When they first came out here at the beginning of the summer, she seemed perfectly normal. Quite friendly too. Busy all the time, but never too busy to stop and say hello. She didn't do much talking, but Fred and I got the impression that she was a nice person. And she couldn't spend enough time with her two little ones." She paused, as if trying to make some sense of what had happened. "Now she's upset herself and upset everyone around her."

Kaiser got up and poured himself another cup of coffee. "What do you think changed her?"

"Her stepfather died." She paused, thinking back. "Before that, everything was very pleasant. They did a lot of entertaining with a certain group here on the island. You know most of them, I'm sure. Important people, and Julian Ferrare seemed to attract them like flies. But everything in quite good taste, you understand. Not like some of the people who come out here for the summer," she sniffed. "Then one unbearable hot August day—I remember the exact day because I had to make a pot of spaghetti sauce for the church supper, and believe me, Patrick, it was hot. Too hot to cook, I know that much. It's times like that when I wish we weren't right here in town. It's so much cooler out at the end of the island. Anyway, I stepped outside to try and catch a breath of fresh air, when up came a cab and out stepped a handsome old gentleman. 'Can you direct me to the Ferrare residence?' he asked, and I recognized his accent right away. Just like his daughter's. 'Right next door.' I pointed. He stepped up then and offered his hand. 'I am Dr. Gustav Stahlberg,' he said. 'Mrs. Ferrare's stepfather.' We chatted for a few minutes, and he was just telling me how much Nantucket reminded him of his native Finland— he had only just arrived from Helsinki that morning—when all at once Francesca came out the front door. She was crying, and she called for him to come quickly. She was upset, almost hysterical, anyone could see." She shook her head.

"And?"

"Not an hour after he went into that house, they carried him out, stone dead. He'd had a massive heart attack. They said he had a history of heart problems, though to tell the truth, none of the Ferrares would discuss it. Not with reporters, not with the staff, not with anyone."

"Was he buried here?"

"Oh, no. Julian flew out to help Francesca make arrangements to have the body shipped to the mainland. Then the family left the island together on the ferry. They fired the staff, locked the house up tight. As if they were never coming back."

"But they did," Kaiser said.

Mrs. Minstrell nodded. "They came back all right. A few weeks later. That's when they brought Julian's sister Elise with them . . . to take care of Francesca. They hired a few people on a part-time basis, just to take care of the household chores—a cook, a maid and the like. But no live-in help. That was Elise's job—to take care of Francesca when no one else was there."

"To take care of her?" Mrs. Minstrell looked upset, and Kaiser wondered what the Ferrares had done to cause such concern.

He didn't have long to wonder. "I'm not the one to make judgments, Patrick," she said sternly. "But there are some people I have no sympathy for. Life is tough, but for some things there is no excuse. The night they left the island, Francesca Ferrare tried to kill herself. And if that wasn't bad enough, she tried to kill those two innocent children along with her. She pushed them right off the ferryboat just as it rounded the bend coming into Hyannis. Then she jumped in after them . . . in the dead of night, if you can imagine anything more frightening. They wanted to put her away, but Julian wouldn't allow it." She looked over at

Kaiser and shook her head. "He adores that woman. And from what I hear, she hasn't a kind word for him. And to think that he moved heaven and earth to keep her out of a lunatic asylum. So now, instead of being in a hospital where she belongs, she's back here, hiding in that house, waiting for her chance to do who knows what to who knows who."

Mrs. Minstrell was indignant, but underneath it Kaiser could hear a trace of fear. "It makes a body nervous, Patrick, to have someone like that living right next door. Julian finished his concert tour in August, but even so, he doesn't spend a lot of time here. Seems like he flies around the world on a whim, as casually as if he were going to the supermarket. If there's a concert in Vienna that he wants to attend, off he goes. Or a recital in Warsaw." She threw her hands up in the air. "Since September he's been gone at least three or four times, and he leaves his sick wife here. With poor Elise to care for her. The servants say that it's only when Julian is away that Francesca goes off the deep end. I guess that's what those prescriptions are for that Elise has filled every week. Some kind of medication to keep Francesca calm. But Pop Avery down at the pharmacy says that it doesn't make sense. He says those drugs are serious business, not something you'd take just once in a while. He has to order them special." She put her hands on her hips. "It's no wonder the little boy is so nervous. It's no kind of place to be raising a child. No place at all."

"You said there were two children. Where does the other child live?"

"Hildy? She lives with them, but whenever Julian leaves the island, she goes along. Part of her musical education, her father says. And you should hear her play the piano. Sometimes Fred and I sit out in the garden and listen to her for hours. She's only eleven years old, but what talent she has! I can understand why he wants to do whatever he can to encourage her. Someday she's going to be famous, you just mark my words." She frowned. "What I can't understand is why he leaves little Christian behind. You'd think he didn't care about the boy at all, leaving him alone with a woman who tried to kill him."

Kaiser raised his eyebrows. The picture he was getting of the Ferrare family wasn't pleasant, but it certainly wasn't boring. "Does anyone ever see Mrs. Ferrare in public?"

"Oh, sure. You'd think there was nothing wrong with her when Julian is around. It's as if nothing had ever happened." She stood up and stoked the fire, sending little clouds of sparks swirling up the chimney. "It's been only two months since Dr. Stahlberg died, but it seems like a year. I don't sleep well at night, worrying about those children and that poor man. It just goes to show you that fame and fortune aren't everything." She sat back down. "I don't wish them any unhappiness, Patrick, but I do wish they'd go back to wherever they came from so I wouldn't have to worry about them anymore."

Kaiser had a dozen or more questions to ask, and he was just sorting them out in his mind when they heard a rustling sound outside. "An animal?" he said, getting up to look.

Mrs. Minstrell got up too. "Probably somebody's poor old cat," she snorted. "People bring them out here in the summer, then up and leave the island without them. I spend half my life feeding the poor things."

They opened the back door and stood looking out through the swirling mist, but there was no sign of life. Then, from across the way, came the sound of sobbing, the same endless flow that Kaiser had heard the night before.

"Who is it?" he asked Mrs. Minstrell.

She shrugged. "It's been going on since the doctor died. Fred and I haven't figured out who it is yet, but I guess it really doesn't matter. It seems like any one of the Ferrares has plenty of reason to cry."

3

Kaiser walked down Broad Street and turned onto Easy Street, past the rows of weathered, gray-shingled buildings, a number of which had been closed up for the season. There was still some quiet activity in the center of town, but as he headed down toward Straight Wharf he could feel the eerie stillness that comes to most island communities with the passing of summer.

The wind had picked up, coming cold from the sea. Even in the shelter of the harbor it was turning the tops of the waves icy white. There was an edge to the air that reminded Kaiser that winter was not far off. He wondered how long it was going to take to get his boat repaired. Just before he had left the marina in Noank, he'd been reminded that they were going to dismantle their hauling equipment on the fifteenth of November. That meant that if Kaiser wanted *Seabird* in drydock for the winter, he'd have to get her back before that.

He pulled the hood on his sweatshirt up over his dark hair, and crossed the cobbled street onto the wooden walkway that ran the length of the wharf. In season every boat slip in the area was filled, but now only a few commercial fishing boats remained at anchor. As Kaiser came closer, he could see that nothing had been done to his boat. But he wasn't really surprised. The islanders had a different outlook about time. Nothing wrong with tomorrow was the general philosophy. Kaiser knew, too, that in some native circles it didn't really matter who you were or what you needed done. You had to wait your turn. If you didn't like the service, you could take your business elsewhere. The trouble was that on this island, there was no elsewhere.

Kaiser looked around for Hank, the fellow who had helped him take the sail down last night. Hank had assured him that he would have it repaired. He was also going to take care of the rest of *Seabird*'s problems, but today was Saturday and the dockyard was deserted except for two young boys fishing.

Kaiser took a look in their bucket as he came up from behind. "What're you after, guys?" he asked.

"Eels."

"What are you going to do with them?"

"Sell 'em to Mrs. Gladwyn," said the smaller of the two.

"What does Mrs. Gladwyn do with them?"

Both boys made faces. "She eats them."

"Ugh," Kaiser said.

"Yeah. You said it."

Kaiser pointed up the wharf. "Do you boys know where Hank is?"

"He just went up to Downy Flake for a cup of coffee. He should be right back. Do you want us to tell him anything?"

"No, thanks. I just wanted to see when he's going to work on my boat."

"Where's your boat?"

Kaiser pointed.

"Nice," said one of the boys.

"It was," Kaiser said, "but it needs work."

A commotion below in the water drew both boys' attention, and Kaiser turned away to see if he could spot Hank. It was then that he saw the child.

Christian Ferrare was standing alone at the edge of the

wharf, watching intently as the other boys struggled to land their catch. He had on a yellow rain slicker at least two sizes too big for him, but no one had bothered to turn up the cuffs. It made him look like a waif, a child no one cared about. *I know you aren't Jamie,* Kaiser thought suddenly, *but I care.* He raised an arm and motioned, but the child remained where he was.

"Come here and take a look at this," Kaiser called as the boys dropped the squirming eel into the bucket of salt water.

Christian took one halting step forward, then unable to resist the temptation, ran to Kaiser's side to peer fascinated into the bucket.

"Ugly fellow, isn't he?" Kaiser said.

The boy nodded but didn't look up.

"Do you like to fish?" Kaiser asked.

"I don't know how," he said quietly. "Besides, Julian says it's a foul sport."

"Who's Julian?" Kaiser asked, though he knew.

"My father," the boy replied, looking up at Kaiser for the first time. All at once he seemed to realize he was somewhere he wasn't supposed to be. He turned with a jerk and was about to run off when Kaiser heard a voice behind them.

"Child, *where* have you been?" The voice was just barely controlled.

Kaiser turned to see a woman coming toward them. He guessed she was Elise Ferrare and was intrigued. He hadn't had a clear look at her the day before in the garden, but somehow, from the sound of her voice and from what Mrs. Minstrell had told him, he'd expected someone thin and frail-looking.

Elise Ferrare was far from frail. She was almost as tall as Kaiser, a handsome woman in her late forties and surprisingly youthful, except for her hair, which she wore straight back from her face, plaited in a single gray braid. It gave her a severe, no-nonsense look that was betrayed by the near hysteria in her voice.

She was wearing a heavy black overcoat that hung almost to her ankles, as ill fitting a garment on her as Christian's slicker was on him. Standing side by side, they looked almost comical, but somehow Kaiser knew there was nothing funny about the situation. He had a sudden, striking premonition of impending disaster. Then it was gone. Elise's hand flew to her throat then darted out to take hold of the little boy, who was standing frozen in place beside Kaiser.

"You ran from me," she said without a word to Kaiser. "I am very angry."

"No harm done," Kaiser said pleasantly. "He just wanted to see the eel." He was about to introduce himself, but Elise Ferrare took the child by the hand and began to make her way toward Main Street. Francesca Ferrare had come around the corner and was standing motionless on the wooden walkway leading to the wharf. Spotting her, Christian suddenly broke free and ran to bury his face in his mother's skirt. From where he stood, Kaiser could see her face clearly. She seemed at least thirty, not as young as he'd first thought, but she was certainly as beautiful, with delicate, finely-chiseled features just short of being too perfect. Her hair, loose now, framed her face like a golden cloud, darker than the boy's but more striking in contrast to her pale skin. She had on a long, white dress, elegant and painfully inappropriate, and a short wool jacket that seemed like an afterthought.

Elise had come up to her and was talking with quick, agitated gestures, but Francesca Ferrare did not seem to notice. She stood trancelike, her arms around her small son, staring past Kaiser toward the open water.

Kaiser walked quickly up the pier. As he came closer, Francesca Ferrare suddenly saw him, her eyes touching his for an instant like the fluttering of a bird's wing. In that

fleeting second Kaiser saw something so terrible in her face
that he was stunned. He stopped and stared, but her gaze
had drifted past him and was lost once again somewhere out
to sea.

"Come, Francesca," he heard Elise say. "There's nothing
for you here."

Kaiser watched as the three made their way back toward
the center of town, Francesca moving in a rigid, robotic
gait, with Elise holding her firmly by the elbow and
Christian just behind, holding tight to his mother's hand.

"Quite a trio," Kaiser heard someone say, and he turned
to see Hank standing behind him, sipping a cup of coffee.
He was a sour-looking man with a gray, washed-out look, as
if someone had left him out in the rain and had forgotten
about him. His voice was gray, too, and flat, without a trace
of inflection. "Quite a trio," he said again. "An Amazon, a
spastic little kid, and a tutti-frutti."

"How do you know she's a tutti-frutti?"

Hank shrugged. "Everybody knows. She tried to kill
herself. Her two kids too. Jumped right off the ferryboat.
Now maybe you don't think so, but only a nut would jump
off the Nantucket ferryboat. A nut or one of those crazy
college kids. Besides, you just saw what a zombie she is."
He took another sip of his coffee. "Too bad too. She used to
be a nice lady. At least that's what they'd like everyone to
think."

"I take it you don't approve of the Ferrares."

"Can't say I do, can't say I don't. Never met them. I only
know what I hear."

Kaiser was irritated, and wondered why. After all, he
hadn't met them either. Maybe I should, he thought. As
their next door neighbor it wouldn't be out of order for him
to introduce himself. He decided that he was going to do
just that, but first, since he had nothing better to do, he'd
visit the newspaper office to see what the official story was
concerning Francesca Ferrare's suicide attempt.

There was something about the Ferrares that intrigued him. It went beyond the fact that Francesca was breathtakingly beautiful, and beyond the fact that whenever he saw Christian he couldn't help but think of his own son. His instinct told him his fascination had something to do with the terrible sadness he sensed in them—sadness, and a sense of utter despair.

He turned to Hank and asked a question he knew was pointless. "When do you think you'll start working on my boat?"

"Took the sail over to the sail maker's this morning. But I won't be doing much else. At least not today, that's for sure. Too busy."

Too busy doing what? Kaiser wondered, looking down the deserted wharf. Even the two young fishermen had gone. Nevertheless he decided not to press Hank, because if he irritated him, he probably wouldn't see *Seabird* fixed before the spring. "How about tomorrow?" Kaiser suggested.

Hank looked at the sky. "If the weather holds, maybe."

"That would be great," Kaiser said. "I'll check back tomorrow."

"Don't bother if the weather is bad," Hank said, and moved off down the pier.

Kaiser wondered what Hank considered bad weather as he headed away from the dock, looking for a cab to take him to the newspaper office.

The story in the *Inquirer and Mirror* was only a single column long and said exactly what Kaiser had already been told. Francesca Ferrare left Nantucket Island with her husband and two children on the evening of September third, and just before the boat was due to dock in Hyannis, she allegedly jumped with the two children from the foredeck of the ferry. A passing fisherman pulled them from the water. "The lady fought like a tiger," said Henry Peabody, "but I managed to subdue her and get the kids on board." Julian Ferrare had no comment, except to say that his wife had been distraught after the sudden death of her stepfather, and that she would be given the best possible care.

In the September twentieth issue of the same newspaper, a brief note in the "About Town" column reported that Julian Ferrare and family had returned to the island to spend the winter. After that, except for an occasional bit about a party given or a function attended, no further mention was made of the Ferrares.

As a by-product of his investigation, however, Kaiser did learn that the Gledhills, two old friends of his and Toby's, were staying on the island for the winter. He had always liked the couple, and decided that if he needed some company he would give them a call. Besides, Emma Gledhill was the world's foremost information gatherer, and was bound to know quite a bit about the Ferrares.

4

The next morning Kaiser couldn't find Mrs. Minstrell, but her husband Fred turned out to be an unexpected source of information. Normally Fred was a man of few words and even fewer opinions, his conversation as lean and spare as the flesh on his bones, so Kaiser was surprised at Fred's flood of words when he was asked about the Ferrares.

"The phone over there had been disconnected that morning," Fred said, leaning on his rake, "so after Dr. Stahlberg's attack, Maude—she was their housekeeper, you know—Maude came over here to call an ambulance. That was before the fence was put up." He pointed, and for the first time Kaiser noticed the chain-link fence that ran along the top of the brick wall, down the side of the cliff, and out to the end of the jetty separating John's strip of beach from Julian Ferrare's. The jetty had been there for as long as Kaiser could remember, obviously built by some previous landowner to keep what little beach there was from washing away entirely. The jetty belonged there, but the fence looked so alien and menacing, bristling along the breakwater, that Kaiser was amazed he hadn't noticed it before.

"Who put it up?" he asked.

"Julian Ferrare did." Fred shrugged. "We can't figure out whether it's to keep people out or to keep people in.

Anyway, that morning Maude came over here banging on the door, wanting to use our phone. I went over to see if I could help. We knew that Julian was off the island."

He paused to shift his weight from one foot to the other, and continued to lean on the rake, but when he began to speak again, his normally unemotional tone had changed. He was obviously still shaken over what he had witnessed. "I didn't know Mrs. Ferrare well, but she seemed to be a nice lady. Friendly, too, and a wonderful mother to those two kids. Anyway, when I went over there that morning . . ." He shook his head. "I swear, Kaiser, and I'm normally not a swearing man, but the look on Mrs. Ferrare's face would have rattled the hangman. She never said a word to me, not to anyone. She just knelt there on the floor by her stepfather's body. Even after they took him out she stayed there, kneeling on the floor all by herself. I wasn't surprised later when they told us she'd tried to kill herself."

"Have you seen her since they came back?"

"Only from a distance. She stays inside most of the time. Especially when he's away."

"Is Maude still with them?"

He shook his head. "They don't have a housekeeper anymore. Just some part-time help. My wife's cousin is cook over there. What little we know about what goes on comes from her. They let Maude and the rest of the staff go the day after the doctor's death. Closed the house up tight, like they weren't ever coming back. Then two weeks later back they come, lock, stock, and barrel." He frowned. "I'm not one to snoop around. That's my wife's department. But I know one thing—something's not right over there. Not right at all." He began to rake around the shrubs, then stopped suddenly and looked hard at Kaiser. "You're an educated man, Kaiser," he said. "Do you think you have to be crazy to try to kill yourself?"

It took Kaiser by surprise. "Why do you ask?"

"Because I don't think that lady over there is crazy. I think she's fighting for her life."

Kaiser's intention had been to go directly to the study on the first floor and work on his book, but instead he made his way to the room on the third floor, hoping for a glimpse of Francesca Ferrare. He was so busy arguing with himself over what seemed to be becoming a nasty habit of spying on the next door neighbors, that at first he didn't see her.

She was standing on the edge of the cliff with her back to the house, staring out to sea. He wondered if she was looking at something or if her eyes were glazed over, unseeing, as they had been the day before, on the dock.

She turned suddenly and began to pace rapidly back and forth along the cliff's edge, without any evidence of the dazed shuffle he had observed before. She clasped her hands together again and again. Her distress was so painful to watch that Kaiser wanted to shout out the window that he would help her. Why in hell, he wondered, after the sudden death of her stepfather, had Julian Ferrare brought his wife back to this house, to live in an atmosphere where it would be impossible for her to forget? He was sure this had to be the worst place in the world for Francesca Ferrare. On the other hand, he thought, if she really required confinement, the kind of seclusion the island offered would be hard to find elsewhere.

He made a quick decision to go next door, and on the pretext of being neighborly, learn what little he could about Francesca and her sister-in-law Elise. Within minutes he was at the Ferrares' front gate. From the road, little could be seen of the house itself. Nothing but gables and chimneys, but as Kaiser walked up the drive he could see a wide veranda that ran along the two sides of the house, facing away from the ocean. Three steps led down to the meticulously groomed lawn—clearly the product of a constant battle with the elements. He walked up the steps and was about to lift the knocker when the door opened and he found himself face to face with a radiantly transformed Elise Ferrare.

The woman who yesterday had impressed him as nervous and severe, stood before him glowing with such eager anticipation that it took his breath away. He opened his mouth to speak, but before he could say a word all life drained suddenly from her face, leaving her drab and colorless. Obviously he was not the person she'd expected, and for a second he thought she was going to slam the door in his face.

"I'm Patrick Kaiser," he said quickly, "from next door. I wanted to stop by and introduce myself, since we're neighbors."

Elise Ferrare said nothing, and Kaiser had the eerie feeling that whoever had answered the door had gone away, leaving only a lifeless automaton in front of him. He tried a smile. "Are either of the Ferrares home?"

Her hand fluttered to her throat and she seemed to be struggling to fix her gaze on something substantial. "Mr. Ferrare is away," she said woodenly, "and I'm afraid Mrs. Ferrare is not feeling well. She is confined to her bed. But I'll tell her you called."

"Thank you." His smile was automatic. He knew that Francesca Ferrare was not confined to her bed. He had just seen her outside in the garden. He stood for a minute, not certain what he was going to do next, but Elise Ferrare made the decision for him. She closed the door.

Kaiser shrugged and started down the drive. Weird lady, he thought, and something told him that *weird* was an understatement. Just as he reached the road a car pulled up to the gate and Julian Ferrare and his daughter got out.

Ferrare was a handsome man, still youthful-looking in spite of his fifty-eight years. His hair had the same silver-gray streaks that were so prominent in his sister's hair, but where hers marked aging, his made him look more distinguished. He was not a tall man. In fact, he was considerably shorter than Kaiser, yet he gave the impression of commanding stature—self-possessed and faintly patronizing. He was casually dressed in a turtleneck, a tweed sport jacket, and slacks, but he carried himself as if he were in full military uniform. Kaiser felt an absurd urge to salute.

For a moment, Ferrare seemed shocked to see Kaiser standing there, then an amiable expression crossed his face. "Can I help?" he asked. Kaiser was immediately conscious of the perfect modulation of his voice.

"I'm Patrick Kaiser," he said, extending his hand. "John's brother."

"Of course." Julian Ferrare's smile was brilliant. "The celebrated journalist. I had the pleasure of meeting your brother this summer. How is he?"

"In perfect health as far as I know."

"And his family?"

"The same."

Julian Ferrare nodded and turned away, apparently indicating that the conversation was at an end.

Kaiser had no intention of letting Julian Ferrare escape so easily, and was about to pursue his quarry when Julian turned back suddenly and surprised him by saying, "Won't you come in and meet my wife? She loves company."

"I'd be delighted," Kaiser said, covering his astonishment with a quick smile.

"May I go in, Julian?" A small voice made Kaiser turn to look down at the young girl who had been standing quietly just behind her father. She was about eleven years old, and she had the face of an angel. Her hair was as dark as her mother's was pale and her eyebrows even darker, but her eyes were turquoise, and against her fair skin the contrast was startling even in one so young. She was a slender girl, a child still, but Kaiser could tell that Hildy Ferrare would become a beautiful woman.

"This is Patrick Kaiser, Hildy," Julian said. "*The New York Times* Kaiser—among other things."

"How do you do, Mr. Kaiser?" the girl said, holding out her hand. She was incredibly poised, but there was a gravity about her that went far beyond what Kaiser considered natural, even given her father's position as the foremost classical pianist in the world.

Kaiser took the small hand and smiled. "I'm pleased to meet you, Hildy," he said.

"The pleasure is mine," she said solemnly, then turned to her father. "Now may I go ahead?"

"Of course, my darling," he said. "I know you're eager to see Francesca."

The girl turned and took two slow steps, then unable to restrain herself, she ran up the drive and into the house. Julian Ferrare picked up the single suitcase, and Kaiser, determined not to miss this extraordinary opportunity, followed.

They were met at the door by his sister, and Kaiser could see from her radiant expression that Elise Ferrare had been expecting her brother earlier. She made no move to embrace him, but simply stood looking at him in silent adoration.

"Elise, my dear," he said, setting the suitcase down at her feet, "please tell Francesca we have company. We'll be in the library. Come, Kaiser." He stopped, and Kaiser assumed that he would be introduced to Elise. Instead Julian said, "How rude of me, calling you Kaiser. Would you prefer to be Patrick? Or Mr. Kaiser?"

"Just plain Kaiser is fine."

"I thought so," Julian said. "I know people. I know what they like. I have a sense about these things." He crossed the hall and Kaiser followed, conscious of the man's powerful personality. Ferrare was no doubt a supreme egotist, but an intriguing one, and curiously, one almost impossible to dislike.

Kaiser followed Julian across the foyer, taking note of the architectural similarities between this house and John's. But there the similarities ended. Where John's house reflected the casual, at-home style of his own life, the Ferrare house was a living tribute to the elegant refinement of the nineteenth century. The original paneling, meticulously restored, lined the walls on both sides of the hallway, which was furnished only with period pieces of the finest quality. Kaiser had been in many places as faultlessly preserved as this one, but there was something here that he found unsettling. It seemed a pretense, as if it were nothing more than an elaborate set for some stage play.

As they entered the library Kaiser smiled to himself, wondering what Julian Ferrare would say if he knew what he'd been thinking. And worse, that he'd been spying on the whole family, conjuring up all kinds of grim horrors. Again the journalist in him sneered at the novelist.

"What will you have?" Julian asked, crossing the room to an open bar that stood along one wall.

"A beer will be fine."

Ferrare took a bottle from the refrigerator and poured. "I would have guessed gin."

"Not at three in the afternoon."

Julian Ferrare held out the glass, poured himself a gin on the rocks, and drained it before Kaiser had even skimmed the foam from his beer. "A long trip," Julian said casually, by way of explanation, and poured himself another. "Make yourself at home." He gestured to a chair.

Kaiser was about to sit when the door opened, and like a soft breath, Francesca Ferrare came into the room. She was wearing a plain gray dress whose simplicity made her seem even more lovely. Her hair was pulled back straight from her face, knotted behind her head, and Kaiser could see now that her eyes were the same startling shade of turquoise as her daughter's.

She studied Kaiser for a minute, without a smile, her face still and watchful. Then she said, "Mr. Kaiser, I'm pleased to meet you." But she did not extend her hand. Her voice was low, controlled, matching the expression on her face, but there was a peculiar lifelessness about her—as if she were nothing more than another piece of exquisite Ferrare furniture, Kaiser thought. She had the faintest trace of an accent, one he supposed was Finnish.

"I've been looking forward to meeting you, Mrs. Ferrare," he said quietly.

"Please, call me Francesca," she said, moving toward the bar. "Everyone does. Even my children. At least they're supposed to. Calling a person Mama is a sign of weakness. Isn't that right?" She looked at her husband but didn't speak his name. In fact it was the only acknowledgment she gave that she was aware of his presence.

"It's a good way to teach them independence at an early age, my dear," Julian said, seemingly unaffected by her coolness. "May I get you a drink?"

"No. I'm perfectly capable." There was an unmistakable edge to her voice.

"I know that. I only meant—"

"I know what you meant." She poured herself a glass of gin, then turned to Kaiser. "To happier times," she said, but her face was hidden in shadow and he couldn't see her expression. It didn't matter. He knew she wasn't smiling, and he felt uncomfortable.

There was a tension in this room which was almost visible. And what puzzled Kaiser even more was the dramatic change in Francesca Ferrare. This woman, cool and self-possessed, bore no resemblance to the zombie he had seen the day before, shuffling along beside her sister-in-law, nor was there any evidence of the awful, hand-wringing despair he had witnessed earlier in the garden. This lady was the picture of cold control.

"How did you spend your day?" Julian asked. Kaiser shifted his attention to his host, wondering why he'd been invited here, since no one was paying any attention to him. Ferrare's tone was casual, but his dark eyes were riveted on his wife's face with an intensity of expression Kaiser found puzzling, considering the offhanded nature of the question.

Francesca did not answer at once, and Kaiser got the impression that she was gathering her thoughts. "The usual," she said coldly. "What did you expect?" It was as if Julian was someone she hardly knew and she was offended by his interest.

Julian shrugged. "I had hoped you would visit old friends."

She seemed on the verge of answering, then turned instead to Kaiser. "How long are you on the island, Mr. Kaiser?" And without waiting, "I hope we have pleasant weather. November can be a lovely month." She paused. "On the other hand, it can be hellish. I hate the fall, don't you? Everything dies." There was a sudden quiver in her voice that threatened her earlier calm.

Julian cut in. "We're having a dinner party this evening, Kaiser. Will you join us? Nothing fancy, just a few old friends."

Kaiser took the shift of mood in stride. "I'd be delighted," he said, and did not look at Francesca. She was still in shadow, silent, but he had the uncomfortable feeling that she was fighting for control.

He got up and crossed to the bar, setting his empty glass down. "I'll be going," he said. "You both must have many things to do." He turned to Francesca and on impulse held out his hand. "It was a pleasure meeting you."

She moved toward him, about to take it, then changed her mind, her arm falling lifeless to her side. She smiled a cool smile, one of the least friendly Kaiser had ever seen.

"It was kind of you to visit," she said. "We look forward to seeing you this evening."

You could have fooled me, Kaiser thought, and again had the impression that none of this was real, that he was in the middle of an elaborate stage play. But who are the actors, he wondered, and who is the audience? He reached up and touched the side of his face, trying to concentrate. He needed to regain some sense of detachment, some critical objectivity, when all at once he realized that that wasn't what he wanted at all. As bizarre as this all seemed, he was beginning to enjoy himself. The more he saw of the Ferrares, the less he seemed to be concerned about Toby, or anything else for that matter.

"Till this evening then," Julian was saying with sincerity. "About seven. Is that too early?"

"Not at all," Kaiser said.

He caught a last glimpse of Francesca, still standing in the middle of the room, coolly sipping her drink, as he followed his host out.

"You must forgive my wife," Julian said.

"For what?"

"She's been through a bad time." Julian looked grim. "Thank you for coming. It seems to help."

As Kaiser made the short walk to his brother's house he wondered how he could find out more about the Ferrares. Perhaps tonight at their party some new source of information would turn up. Until then he would have to try and forget about them.

Just as he reached the front door, on impulse he turned back. To his surprise he caught a quick glimpse of two small faces peeking at him through the hedges. He raised his arm and waved, but the two children, obviously startled, disappeared behind the wall.

5

"He saw us." Christian was frightened. "Do you think he'll tell Julian?"

"I don't think so, Christian. Mr. Kaiser seems like a nice man. Besides, we weren't doing anything wrong." Hildy took her brother by the hand and led him around to the garden.

It was sheltered there in spite of a cold afternoon wind that was sweeping in from the northeast, a wind carrying dark clouds on its back. Hildy smelled rain.

"Were you a good boy while Julian and I were away?" she asked.

Christian shivered and hung his head. "I hope Mr. Kaiser doesn't tell that he saw me on the old beach road."

"Christian," Hildy said sharply, "what were you doing there? You know we aren't allowed."

"I know," he said miserably, "but Mama's sickness came again, and I was left alone with Elise. Elise hates me, you know."

"She doesn't either."

"She does. She told me so herself. She said I was wicked because I have golden hair. That's probably why she likes you. Your hair is brown."

Hildy laughed. "That's the silliest thing I ever heard."

"It's not." Christian's lower lip began to quiver. "It's the

42

truth. And then Elise started turning into a witch, so I ran out and hid."

Hildy shook her head. "Christian, how many times do I have to tell you, people don't turn into witches."

The little boy looked at his sister, his dark eyes filling with tears. "Elise does," he said in a whisper.

Hildy knew that Christian was about to cry. She changed the subject. "How long was Mama sick?" she asked, not sure she wanted to hear the answer.

"Till this morning."

Hildy was silent. She didn't know what this "sickness" was that her brother kept telling her about. She had never seen it. It happened only when she and Julian were away. Three times since Grandfather died, Julian had taken her to Europe. And that's when Christian said the sickness came. Hildy frowned. Imagined or not, it was very real and very frightening to Christian. She hadn't told Julian about it because she knew he would get that terrible black look behind his eyes and then punish Christian for having too much imagination. She decided that the first chance she got to be alone with her mother, she was going to ask her about it.

"Julian thinks everything I do is wrong," Christian said, breaking into her thoughts. There was no complaint in his voice. He was making a simple observation.

Hildy didn't contradict him. It was only too true. She sat down in one of the wicker chairs and pulled him close. "I'll tell you a story."

Christian snuggled next to her, happy that she wasn't angry with him for going down to the beach, happy to have her back again. "The Wild Swans," he said. "Tell me about the Wild Swans."

"Oh, Christian," Hildy said, putting her arm around him, "don't you ever get bored with that one? I get bored telling it."

"It's the best one, Hildy," he said. "The beautiful princess loves her brothers so much."

"Like I love you, silly," Hildy said. It was a ritual with them. He would always tell her how much the princess loved her brothers, and Hildy would always reply in the same way: "Like I love you, silly."

She began to tell the story, and when she had finished she was quiet for a minute, thinking. Then she straightened up, pushing Christian gently away. "I have to talk to you, Christian. Serious talk."

His eyes grew dark, like his father's did when he was displeased. "About what?" he asked, on guard.

"About Mama."

"You know you're not supposed to call her that."

"I'll call her that if I want to."

"But Julian says we aren't supposed to."

"I don't care," Hildy said with a rare show of rebellion. Then she thought about Julian's black anger and softened. "Well, at least I'm going to call her Mama when he's not around. You know she likes us to."

"Then why doesn't she just tell him?"

"She doesn't want to displease him." She paused, and a tiny frown traced its path between her dark eyebrows. "At least she didn't used to want to. Before."

Christian nodded. "She doesn't like Julian anymore."

"I know."

"Do you know why?"

Hildy shook her head. "He must have done something terrible," she said quietly.

"Is that why Mama is always crying?"

"I guess so."

"Do you think we're all going to be divorced?"

"No," Hildy said emphatically. "I heard Julian tell Mama that he would never allow it."

"Why did Grandfather have to die?" Christian asked suddenly.

Hildy shivered. Christian persisted in asking that question even though she had no answer. She shook her head but didn't speak.

All at once, as if he had thought enough unpleasant thoughts, Christian jumped up and ran to the edge of the cliff. Late afternoon shadows were stretching themselves across the garden and the air was chill, but the boy didn't seem to notice. He was busy staring down at something below on the beach. "Hildy," he called excitedly, "come here and look. There's an animal down there."

She crossed to his side.

"Let's go down and look."

She shook her head forcefully. "You know we aren't allowed, Christian. Why do you always want to go looking for trouble?"

"I guess it's because I'm bad, just like Julian says," Christian said, and ran up to the terrace, flopping down on his knees. He began to probe a deserted ant hill with the tip of his finger. "I wonder if Julian will ever take me on one of your trips?"

"Would you like to go with us?" she asked, knowing the answer would be no.

"If he liked me, I would. But he doesn't."

"If you would try harder, maybe he would."

"I hate playing the piano, Hildy. I'm no good at it."

Hildy sank to her knees beside her brother. "I know, Christian. But Julian would be so much nicer to you if you would try harder."

"I do try." Christian was close to tears, and his sister glanced toward the house, fearful. She knew that there was nothing Julian detested more than to see his son cry.

"Hush, silly," she said, brushing a tear off his cheek, trying to staunch the flood before it came. "I know you do. It's just that you'd rather be looking for sand crabs, right?"

He nodded, and his eyes grew bright. "You know what I saw yesterday, Hildy? An eel." He stretched the word out a mile, and although she wasn't much interested in eels, she breathed a sigh of relief, sensing the passing of the storm. "Come on, Christian, let's count waves," she said, and together they walked back to the edge of the cliff and sat down on the dry, brown grass.

In the fading light Christian began to count. Hildy knew he would get to thirty-three and then begin again, but at least it kept him busy. She fervently hoped that he had practiced his piano lesson while she and Julian had been away. It wouldn't be long before he'd be summoned inside to perform, and Hildy used one of her magic wishes to help him get through the ordeal. It always amazed her that what came so easily to her was so difficult for her brother.

Hildy had four loves in her life, none of which included eels: first was her mother Francesca, the center of her universe, infallible, indestructible, all-loving. Hildy frowned. At least she had been until Grandfather died.

Second in her life was her little brother Christian. She had adored him from the minute of his birth, a small, golden-haired baby with the same black eyes as their father. But where Julian's eyes frightened Hildy at times, Christian's were always filled with a puppylike eagerness to please. And when he looked at her, she knew that he loved her best in the world, even more than he loved Mama.

Her third love was her music, music that filled her soul. She wasn't a bit like Christian, always wanting to look under rocks and pick up slimy things. All she needed to make her happy was music. She loved to listen to Julian when he played the piano. She loved to play herself. Everyone said she had his genius in her hands. Even Julian said so. She wouldn't have believed it from the others, but when Julian said it, she knew that it had to be true. Julian knew all there was to know about music. He felt it in a way Hildy could understand, and for that reason she loved him too. At least she thought she did.

"Thirty-two, thirty-three," Christian sang, then stopped,

as Hildy had known he would. She waited. "One, two, three . . ." Christian began again. Hildy wished they could all begin again, that Grandfather would come back and make her mother smile.

Ever since Hildy could remember, her grandfather had played a central part in her life. She only saw him three or four times a year, when her mother would take them to visit in Helsinki, but it was time enough to make Hildy love him. She remembered asking her mother once if it was a sin to love Grandfather more than she did Julian, and her mother had told her that people who deserve to be loved *should* be loved. Grandfather surely deserved to be loved, of that Hildy was sure. He was never too tired to spend time telling them all kinds of wonderful stories. About shipwrecks and faraway places, about Hannibal bringing the elephants across the Alps, and the Great Wall of China, and Mary Queen-of-Scots' bloody head. And more than anything, Grandfather never seemed to care that Christian couldn't play the piano. Hildy had loved her grandfather, and so had Mama. Now there was something about her mother's face that it hurt Hildy to look at. It was as if she were bleeding.

"Christian! Hildy!" Hildy heard Elise call, and she sighed. Elise had been living with them for almost two months, and though she certainly wasn't a witch, Hildy did think she was kind of strange.

"She's only nice when you and Julian are here," Christian had told her once. "But everytime you and him have gone—"

"You and *he*, Christian," Hildy had interrupted.

"He, what?"

"It's you and *he*, not you and him."

"Gee, Hildy, aren't you even paying attention?"

"Of course I am, silly. It's just that you have to learn to speak correctly."

"Well, I'm not silly about Elise. It's true. When Julian

isn't here, Elise turns into a witch. She casts a spell on Mama and then Mama gets sick." He had rolled his eyes up under the lids so that only the whites showed.

"Stop it," Hildy had said. "That's gross."

"Elise is what's gross," Christian had whispered. "She really is, Hildy. She may be nice when Julian is here, but when he goes away . . ."

Hildy could remember vividly the look on her brother's face, and she had shivered. She knew that Christian was genuinely afraid of Elise, and wondered why.

"The wicked witch is calling us," Christian whispered, bringing her back to the present.

"There's no such thing as witches," Hildy said sternly.

"Someday you'll believe me, Hildy," Christian said tearfully. "Someday she'll put me in the oven and cook me and then you'll know."

Elise called again, and Hildy jumped up, brushing the dried grass from her leotards. She took Christian's hand. "Don't worry, silly," she said cheerfully, but had a funny feeling in her stomach. "I won't let her cook you. Come on. It's suppertime." She started to walk toward the\house. "By the way," she said, crossing the fingers of her free hand, "did you practice your piano lesson while we were away?" From the look on her brother's face, she knew he hadn't. She shivered, dreading the moment when Christian would be asked to perform, cringing mentally at what she knew Julian's reaction would be.

She looked down at the blond head bobbing along beside her and tightened her grip on his hand, saying her secret prayer that somehow Christian would not be asked to play. Or if he was, that somehow God would help his fingers find the right notes. If I were God, she thought, I'd make Christian play like a genius. The best in the world. Then Julian would love him. And I'd make Grandfather come back so Mama wouldn't cry anymore. And then we'd all be happy again.

When they stepped inside the back door, Hildy knew that God had heard at least part of her prayer. Julian and Mama were expecting company, so if all went well, Christian would not have to perform, not tonight anyway. She gave her brother the secret pinch that told him everything was going to be all right and that she would protect him whenever she could.

"Wash your hands, Hildy," Elise said, smiling down at her. "You too," she said to Christian.

"See?" Hildy whispered to him as they went into the bathroom, "she's perfectly nice. You're just imagining things." But she had to admit, if only to herself, that Elise *was* a little bit scary.

Hildy had overheard a conversation between her mother and Julian right after Elise had come to live with them. She hadn't been eavesdropping—Julian hated eavesdroppers—she'd simply been in the wrong place at the wrong time, sitting in her secret spot behind the stairs, reading *Jane Eyre*. Her friend Pamela had given the book to her, but when Julian discovered it, he'd thrown it in the trash. "Pure, unadulterated tripe," he said.

Later, after much soul-searching, Hildy had sneaked out behind the house to the garbage bin and retrieved the book, but had suffered great pangs of guilt which she later confessed to her mother. She remembered what Francesca had said: "Sometimes, my sweetheart, we need a little of that kind of 'pure, unadulterated tripe,' as your father so colorfully labels it, to help us survive the real thing."

Hildy had almost finished reading the book when suddenly she'd realized that Julian and her mother had come into the back entry and were arguing about Elise. She didn't understand most of what she heard, but did learn two things: her mother didn't want Elise to live with them, and her mother said that Elise was a schizophrenic.

Hildy didn't know exactly what the word meant, and she'd put it out of her mind. But now that Christian was so upset, she decided to look the word up in the encyclopedia. Maybe it would help explain why her brother was so frightened.

Right after supper Hildy went to the study, took the encyclopedia off the shelf, and paged through it until she found the word. It took her a few minutes because she wasn't sure of the spelling, but once she found it, she read quickly.

"Schizophrenia," she read, "is the most common form of mental illness, characterized by rich development of delusions, accompanied by manifestations of persecution. Auditory hallucinations, 'voices' that may compel the victim to act. Progressive disorganization and confusion, resulting in bizarre actions, i.e., inappropriate laughter or movement." Hildy didn't understand all of what she was reading, but one sentence stuck in her mind. "In its paranoid form, persons afflicted are commonly referred to as maniacs."

6

At seven-forty Kaiser lifted the knocker at the Ferrares' front door. He was so curious about the Ferrares that he'd been dressed and ready for almost an hour.

Julian Ferrare answered the door, generating an almost electric atmosphere of cordiality. Every bit the perfect host, he led Kaiser to the living room where the other guests had already assembled. Kaiser was not surprised to find that he knew a number of them. The year-round population of Nantucket Island was small. Those non-natives who remained for the winter out of choice had spent most of their lives somewhere else, before deciding that solitude and privacy were worth the price. They were a distinguished if bizarre group, tied together by a single, common thread: the island and the kind of protected existence it offered.

Kaiser took his time mixing himself a drink as he scanned the room. He saw Emma and Sam Gledhill. Emma was talking, and gesturing as usual with her hands, to an aging sculptor Kaiser knew only as Monaste. Kaiser had known the Gledhills for years—first in Paris, when Sam was at the American Embassy, later in New York, before Sam had retired to the island. Emma had been an artist of sorts, though most of her paintings hung on her own walls. Kaiser had never determined whether it was because no one else liked her work or she simply could not bear to part with her

51

own creations. He liked the Gledhills. If all else failed, he would spend the evening renewing an old acquaintanceship.

Kaiser saw John Abraham, retired cosmetic czar, standing close by the hearth, where a fire added the ultimate touch to the ambience of the room. He was smiling tolerantly down at an attractive young woman in a red chemise. With them were the three island dowagers: Mrs. Wilkie McLennan, Miss Anna Limmeridge, and Mrs. Percival Halcombe-Dempster. Kaiser's brother John had known Percival Halcombe-Dempster for years. They had worked together in Boston for the same law firm, so it had been a happy coincidence when John had discovered Percival's widow living on the island. Kaiser's nephews adored her, and he suspected that it was in large part because they never tired of saying her name; in fact John's children had named their last dog Percival Halcombe-Dempster.

Kaiser sipped on a Scotch, his line of vision moving past the Abraham group to Julian Ferrare, who stood talking with his sister and a middle-aged couple Kaiser did not recognize. Kaiser moved toward the group, then changed his mind and decided to speak first to the Gledhills, all the while keeping his eye peeled for a first glimpse of Francesca Ferrare, who had not yet appeared.

He was halfway across the room when he saw the Ferrare children out of the corner of his eye. They were sitting on a small bench beside the piano, hands folded in their laps, not moving. Hildy was wearing a pastel pink dress with white lace at the collar and buttons running down the front to disappear under a wide, pleated waistband. Christian had on a navy blue blazer with brass buttons, gray wool shorts and knee socks. They looked like two priceless porcelain figurines.

Kaiser walked over. "How's it going?" he asked.

Neither spoke at first. Then the girl smiled politely and said, "Everything is just fine, thank you."

"Are you joining us for dinner?"

"Oh, no," she said quickly. "We have already eaten."

The boy was silent, looking down at his hands.

"Have you told your sister about the eel you saw yesterday?"

Christian nodded but did not lift his head.

The girl answered for him. "He told me. Christian really likes such things."

"Don't you?"

She made a face. "But there's nothing wrong with liking them," she added quickly. "It's all a matter of taste."

"I knew a girl once who really liked eels," Kaiser said. He thought Hildy was going to respond, but instead she dropped her eyes, and Kaiser had the feeling that he had been dismissed. "Am I bothering you?" he asked.

"It's just that we were hoping that Julian would forget about us," she said without looking up.

"Why is that?"

Hildy lifted her head and took quick measure of Kaiser. "You won't tell?"

He shook his head.

"We are going to be asked to play the piano, and Christian hasn't done his lessons." She stopped and glanced over to the spot where Julian still stood talking. "Julian won't be pleased."

"I see," Kaiser said, wondering just how displeased Julian would be. "Will he yell?"

For the first time Christian lifted his head, his dark eyes filled with unshed tears. "He'll *hate* me," he said with conviction.

Startled by the child's choice of words, Kaiser was about to question him further when Julian's voice cut across the room. "I think it's time for your recital, don't you, Christian?"

Kaiser turned, but not before he saw a tremor pass through the child's thin frame. He felt a sudden, overwhelming urge to protect Christian.

Hildy stood up quickly, straightening the folds of her dress. "I'll play, Julian," she said, and walked to the piano. "I've been working on the Brahms piece."

"Later, my darling," Julian said, holding up one hand. "First we must hear Christian."

Kaiser frowned. There was a malicious quality to Julian's tone, and Kaiser sensed a sudden uneasiness in the room, as if these people had all seen this happen before. Julian had not moved, but Kaiser could almost feel a tightening of the man's muscles, and the dark eyes that had been so filled with warmth and vitality were now cold and still.

I don't think I like this guy, Kaiser thought. "Come on, Christian," he said loudly, putting his hand on the child's shoulder. He could feel a pathetic quivering, like a small animal cornered with no place to run. "I used to play the piano myself as a youngster." He made a face. "I was awful, and I promise if you aren't worse than I was, I'll take you fishing tomorrow." He looked over at a motionless Julian. "That is, if your father will let you go."

No one in the room spoke. They all stood frozen, as if suspended in the midst of their sentences, leaving only Julian Ferrare unaffected. The man didn't move, nor did he speak, but Kaiser could feel a terrible anger in him, an anger out of all proportion to what had just happened. His sister Elise stood at his side, strangely rigid. Kaiser opened his mouth to say something, to try to restore some sense of balance, when he heard a voice from the doorway.

"Of course Christian may go fishing with you, Mr. Kaiser. How kind of you to offer. Mr. Ferrare doesn't seem to realize that times have changed. You'll have to excuse him. Now off to bed," she said to the children. "Both of you. It's long past your bedtime."

Kaiser turned to see Francesca Ferrare standing in the

doorway. She had traded her plain gray dress in for one the color of faintly tinted glass. She made everyone else in the room look vulgar. In profile the lines of her face seemed to have been lifted from a cameo, fine and classic, but when she turned, the effect on Kaiser was staggering. He felt a sudden sense of anticipation, as if he were on the brink of an incredible discovery. He heard her laugh, like a young girl, lighthearted and almost breathless.

As if they had all been given permission to breathe again, the company came alive. Emma Gledhill came rushing across the room, hugging Kaiser against her ruffled bosom. "Kaiser, you rascal," she said. "When did you get on the island? Is John here too?" She didn't wait for an answer. "Do you know all these lovely people?" She waved her arm around the room. "For shame, Julian," she said to the man who still stood unmoving by the fire. "Here we have the most handsome and—correct me if I'm wrong—the most recently eligible bachelor on the coast, and you, sir, haven't even introduced him to some of these charming ladies."

Kaiser took one moment to look over at Christian, who with his sister had moved to their mother's side. Francesca bent and kissed them, but before they left the room, Hildy turned back and flashed Kaiser a smile so fleeting that he almost missed it. Still, it promised that she would never forget what he had tried to do for her brother.

"Do you know our resident sculptor?" Emma was saying as she led him across the room. "Of course you do." She stopped suddenly, as if to catch her breath. "Well," she said in a whisper, "we shall all be eternally grateful to you for that reprieve. It's a shame, really, but then who am I to judge what other people do with their children?" She glanced over toward Julian, who had moved to the door, where his wife still stood.

Kaiser heard Francesca laugh again, but this time it had a hard, mocking sound. "What's going on here?" he asked Emma.

"My dear boy, now is not the time nor the place to get into that. Suffice it to say that . . ." Whatever Emma was going to tell him, Kaiser never heard, because at that moment the inhuman sound of something mortally wounded filled the room, and Elise Ferrare folded up and fell to the floor like a puppet whose strings had been cut.

7

Where are you? Go slowly now. If you go slowly, you know you'll remember. She kept her eyes shut tight as reality trickled into her mind like water through a tea strainer. You are in Julian's house, she said to herself. Your brother has brought you to live with him and that is where you are.

She opened her eyes to see Julian bending over her, their father's eyes staring out at her from Julian's face. She tried to say something but couldn't speak.

"Elise," he was saying, his voice low, intimate, so that only she could hear, "can you pull yourself together?"

She nodded, but it was still too soon to be able to speak. She closed her eyes again. She hadn't had enough time. Dread still lingered around the edges of her mind. But at least her voices were quiet. Not even Coriander spoke. But she knew he would. Eventually. Coriander always spoke eventually. Dr. Bryson said that Coriander was nothing more than an auditory hallucination, one of the most striking manifestations of her illness. But Elise knew better. How could Coriander be part of her illness when it was his voice that kept her sane?

She forced herself to float, something she had learned to do in the sanitarium. It helped her pick up the fragments of thought, putting them carefully in place like pieces of a puzzle.

"Elise?" Julian's voice again. Always so patient. So loving. Not ashamed of her. Never ashamed. All her life people had been ashamed of her, but never Julian. Dr. Bryson said that her perceptions were distorted. Maybe they were. But not where Julian was concerned. Even when it appeared to outsiders that Julian was cold, even cruel to her, Elise knew better. Julian was her salvation, the one person in the world who understood her.

"Elise?" Julian's voice again.

"I'm all right," she said. "Just dizzy. How foolish of me." She smiled, not aware of the tears running down her cheeks.

"Shall I call Edward?" she heard someone ask. She frowned. Who is Edward? she wondered. *Edward is the family doctor*, Coriander said, speaking to her from inside her head.

"I don't think there's any need for a doctor," Julian said. "She seems to be coming around."

"I'm fine," she said, and sat up, clutching herself tightly.

"What happened, dear?" someone asked.

Elise looked across the room to where Francesca stood in shadow, and she suddenly remembered. It had been Francesca's mocking laughter that had caused her to faint. "It must be because I've not eaten all day," she lied, forcing herself to smile. She turned to her brother. "We ought to have dinner, don't you think?"

Julian nodded and helped her to her feet. She stood holding on to him for a moment, balancing as if on a tightrope. She looked around at the company, but they were far, far away, the distance between them too great to be measured. She looked across the room to where Francesca stood. She looked so innocent, but Elise knew better. *She wants to send you away*, Coriander said. *Like she did before. And you won't be able to stop her because you're crazy.* Elise shivered, but then heard Julian speak and was pulled back toward his words.

"Let me get you something to eat," he was saying. "You'll feel better." He helped her into the dining room, where the servants had set up the buffet. The rest of the guests trailed after them. She felt Julian's arm around her, and tonight it was enough to give her the strength she needed. She was grateful. She remembered all too well the other times, when no one had been strong enough to save her.

"Sit down, Elise," her father had said, and she had obeyed; in the corner of the darkened room, watching the people whispering past, their voices muffled, their eyes thick with tears. Up the stairs she heard them move, heavy footsteps going down along the hall, doors closing.

She put her fingers over her nose, cupping them to catch the alien smell. In all the five years of her life there had never been flowers in the house before. Why now? she wondered, and looked down at her shoes, which had black ribbons on the tips. She felt cold. The black tights casing her chubby legs itched, and she wiggled uncomfortably in the chair.

Her father came back into the room, and she prayed for a smile to warm her, but as usual his face was hard, his dark eyes dry. Yet somehow she thought he'd been crying. "Where's Mother?" she asked.

He said nothing, but motioned for her to come with him. She felt suddenly afraid.

Together they went up the stairs and down along the cold, dark hall. "Please, Father," she whispered. Her throat was dry with fear of something she couldn't understand. "I don't want to."

He didn't answer. He opened the door and went in, but she didn't follow. She couldn't. Her legs were too heavy. The grandfather's clock in the hall downstairs began to chime. One, two, three. She stood where she was, sinking into the floor, her hands, sticky from the jelly rolls she had eaten earlier, hidden in the folds of her dress, her small fingers stuck together as if they were webbed.

Her father came to the door. "Come here, Elise," he said, and there was no comfort in his voice. Stiff-legged, she walked to him. There was no thought of disobeying. Beyond his legs she could see banks of flowers in the flickering light. And now, above the scent of the flowers, she could smell hot wax from the candles. She saw her brother Julian and felt a moment's relief. Everything would be all right now that Julian was here. After all, Julian had just turned thirteen. Now he was an adult.

But then she looked past him, and felt the jelly rolls coming up in her throat. She choked them back. Father would be furious if she were to shame him in front of all these people, people who stood silently watching, waiting. She wondered what they were doing here in her house. "Thank all our good friends who have come to pay their last respects, Elise," her father said.

She didn't know what he was talking about, but she said thank you anyway. Curiosity pushed back her fear a little and she moved cautiously into the room, feeling her way. Then her father turned and lifted her up to see. "Say good-bye to your mother, Elise."

In the dim light, so close that she could have reached out her hand to touch her, lay a lady. Elise knew that she was dead. But it was not her mother. How could her father lie and say it was her mother? Mother had been beautiful, with rosy cheeks and dark, curling hair. This lady was hideous, with the sunken, withered face of an old apple doll.

"Say good-bye," her father commanded.

The child opened her mouth to speak but no words came out, only a hot rush of vomit. As she fell from her father's arms, Elise felt the first swift moving of swallows' wings, bringing the awful, smothering darkness that was to be such a terrifying part of her illness.

* * *

Elise looked around the table and put on her listening face to give herself time. *Think, Elise, think*, Coriander said. *Try not to hear anyone but Julian*.

She did as he told her. She said "Absolutely" once, and watched the faces of Julian's guests closely to see if anyone looked puzzled. No one seemed disturbed. Or did they? She couldn't tell.

You forgot again, didn't you? Coriander said.

Forgot what? she asked, and the answer slipped down through her mind.

Your pills, Elise. Your key to sanity, Coriander said. *How can you keep Francesca from sending you away if you don't take your pills? You know what Dr. Bryson said. Your pills keep you calm. They keep you from falling into the pit.*

Elise tried to concentrate. Coriander was right. She had forgotten to take her pills, and when she did, the slightest upset could mean disaster. At the least she might spend hours staring at a light switch, wondering what its position was in the world. At the worst she might find herself falling senseless, out of control, without memory, without mind. That was what had happened to her when she'd heard Francesca laughing.

Elise looked down the table to where Francesca was sitting and shuddered. How can I keep you from sending me back like you did before? she asked. She felt the fear coming like the beginning of a hiccough. She swallowed hard, holding her breath. Then she felt Julian put something in her hand.

She looked down and gratitude flowed as if someone had opened a window to let the breeze flow in. Her medication. Coriander had been unhappy with her, and rightly so. In all the confusion of the day, she had forgotten to take her pills. But Julian had known. He always knew.

She put one pill in her mouth, then another, and

swallowed hard, hoping that it wasn't too late. She didn't know exactly what she was taking. Thorazine or Stelazine or Navane? It didn't matter. She had taken them all before from time to time.

She should have known there was going to be trouble. There was always trouble when Julian went away, because she couldn't take her own pills then. Instead she had to slip them into Francesca's tea. The pills that calmed Elise and allowed her to exist in the real world put Francesca to sleep. And if Francesca slept, she couldn't send Elise away when Julian's back was turned. But Elise always paid the price for not taking her own medication. It destroyed her memory, so that even when she didn't have to give her pills to Francesca, she would forget to take them herself. Like this morning. She had been sipping her tea and suddenly it had been evening and time for their guests to arrive. She didn't know where she'd been all day. But one thing was certain—she'd forgotten to take her medication.

Elise looked across the table at Sam Gledhill, and had the strangest feeling he was repeating himself, that he'd asked her the same thing only minutes before and she hadn't heard. She saw his hand go to his plate, watched closely as the small bit of food went into his mouth. The maid was offering something to Elise now, but she didn't know what. *You should have taken your pills earlier,* Coriander said. *Then you wouldn't be so confused.*

Elise looked quickly to see if Sam had heard Coriander, but he didn't look alarmed. Someone across the table had mentioned being bright as a button, and she looked quickly down at the buttons on her dress, wondering which button they meant. They were very nice buttons, all of them, but not at all bright. Quite the contrary, in fact. She frowned.

She tried to speak, but although she hadn't been drinking, she felt as if she were drunk. "Leave me alone," she said, not looking at anyone in particular, and her voice was loud, angry. Then she said it again, but the second time it was a plea.

She was dimly aware that Julian was beside her, leading her out of the dining room. Elise looked back for a minute and saw Francesca walking around the end of the table. *If you don't do something, she's going to send you away,* Coriander said. *And then you'll never see Julian again.*

Kaiser leaned back in his chair and looked down the table at Julian's sister, who had just staggered to her feet, shouting. Julian, clearly annoyed, had excused himself and escorted her from the room. Only moments earlier Kaiser had noticed Elise staring with a glazed expression past Sam Gledhill's right shoulder. There was something about the woman that Kaiser found disturbing. It had nothing to do with the fact that she had fainted; it had to do with the irrational look of terror he'd seen in her eyes when she first regained consciousness. And the terrible tracklike scars he'd noticed on the inside of her left arm.

"It was kind of you to help Christian earlier." A cool voice beside him made him turn. "I'm afraid I have allowed too much of that sort of thing to go on." Francesca Ferrare had come up from behind and seated herself to his left. "Thank you for coming to his rescue."

"I was young once myself," he said, "though you might have your doubts." He smiled, but her face remained impassive.

"Were you only being kind?" she asked, her voice tinged with suspicion. "When you said you would take Christian fishing?"

"I wasn't being kind. I'd love to take him. If you want, have him ready tomorrow morning at nine sharp."

A genuine smile crossed her face, and it was all the reward Kaiser needed. She truly was a beautiful woman. "He'll be ready, Mr. Kaiser," she said.

"I'll take him out to Esther Island," Kaiser said, thinking aloud. "He might get a blue."

She became suddenly tense. "Esther Island? Then you'll need a boat."

Kaiser nodded. "I'll have to rent one. I'm afraid my own is still in sad shape." He could see that she was considering something. "I can assure you he'll be perfectly safe," he added.

"Oh, I'm sure," she said offhandedly, and then was silent, lost once more in her own thoughts.

Kaiser made a last attempt at conversation, but whatever interest Francesca Ferrare had shown in him was gone. The meal over, she sat idly stirring her coffee, seemingly unaware of the company around her.

Toby was right, Kaiser thought wryly. I really knock 'em in the aisles. He turned his attention toward the door and Julian, who had just returned to the room. "You must forgive my sister," he was saying in his perfectly modulated voice. "I think she had a bit too much champagne."

"Aren't parties at the Ferrare home amusing?" Francesca said. "Julian and Elise certainly do know how to entertain."

8

Kaiser couldn't get the Ferrare children out of his mind, especially Christian. It wasn't because the child made him remember Jamie. If anything, Kaiser always steered clear of things that reminded him of his dead son. He also made it a point not to become involved with things that were none of his business. But Christian touched him in a way that was unique, made him want to help, even if it *was* none of his business.

Kaiser, at the Ferrare front door precisely at nine the next morning, was met by an anxious Hildy who told him that Christian had to finish his oatmeal but then he'd be right out. Would Mr. Kaiser please, please wait? He assured her that Christian had plenty of time to finish his oatmeal. He would wait. Relieved, Hildy disappeared.

Kaiser stood alone in the hall, listening to the silence. It was not a comfortable silence, and it made him wonder what, if anything, had transpired last night after the guests had left. He had other questions too. Was Julian Ferrare really as cruel to his son as he had seemed? And what about the strange-eyed Elise? Julian had returned to the group with apologies about his sister's overindulgence. However, Kaiser didn't believe that she'd been drunk. But one question took precedence over the others: What was wrong with the beautiful but haunted Francesca Ferrare?

Hildy soon returned with Christian by the hand. Kaiser was relieved to see that he was appropriately dressed for a change. The boy hung back, shy, obviously reluctant to leave his sister. "Go along, silly," she said. "You'll have a wonderful time."

"This is going to be the most amazing fishing trip ever," Kaiser said. "And if it's as good as I think it's going to be, maybe next time Hildy will come too."

"Can't she come with us today?" Christian asked.

"You know I can't," Hildy said. "You know Francesca and Julian want me to go with them."

"Next time," Kaiser said. "First I have to teach you all my secret tricks. Then you can show your sister."

Christian brightened noticeably. "Do you really think I'll catch anything?"

"Guaranteed," Kaiser said. "But you can't catch a fish if your line isn't in the water, so let's go." He held out his hand, and after a slight hesitation the boy took it and held it tight.

"Aren't you going to give me a kiss before you leave, my little Christian?" Francesca said from the stairs. There was a ragged edge to her voice. "For luck?" She seemed close to tears and again Kaiser was surprised by her shifting moods. One minute she seemed cold and hostile, the picture of perfect control, the next so desperate and vulnerable that he wanted to do anything he could to help her.

Christian ran to his mother and threw his arms around her neck. "I'm going to catch the biggest fish in the ocean, Mama," he said, "and give it to you."

She closed her eyes and hugged him tight, then turned back toward the stairway.

"I'll have him home before dark," Kaiser said, but she didn't answer.

* * *

Hildy ran up the stairs after her mother. "Where are we going today, Mama?" She was so excited she could hardly contain herself.

"To Esther Island," her mother said quietly. "Now run and get dressed."

Hildy had heard of Esther Island but wasn't sure where it was and didn't care. All she cared about was that her mother and father were going on a picnic, the first since summer, and she was going with them. It was going to be a wonderful day, she mused, then frowned. It was too bad Christian wasn't going to be there to enjoy it.

She skipped down the hall to her room. Julian had been so pleased when Mama had suggested a picnic, and not even the terrible look on Elise's face had dampened his high spirits.

Kaiser steered the boat around to the westerly tip of Esther Island, where the waves broke low and gentle, and he let the surf carry them in. They had spent the morning doing very little talking and a lot of fishing. Christian learned quickly, but his almost pathetic eagerness to please had disturbed Kaiser. Christian seemed to expect disapproval, as if no matter what he did, he could never do well enough. It made Kaiser furious, made him want to praise Christian, to let him know that he was the boy's friend.

Christian sat in the bow of the motorboat, his fish across his lap, unable to believe that he had really caught such a magnificent creature. For a small boy, he'd shown surprising strength and determination. Except for some help Kaiser had given reeling the blue in, it was truly Christian's catch.

As soon as they scraped the sand, Kaiser jumped over into the knee-deep water and pulled the boat to shore. He grabbed the basket Mrs. Minstrell had packed for their lunch and headed up the beach.

"Can I bring my fish?" Christian called.

"If you want to," Kaiser said.

The boy came behind him, dragging his prize. When they reached the point where the beach narrowed to a V, bordered on two sides by a high ridge of sand, Kaiser stopped. He'd been here before. Sheltered from the wind, it was a good place to picnic.

"Cover him with seaweed." Kaiser pointed to the fish that Christian had laid carefully beside him in the sand. "It will keep him cool."

As Christian complied, Kaiser unpacked the picnic basket. "What's your choice? Ham and cheese or roast beef?"

"Roast beef is my favorite," Christian said, smoothing the seaweed in a careful mound over the blue.

"Side order of Fritos?"

The child knelt in the sand beside Kaiser and looked into the basket. "Is all of this for us?"

"I think Mrs. Minstrell wanted to make sure we wouldn't starve if we got stranded."

As they ate, Kaiser tried to encourage Christian to talk about his life, not out of curiosity but from a nagging concern. "What do you and Hildy do about school?" he asked.

"I'm still too little, but Hildy has special teachers back in New York."

"Is that where she went last week with your father?"

"No. They were in Vienna." He began to count on his fingers. "And the time before that they went to Warsaw. And before that England."

"And did you stay and take care of your mother?"

The little boy frowned. "No. Elise takes care of Mama when Julian is away." The forced casualness in the way he said it made Kaiser raise his eyebrows. It sounded to him as if Christian were afraid. "Do you like Elise?"

Christian looked up from his sandwich. "Sure I do. She's

my aunt. You're supposed to like your relatives." Then he ducked his head and began to inspect his roast beef.

"Honest to goodness? You really like her?" Kaiser said, letting a hint of disbelief tinge his voice, hoping to encourage Christian to talk.

"Don't you?" the boy replied.

"Well, I don't know her very well, but she seems sort of . . . well, promise you won't tell?"

Christian's eyes grew round. He nodded, but Kaiser could tell that he was nervous.

"I think she's sort of creepy," Kaiser whispered.

Christian eyed Kaiser, but said nothing. Instead he hunched over and went back to inspecting his sandwich. Kaiser took a breath. He'd been right—the boy was afraid.

"Hildy didn't believe me," Christian mumbled, still hesitant.

"About what?"

Again Kaiser felt himself being studied by the dark, serious eyes. "Will you tell?"

"I told you I thought Elise was creepy, so if I tell on you, then you can tell on me," Kaiser said.

Christian seemed to relax a little. "I don't like her," he said.

"Why not?"

Christian shrugged.

"Is she mean to you?"

The child didn't answer right away. "No," he said finally. "She isn't mean."

"Well, what then?"

The child jumped up and came over to Kaiser. He dropped to his knees and looked up into Kaiser's face. "She scares me," he said in a rush. "I think she's a witch. Hildy says there's no such thing, but I know better." He looked to see if Kaiser was smiling, but he wasn't. "She has witches' eyes," he said quietly.

"I know," Kaiser said.

"You do?" Christian was excited.

"I don't think she's a witch, mind you," Kaiser said, pulling the boy close. "I'm inclined to agree with Hildy that there's no such thing. But I can see why her eyes frighten you."

"She talks to herself too." Christian shivered. "And something else. If she ever finds out that I told about it, she'll get me. Promise you won't ever tell?"

"I promise."

"Cross your heart and hope to die, raise your right hand to the sky?"

Kaiser performed the ritual.

"Elise told me I was wicked because I have blond hair. And that same night," Christian whispered, "she came in my room and cut some of it off."

Kaiser felt a cold chill at the base of his skull, but he kept his voice calm. "What did you do?"

"I ran and hid. Julian and Hildy were gone, and I couldn't make Mama wake up, so I hid behind the drawers under the bunk bed."

"And you never told anyone? Not even Hildy?"

Christian shook his head violently. "I told Hildy that Elise hates me, but I didn't tell her about cutting my hair off because then she'll get Hildy too. You're stronger than Elise so maybe you'll be safe."

Kaiser was concerned. How could the Ferrares allow an obviously neurotic woman to scare the hell out of a little kid?

"And now that I've told, she'll be waiting for me when I get home. She'll get me, just like she said." He shuddered.

"Your aunt isn't going to get anyone, Christian, and that's a promise."

Christian looked uncertain.

"Does your mother know that Elise scares you?"

Christian shook his head. "It only happens when Mama is sick."

"How do you mean, sick?"

"She stumbles and she doesn't remember anything. And sometimes I can't wake her up."

"Does she go to the doctor?"

Christian shook his head. "She's only sick when Julian goes away, when Elise is taking care of us. It's happened three times now. When Julian comes home she gets better, but she cries a lot."

"I guess she misses your grandfather."

Christian nodded. "We were all happy before he died." He paused and his eyes clouded over. "Except when Julian was mad at me."

"Why does Julian get mad at you?"

"Because I don't play the piano very well," he said miserably.

"There are other things besides playing the piano," Kaiser said.

"Not for Julian there aren't." He jumped up suddenly and ran to the spot where his fish lay buried under the seaweed. "I almost forgot about him," he said happily. "He's the best thing that ever happened to me."

Kaiser wanted to hear more about the Ferrares, but it was clear that it would do Christian more good to forget about his family than to talk about them. "Let's see if we can catch another fish," he said, glancing at his watch. "The tide should be just about right. Come on."

The child needed no encouragement. He helped Kaiser pack up the remains of the lunch, and together the two headed back along the edge of the sand, toward the spot where they'd left the small motorboat Kaiser rented that morning.

"When I push off," Kaiser told Christian, "you steer that way." He pointed north.

The child hopped into the boat, and Kaiser bent to roll up his pant legs. "Ready?" he asked Christian.

"Ready."

But before Kaiser could shove off, a call from above stopped him. He looked back along the ridge and saw two figures, hand in hand, scrambling down the bluff toward them. "It's Mama," Christian yelled, jumping up and down. "Mama and Hildy."

Kaiser stared, stunned, as the two ran the last few steps to the edge of the water, then waded in. "Take us to town," said Francesca Ferrare, breathless. "Please. Hurry!" The frantic urgency in her voice caught Kaiser off guard.

She pushed Hildy toward the boat. "Get in, child," she commanded, and without concern for her clothing waded knee-deep into the cold water and climbed in, sitting down hard between Christian and Hildy, pulling them close beside her. "For God's sake, hurry!" she screamed at Kaiser. "Don't just stand there. Hurry!"

The sharp tone of her voice annoyed Kaiser. She might be beautiful, he thought, but he was not her slave. He was about to tell her that when he saw the deep circles under her eyes. She looked haggard. But it was what lay beyond her eyes that mobilized him; it was a silent, frantic cry for help.

He pushed off without a word and started the motor. No one spoke on the way back to town. The two children sat tense and wide-eyed. Christian obviously had no idea what had caused their sudden appearance, but he wasn't asking. Hildy knew, and as Kaiser headed north, he could see the silent tears sliding down her cheeks, dripping off her chin.

Francesca Ferrare, however, sat dry-eyed and alert, looking back over her shoulder every few minutes, as if expecting something.

The tide was running, so it took only twenty minutes to reach the mouth of the harbor. Kaiser headed toward the marina, but Francesca stopped him. "Dock at the old north wharf," she said, her voice brittle. "Do you know where it is?"

He nodded. "But it's falling down," he said. "I don't think it's safe to walk on."

"Just do as I say."

Again Kaiser bristled at her tone. He was about to tell her off when she reached out suddenly and touched his arm. He looked over and again, beyond the mask, saw such silent pleading that he was disarmed. "Whatever you say," he responded.

She didn't wait for him to help them out of the boat. The moment he touched the edge of the ancient dock, she scrambled up, pulling Hildy after her. Christian, still clutching his fish, began to follow, but she stopped him.

"You can't bring that, Christian," she said, trying to be gentle in spite of her frenzy. "We haven't any place for him where we're going."

The child opened his mouth to protest, then closed it, letting the bluefish slide back to the bottom of the boat.

"Don't worry, Christian," Kaiser said. "I'll take care of him for you. Cross my heart."

Kaiser could see the rotten dock sway as the three moved toward dry ground, and his breath caught in his throat as Francesca Ferrare, holding her two children tight by the hands, began to run. She was almost on shore when, in the midst of her headlong flight, something made her stop dead in her tracks. It was Julian Ferrare.

For a minute Kaiser thought she was going to turn back. Instead she dropped her children's hands and slowly began to walk toward her husband. "How wonderful that you've found us," Kaiser heard her say. "We thought we'd lost you. Didn't we, Hildy?"

And together, without so much as a backward glance at Kaiser, the four moved on up to the road, where Julian had a car waiting.

Kaiser watched, incredulous, as Julian and his family

drove away. The more he saw of the Ferrares, the more bizarre their actions seemed. What in hell had Francesca Ferrare been doing on Esther Island, when last night it seemed she hadn't even known where it was? And why had she been so frantic to get away from the place? Kaiser shook his head and turned the motorboat back down toward the inner harbor. He was almost to the marina when something suddenly occurred to him. Clearly, the last person in the world Francesca Ferrare had expected to see on the old wharf was Julian. But why? Could it possibly have been Julian from whom she was running?

"There have to be some answers somewhere," he muttered to himself. "And I don't care if it isn't any of my business. I'm going to look until I find some."

9

Hildy lay on her back on the attic floor and looked up through the leaded windowpanes. The old bubbled glass made everything look wavy and slightly distorted, as if the world outside were underwater. As she moved her head from side to side the trees stretched and twisted through the imperfections. If she moved her head back, they grew long and thin; forward, they squashed down into shapeless lumps.

Normally this was enough to take her mind off her troubles, but not today. She could hear the faint sound of Christian practicing his lessons over and over again. She stuck her fingers in her ears. He'd been at it for hours now, ever since they came back from the island. She wondered how much longer Julian was going to make him play, and prayed it would end soon.

She had her ears blocked so tightly that she didn't hear her brother until he snuggled up beside her on the attic floor. "Christian," she said, sitting up. "Thank goodness. Are you finished?"

Christian didn't speak.

"Was Julian angry?" Hildy asked in a low voice.

Christian nodded, the tears sliding silently down his cheeks.

Hildy pulled him close and rocked him. "Mama would

have helped if she could have," she whispered, hoping it would be some small comfort. Hildy had never seen her mother as upset as she'd been when Julian brought them home. She'd gone to her room and no one had seen her since, but Hildy had heard her crying.

And then there was Christian. She felt a wave of nausea wash over her as she visualized her father standing beside the piano, his baton in his hand, banging out the time like a human metronome while poor Christian tried frantically to strike the right notes. Sometimes, she knew, Julian brought his baton down with a terrible whistling sound only inches from Christian's fingers if he made the smallest mistake.

She forced herself to look at Christian's hands. Never after one of these sessions had she seen any evidence that her father had actually hit Christian. Still, she had to look. She picked up one of his hands and let her breath out slowly. She could see no marks, but she knew that inside her brother there were scars that would never heal, and she hated her father for it. She would never be able to understand his cruelty, or forgive him for it. She didn't even know anymore if she loved him.

"Would you like to go downstairs and look in my treasure box?" she asked. Christian loved Hildy's treasure box. It was where she kept all her most valued possessions: a bit of lace, a piece of purple glass, an 1892 silver dollar, a baby tooth, a lock of her own hair. Everything she'd ever thought worth saving was in that box.

Christian shook his head.

Hildy was shocked. When Christian didn't want to look in the treasure box, he was really upset. She tried another tack. "How was your fishing trip?"

At first she didn't think he'd heard, but then he lifted his head and looked up at her, his dark eyes filled with tears. "I didn't get to bring my fish home."

"It's okay, Christian. Mr. Kaiser promised he'd take care of it for you, and I know he will."

"How come you and Mama were out there?" Christian asked, suddenly remembering who had been responsible for the ruined afternoon.

"We went on a picnic," Hildy said, trying to keep her voice calm. "We were about to eat, but then Mama said she was cold. She sent Julian back to the boat to get her sweater, and as soon as he was out of sight she grabbed me by the hand and we went running through the dunes and down to the beach."

"Did you and Mama know we were there?"

Hildy shook her head. "I didn't, but Mama must have. She seemed to know exactly where she was going." Hildy fell silent. Then in a hushed tone that couldn't hide how upset she was, she said, "Christian, I think we were running away again."

He sat up and looked at her with round eyes. "Again? But why? Why do we keep running away?"

Hildy thought she shouldn't be telling her brother her worst fears. The last time she wasn't sure why they'd done it, but this time she was: They had run to get away from Julian. But he'd caught them. "You are pathetic, Francesca," he'd said in his blackest voice. "Did you really imagine that you could beat me back to the harbor in that pathetic excuse for a boat?" Mama hadn't answered, but Hildy felt her shaking. "And even if you had, just where, pray tell, did you think you could hide?"

Hildy realized Christian was staring at her, so she made herself laugh. "Good grief," she said, "I'm almost as silly as you are. I don't know what I'm talking about." But she didn't feel silly. She felt frightened. From below she could hear the powerful sound of her father at the piano, but the music didn't comfort her. He was playing now as he often did, only for himself, but at times like these Hildy found no magic in the sound. It simply made her more afraid.

* * *

Elise sat in the corner of the room and listened to the piano sounds. She was almost sure it was Julian playing, and that she was in his house. Asked her greatest wish at times like these, and Elise would have answered with one word: sanity. To recognize the reality from the fantasy. Elise knew the word *insane*, and knew what it meant. But knowing didn't change it, didn't cure it, didn't make it any the less hellish.

At least she never saw things that really weren't there, she thought. At the sanitarium she'd known people who hallucinated—like old Mrs. Harding, who thought that trees were space invaders, and Elise had always felt smugly superior to people like her.

But Dr. Bryson had told her that many of her own perceptions, if not imagined, were distorted. And Elise had known that he was right. It was why she now concentrated so hard on small, seemingly inconsequential matters. It was why she needed Coriander to interpret for her. And most of all it was why she needed all of her magical forces—to help create a small corner of order in a world of total chaos.

It had taken Elise most of her life to lay down a few incontrovertible truths: Julian was good. Julian was salvation. Anything that told her otherwise was a wicked delusion. "But how do you know that?" one doctor had asked her years and years ago. "Because I do," she had answered. The doctor had pressed. How did she know that Julian was good? She had searched and searched for an answer. "Because he has dark hair," she had said finally. She hadn't really meant it, she'd only said it to make the doctor stop confusing her. But once said, it had taken hold in her mind. It began to make perfect sense. Every evil in her life had come hidden behind a cloud of golden hair. But Julian had dark hair, and in the labyrinthine tangle of her own mind, this had become an absolute guideline by which to measure reality.

Elise stood up and walked across the room, careful not to

interrupt Julian. (If indeed it really was Julian sitting there at the piano. But how could she know for sure?) She felt the slippery edge of fear touch her, but pushed it back. Just before she reached the place where the window seemed to be, she stopped, closed her eyes, and listened. Everyone was quiet. Not even Coriander was rumbling. She relaxed a bit.

She knew that Francesca was hiding. Julian had been furious when they had arrived home from their picnic, and Francesca had gone straight to her room, locking the door behind her. But she also knew that distance couldn't keep Francesca from screaming insults at her, since Francesca had the ability to project her thoughts without being present. But for some reason, Francesca was leaving her alone today.

Elise leaned against the wall, eyes still closed, and thought about it. Only two people had ever been able to talk to Elise without actually being there—both golden-haired demons. One was Francesca, and the other had been Anna, Elise's stepmother. Elise made herself think about Anna. Sometimes, no matter how painful, remembering the past helped her cope with the present. Sometimes her memories provided her with clues that helped her answer her most frightening questions. She took a deep breath and forced herself to think about the first time she ever saw Anna.

Elise was six years old and she cried all the time. It wasn't just because of the terrible things that lived in her closet. It was because her mother had gone away forever, and a deep sadness drained all the color from the earth. In school the teacher was always scolding her because she was crying, even when she knew she wasn't.

But today everything was fine because Julian was coming home from boarding school for a visit. The world was growing out of its brown and white outline and expanding with all the colors of the rainbow. It made up for the pain her father was causing her.

She walked home from school as quickly as she could, though the sharpness of the gravel on her bare feet was sending bolts of pain up her legs. She carried her new shoes and stockings in her hand. She hadn't bothered to tell her father that the shoes were so ill-fitting that her heels were raw and festering, because she was sure he knew. This was just some sort of punishment for something terrible that she'd done.

She stopped to stare at a daffodil, turned yellow and full now, where this morning it had been brown and flat. She could hear her voices, but they were gentle, speaking today with soft accents which let Elise know they were pleased. They had even been so kind as to let her read in school, and Mrs. Blackstone had been very surprised at her progress. Elise had formed her letters perfectly. Most times it was impossible because they kept changing shape under her crayon, but today they had been still and very well-behaved. Elise had even gone to the girls' bathroom without incident. And all because Julian was coming home. Julian, her protector, her salvation, the only person who understood.

She hurried a little faster, wincing with each step but determined to get home in time to check Julian's room before he got there. Elise spent most of her time at home cleaning Julian's room, seeing to it that nothing was ever out of place, working her magic charms which would keep him safe forever.

Just before the walk that led to her house, she stopped to put on her shoes and stockings. Then, with each step an exquisite torment, she went up the walk and into the house. "Julian," she called. No answer. Good. There was still time to fix his room.

She paused outside the door, clicking her heels five times. Five was the luckiest number of all. That would begin the spell. She crossed to the window above his bed and on tiptoe touched every inch of its wooden frame. That was to help keep the evil spirits out, the ones that had taken her mother away, the ones that lived under Elise's bed.

The voices were still soft in her head, but they were becoming agitated. She wasn't sure what was upsetting them, but it frightened her. She made herself look hard at the corner of Julian's mirror. "I must think about my brother," Elise said aloud. "I must think about Julian." But it was too late because the rushing was coming, carrying with it the all too familiar darkness. But just as she was about to fall, a sound came that lifted her up and carried her back into the light. "Little 'Lise," Julian called, "whatever are you up to hiding there in the corner?"

He crossed to where she was crouching and lifted her gently to her feet. "Come now. Stop crying and give your brother a big hug."

"Julian," she whispered through her tears.

"It's all right," he said, knowing, holding her close. "I'm here."

She watched the darkness roll back and felt the color returning to the world. Although she couldn't make the words yet, she held onto him until she couldn't hear the rushing anymore. Then she looked up at him, and for the first time realized that something was wrong with her. Really wrong. She didn't know what, but she knew that other children didn't have the trouble she had making words. And they didn't have voices.

She had tried to tell her teacher about the voices once, and her teacher had sent her to sit in the corner. Later, when Elise had finally been allowed to go to the bathroom, it was too late—she'd already soiled herself. The teacher sent her home, and Papa had been furious. She tried to tell him what had happened, but the words were squirrels that hid in the treetops. She didn't know what Papa had done then, because she'd gone away and hadn't come back for a long, long time.

All these things made Elise know that something was wrong, something Julian would help her with.

"Hush, Elise," he said. "You're perfectly fine. I'll take care of you." And she believed him.

For the rest of the day she stayed in the safety of Julian's shadow, for he was her salvation, and by the time her father came home she felt almost out of danger. She jumped to her feet and curtseyed as she'd been taught, but her father didn't seem to see her. Instead he turned back toward the door. "Children," he said, "I want you to meet someone very special."

Elise had not been watching the door. Perhaps if she had, her guard would not have been down and she could have cast a spell to stop it. But she'd been looking at Julian when the lady came through the door, all pale and golden and perfect. She was dressed in beautiful silken clothes and had hair the color of the sun.

The lady opened her perfect mouth and Elise heard her speak, a gurgling sound like water running. "Hello, Julian. Hello, Elise," she said. "I'm so happy to meet you."

"Children," her father said, "I want you to meet Anna, your new mother."

Elise was horrified. How could Papa say something so terrible? Her mother had had dark, soft, curling hair. How had this golden-haired demon tricked him into believing that she was their mother? She heard the rushing, and heard Julian's voice, but this time not even Julian could save her.

Elise opened her eyes with a snap and felt a tremendous rush of relief to realize she was standing in the music room looking out the window at Mr. Kaiser's hedge. Julian—it really was Julian—still played. There was no other sound. Time crept by, second by second, sluglike, but she was grateful. She'd learned to cling to each moment of awareness.

When Julian had first come to get her at the clinic—How long ago? Was it only two months?—she'd been apprehensive. At the clinic they knew what she needed. She didn't have to remember how to help herself. When she cried out, they knew what to do. They understood about the confusion, and about the pit.

It had taken Elise a long time to graduate from the sanitarium to the clinic—almost eleven years, most of which she'd spent in and out of darkness. But she had been determined to get out because as long as she remained inside the sanitarium, she knew they would never let Julian in to see her. Dr. Bryson had said Julian was free to come anytime he wanted, but Elise had known better. They were keeping him away. Why else had he never come to see her?

She had worked hard—no one would ever know just how hard—and had learned to knit, to make clay pots, and most important, to recognize the colors on her medicine bottles. Dr. Bryson had said she was one of the most determined patients he'd ever treated. But still, for every small victory Elise paid an immeasurable price. And it had taken her eleven years.

Elise had known what she was working for—to be with Julian again. The out-patient clinic had been the last step. She was convinced that if she made it that far, Julian would come to bring her home. Whenever she'd been sent away before, Julian had always come for her. And she'd been right. On that glorious day two months ago, Julian had come. But instead of taking her back to New York, he took her to their grandmother's house in Nantucket.

At first Dr. Bryson had been reluctant to let her go so far away, but he finally agreed, deciding it might be good for her to try to live in the world again. On an island life would be calm and not too stressful, he'd said; and besides, Dr. Bryson knew how much she loved Julian.

Her doctor knew about Coriander too. But he didn't know about Francesca, didn't know it was Francesca who had sent her to the sanitarium eleven years ago; Francesca who wanted to keep her from Julian, Francesca who was her mortal enemy. Elise knew that if she told him, he would never have let her live on Nantucket.

Elise had worked hard to keep calm when Julian had brought her here two months ago. He said that she was to be a companion to Francesca, a confidante. But how could she be when she knew that Francesca's only wish was to send her back to the sanitarium? Her sister-in-law never said as much, but Elise knew she was planning it— someday, when Julian's back was turned. That's why she gave Francesca the Thorazine: It made Francesca sleep, so she couldn't send her away.

Three times now she'd slipped the contents of her own pills into Francesca's tea. But now Elise was worried. This last time, Francesca had seemed reluctant to drink what she'd prepared, preferring to make her own tea. *She suspects*, Coriander said.

Elise's hand flew to her throat. Could it be true? And then there was Christian. She didn't know what to do about him. A wicked child from the womb of her mortal enemy. Golden-haired, like all the others who had ever tormented her. Once she had tried to cut the color from his head, hoping it would take away his power, but she'd failed. He woke up and then hid from her. Somehow she would have to find the courage to try again—for Julian's sake, and for herself.

Elise sucked in her breath. She wouldn't be afraid. Someday she would do to Christian what she'd done so many years ago to that other golden-haired child. The one that had belonged to Anna . . .

Eleven-year-old Elise skipped down the hall, then dropped her jump rope in the doorway and stared, the hot pain in her throat growing like a tumor. They had destroyed Julian's room, taken all his furniture away and replaced it with baby things.

Her father and stepmother were standing together by Julian's window, and Anna was holding the golden-haired infant in her arms. "We'll put the cradle here," Anna was saying, "so our child can grow strong in the sun." She was smiling, but inside, Elise knew that Anna was mocking her. She was going to bring her evil son into this room to take Julian's place. "Come here, Elise," Anna said. "What do you think, dear?"

Elise crossed the room and stood silently beside them. She looked at the mother and child with her eyes, but inside she had moved away without their knowing. Coriander was telling her what to do with her face to make it seem normal. He would protect her until she could understand what was happening and decide how to fight back.

Anna's mouth was moving but Elise couldn't tell what the words were. They skipped like stones across water. It didn't matter. They would only be more of the same hateful lies.

Elise looked down at her hands and stared. Her fingers were blue. It was summer, but her fingers were blue. She held them up to her face. She heard her father say something about "Elise being impossible to deal with," and she wondered who he was talking about. She heard her stepmother's voice gurgling about "patience" and "try to understand" and "the doctor said," but she could make no sense of it. What she did make sense of was her father's next statement: "I think we ought to send her to Oxnam." Elise knew what Oxnam was. The wicked Anna had sent her there before. It was a prison where they tortured you with ice water and bolts of lightning. She watched her fingers turn from blue to black, and then she went away, but she didn't know where.

Several days later, she returned from the pit just long enough to throw Anna's golden-haired baby boy down the open stairwell to his death.

10

Kaiser sat on the back steps in the late afternoon sun, mending John's fishing net, making himself think about Toby. He had already given up work on his book, finding it impossible to concentrate on Soviet military maneuvers. Now he was finding it equally difficult to think about his ex-wife.

The whole divorce seemed light-years behind him. He'd come out to Nantucket to be alone, if only for a few days, so he could think. But now, after five days, he didn't care if he never thought about Toby again. "Your marriage is over," he said out loud. "You screwed up, but you never really loved her." He listened to the words to see how they felt, but he couldn't tell—the music from across the way was too deafening.

Kaiser decided all at once that it wasn't simply Julian Ferrare that he disliked, it was his music as well. Earlier he'd listened to poor Christian laboring over the same sets of scales and had felt such anger that it had been a struggle for him not to go next door and stop the torture.

Emma Gledhill's words had come back to him. "Who am I to judge what other people do with their children?" she'd said at the Ferrare party. Kaiser made a mental note to call the Gledhills in order to question them on the subject. Making a child practice his piano lessons scarcely qualified as child abuse, he thought, but he felt that Julian was exceeding acceptable limits with his son. And then there was Christian's exposure to the eccentricities of Elise Ferrare. As far as Kaiser was concerned, Julian Ferrare might be a world famous pianist, but as a parent he stank.

Kaiser wondered what Christian was doing now that he had been excused from the keyboard, and he wondered what kind of reception he would receive if he took Christian's bluefish—now frozen solid in Mrs. Minstrell's freezer—over to him. He suspected that Julian might just be in a foul enough mood to tell him what to do with it, so Kaiser decided to leave well enough alone, at least for the time being.

He finished mending the net and held it up, trying to decide whether the old thing had been worth the effort, when Mrs. Minstrell came to the back door. "Telephone for you, Patrick," she said. "Emma Gledhill. They want you to join them for dinner at the club."

Kaiser was delighted. An informative evening with the Gledhills would be timely indeed, so he made plans to meet them at seven.

Sam and Emma Gledhill had been married to each other thirty-five years, a feat that made them celebrities of a sort. Sam had been in the diplomatic service ever since Kaiser could remember, and he looked every bit the part. He was a quiet, aristocratic man with a straightness to his spine that reflected a scrupulous honesty. In his lifetime Sam Gledhill had never been accused of being brilliant, but his reputation for being an honest man made him a treasure. Kaiser respected him, but more than that, he liked him.

He liked Emma almost as well. She was a short, thin firecracker of a woman, as full of passion and energy at sixty as she'd been at thirty, except that now the softness of youth had eroded away, leaving her with a sharpness around the edges.

Emma wasted no time asking about Toby, and Kaiser realized that he no longer felt a compulsion to explain what had happened—not to Sam and Emma, but more important, not to himself. His marriage had been a mistake. Now it was over. Period. End of report.

He let out a long breath. "I was an ass, Emma. Simple as that."

"Nonsense," Emma said. "Toby must have had a mental lapse. Henry Crandall? Unbelievable. We've known Henry for years. Through the Chase Bank, you know, and I don't believe in all that time I have ever heard him say anything worth remembering."

Sam changed the subject. "I don't know why they insist on adding these damned sesame seeds to the salad. Ruin perfectly good lettuce."

"He says the same thing everytime we come here," Emma said to Kaiser. "Why don't you simply tell them to leave them off?" she said to her husband. "You know you hate them."

"You're supposed to remind me."

Emma patted his hand. "I will, dear. The next time." She turned back to Kaiser. "Tell me, how did you enjoy your evening with the Ferrares?"

"Strange family," he said. "What do you know about them?"

"The better question is, What doesn't she know about them?" Sam said. "Emma knows all there is to know on this island, and she'll love telling it, too, if you have several hundred years to listen."

"You make it sound as if I were a gossipy old bitch."

"Not old, my dear. Not old," her husband said, chuckling at his own wit.

His wife chose to ignore him. "The evening is young, Kaiser. Where would you like me to begin?"

"How long have you known them?"

"We've known Julian for years, but Francesca only since their marriage," Emma said. "That was one of the first surprises. Nobody ever imagined that Julian Ferrare would marry. After all, he was forty-seven when he met Francesca, and she no more than nineteen. It was a real fairytale courtship, the kind everyone loves to talk about. It seems she was the protégée of one of Julian's old piano teachers in Helsinki, and when he first heard her play he was smitten."

"She plays the piano too?"

Emma nodded emphatically. "She won any number of international prizes, including the Liszt, if I remember correctly. She was well on her way to becoming a major artist. But she gave it all up when she married Julian. So you can see, Francesca Ferrare is not your ordinary girl." She looked at Kaiser. "Not to mention the fact that she is rather attractive."

Kaiser smiled. "I suppose, if you like utterly gorgeous women."

"Enough said about that," Emma replied. "In any case, I got to know her quite well back in New York. We both belonged to the Opera Guild. She was a delight to be around—sweet, energetic, and above all, a tireless worker. You know how hard it is to find volunteers these days, but Francesca never said no to anyone. And she was a superb hostess in the bargain. Lord knows, married to Julian, there was plenty of opportunity to test her mettle, but she always seemed to land on her feet." Emma paused to take a sip of wine, then added, "Come to think of it, if I hadn't liked Francesca so much, she would have made me sick, she was that perfect.

"When the children came along, nothing was ever too much trouble for her where they were concerned. A devoted mother. Without slobbering over them, if you understand me."

"She tried to kill them," Sam said quietly.

Emma frowned. "She was sick with grief, Sam. You know that."

"Sick with something," he agreed. "But who knows what it was?"

"That's the part of the story I'm interested in," Kaiser said. "How did this fairy-tale couple transform itself into something straight out of a Thomas Hardy novel?"

"You know about Dr. Stahlberg's death, of course," Emma said.

"I know that he had a heart attack. Beyond that, not much."

"Nothing much that anybody knows about that," Sam said. "One day he was on a flight from Helsinki, the next he was dead, and the next Francesca Ferrare was jumping off the Nantucket ferryboat."

There was a lull in the conversation then, as if Sam had summed up all that was known about the Ferrares in one sentence.

Kaiser broke the silence. "And before that? Were they happy?"

Emma shrugged. "Certainly Francesca and Julian seemed to be." She frowned. "We've never approved of the way he treats that little boy. She does her best to shield him, but who knows what effect Julian's cruelty has had on him? Such a sweet child too."

"And where does the strange-eyed Elise fit into the picture?"

"Julian's sister? He brought her here to take care of Francesca," Emma said. "After Francesca tried to kill herself and the children."

"The blind leading the cripples, if you ask me," Sam muttered.

"The lady does seem to have a problem," Kaiser said.

"A problem?" Sam laughed. "That is being too kind."

"What is her role supposed to be?" Kaiser asked.

"According to Julian," Emma replied, "she's a companion—to take care of Francesca when he's away, help her with Christian, and keep her out of trouble."

"And does she do all those things?" Kaiser asked.

Emma shrugged. "I can't see how she could be of any help where Christian is concerned. She doesn't even seem to like him. But she does keep people away from the house when Julian is out of town, I know that. If you don't believe me, just pay a call on the Ferrares when he's away. I promise you, you won't get past the front door."

Sam was frowning. "And even if you do see Francesca, you might as well not have bothered. The last few times Julian went off-island, Francesca disappeared from sight. The few people who did see her said she was a zombie."

"Drugs?"

Sam shrugged. "It looks like it. What's odd is that when Julian is around, Francesca is as straight as an arrow. Cold, but certainly not spaced out."

"She's not having a nervous breakdown either," Emma said. "You can't turn a nervous breakdown on and off."

"Who knows," Sam said, "maybe they have her on some kind of sedative when Julian is away to keep her under control. Then again, maybe she just can't stand life without him," Sam added, tongue-in-cheek. "You've seen the two together so you know that's hardly possible. In any case it's obvious that at times she takes more than sugar in her tea."

"Could it be possible that somehow she blames Julian for her stepfather's death?" Kaiser asked.

"I don't see how she could." Sam shook his head. "According to all reports Julian wasn't even on the island when Dr. Stahlberg had his attack. In fact Julian told me himself that he hadn't seen the man for years." He shrugged. "But then who am I to say what Francesca thinks? Who knows what anyone thinks when they go off the deep end?"

"I saw Francesca the day before it happened," Emma

reflected. "She seemed perfectly normal. Since then I haven't spoken to her except for party talk. Nobody does. She doesn't see any of the people she became friendly with during the summer, and she doesn't seem to want to. Francesca is a different person now, Kaiser. She's unapproachable, cold . . . and I might add that I think it's disgraceful the way she treats Julian. If she is so unhappy with her marriage, for whatever reason, why doesn't she just do the civilized thing and get a divorce?"

"Good question," Sam said. "It would seem to be the sensible solution to an intolerable situation." He turned to his wife. "In fact, why don't you ask Francesca about it? She just walked in the door."

Kaiser turned just in time to see Julian, Francesca, and Hildy Ferrare cross to a table in the back of the dining room. He had a single uncomfortable thought when he saw them: Have they left Christian alone with Elise?

Hildy followed behind Julian and her mother, wishing she hadn't been made to come, that she could have stayed with Christian. He seemed so scared, and no matter how hard she tried to convince him otherwise, he was positive that Elise was going to get him.

Hildy sat down and looked hard at her brand-new black patent leather shoes. Julian had bought them for her in Europe. Hildy had always dreamed of owning a pair of shoes like these, so why wasn't she thrilled? She didn't know, but it made her want to cry.

Julian handed her the menu, smiling. He was in one of his gay moods. "Whatever you want, darling," he said. "Nothing is too good for my beautiful, brilliant girl."

"I'm not very hungry, thank you," Hildy said quietly, and heard her mother take a deep breath.

"You haven't had anything to eat all day, Hildy," Francesca said, concerned.

"They do have potato skins with bacon, Mama," she said, not caring for the moment whether Julian approved of her use of the word *Mama* or not. She loved her mother and knew she was upset. "We could share an order."

"Nonsense," Julian said. "You can have one all to yourself."

"I'd rather share with Mama," she said quickly. "If that's all right with you."

His expression did not change. He still smiled. "I'll tell you what. I'm going to order for all of us. A meal fit for a royal family. What do you think, my love?" he asked Francesca.

Hildy saw her mother wince. "Don't bother to order anything for me," she said. "We're here because you wanted to come."

"I could hardly have left you behind, my dear," Julian said evenly. But there was a hint of something left unspoken, and Hildy wondered if it had to do with what had happened on Esther Island. She still didn't know why they had run off without Julian. "Besides," her father was saying, "Elise wasn't feeling well, so I thought I'd give her a rest. I asked the maid to stay with Christian until we got home, so Elise could go to bed."

Hildy breathed a sigh of relief. If Elise had gone to bed, that meant Christian would be all right.

"What do you mean, Elise wasn't feeling well?" Francesca said sharply.

"She was tired, that's all."

"Are you sure?" Hildy could hear alarm in her mother's voice. Francesca started to say something else, then stopped, seeing her daughter's startled expression.

"Is there something wrong with Elise?" Hildy asked, looking first at her mother, then at Julian. She couldn't forget what she had read in the encyclopedia about schizophrenia.

"Nothing at all," Julian said. "At least nothing a good

night's sleep won't fix. You know what a worrier she is. Little things bother her, and we have to understand that."

Hildy had a sudden urge to tell them that Christian was terrified of Elise, but she held her tongue. It would only change Julian's mood, make those dark shadows drift behind his eyes. Worse, it would upset Mama even more. Hildy wished she was home with Christian.

They ate their dinner in silence, except for an occasional offering from Julian. He was trying so hard to be charming, but it made no difference. Her mother sat like a statue, scarcely eating, and speaking only to Hildy to coax her to finish her supper.

The man at the piano was playing something old-fashioned, and suddenly Julian leaned across the table and asked Francesca to dance.

"Don't make me sick," her mother snapped, and Hildy felt like crying. Her mother and father had always loved to dance. Before.

Julian was silent for a minute, then turned to Hildy. His voice was quiet when he spoke, but still playful. "Would you care to join this old man on the dance floor, my darling?" he asked. "You can try out your beautiful new shoes."

Hildy wasn't sure what to do, but before she could answer, her father had her by the hand and was leading her toward the piano.

"Now's your chance," Emma said to Kaiser. "You wanted to talk to Francesca alone. Well, she's alone."

"You've had too much to drink, Emma," Sam said, but before his wife had a chance to retort, Kaiser was on his feet and across the room to the table where Francesca sat alone in stony silence, her eyes riveted to the spot where her husband danced with her daughter.

"May I speak with you?" Kaiser said as he came up to her table. "Just for a minute?"

She looked startled, then shrugged.

"Would you care to tell me what that business was all about this afternoon?"

"It was simple, really," she said, too smoothly. "So foolish. Our boat drifted away. I never was any good at tying knots."

"Then your husband wasn't with you?"

"No," she said. "Just the two of us."

"Well, then, I'm happy I was there to be of some assistance," Kaiser said. "Though to tell the truth, I thought you were really in trouble."

She laughed, but Kaiser knew she wasn't laughing at anything funny. "We Ferrares are always in trouble, Mr. Kaiser. It hovers over our heads like a dark rain cloud, even when everywhere else in the world the sun is shining."

Kaiser decided to put into words what he had been feeling all day. "I would like to help," he said with a directness that made her look up. Her face was hidden in shadow, but he had the feeling she was trying to read his thoughts, to see if he meant what he'd said. "If you ever need anything . . ."

She looked down at her hands. "That's very kind of you, Mr. Kaiser," she said quietly, "but I'm afraid there's nothing anyone can do."

Kaiser was about to remind her that nothing was impossible when Julian Ferrare and Hildy returned to the table. Kaiser held out his hand to Julian. "Nice to see you again," he said.

The man made no move to shake hands. He stood where he was, a strange stillness on his face.

Kaiser dropped his hand to his side, surprised but not rattled by the man's rudeness. The perfect gentleman of last evening was nowhere to be seen. "Would you care to join us for a drink?" Kaiser said, gesturing toward the table where Sam and Emma sat gawking.

Julian Ferrare still didn't move. "I don't know what your business is with my wife and children," he said with such hostility that Kaiser was dumbfounded. "But I warn you, Mr. Kaiser, keep clear."

Kaiser raised his eyebrows and looked from Julian to Francesca, then down at Hildy. "I'm not quite sure I know what you're talking about," he said evenly. "Perhaps someone can enlighten me?"

"He didn't know we were on the island, Julian," Hildy jumped in, her voice shaking. "He only gave us a ride back to town because we asked him."

"Yes, Julian," Francesca said pleasantly. "You see, our boat drifted away and we were stranded, but Mr. Kaiser was kind enough to offer his help."

Kaiser caught the startled look on Hildy's face, and he knew that Francesca had just lied. But why? Had Julian, in fact, been on the island? Was he the one Francesca had been running from?

Julian Ferrare moved quickly to recover his balance. He laughed and put an arm around Kaiser's shoulders. "Can't blame me for worrying, can you, Kaiser? It isn't every man who is fortunate enough to have a wife as lovely as my Francesca. And how kind of you to invite us to join you. Of course we will, won't we, my dear?"

"Whatever you say, Julian," she replied.

11

Elise had a dream once. It was Christmas and she was the infant Jesus, all golden and loved in her mother's arms. Only it wasn't her mother. It was her father, his face adoring, his dark eyes shining. And everyone had gathered around to worship the beloved child on their knees. But when she opened her eyes, they weren't praying, they were laughing, and she wondered what she'd done to seem so ridiculous. Elise had had her share of nightmares in her life, some while she was wide awake and some were so frightening that she vomited, but none of them ever made her feel as worthless as her Christmas dream.

She lay in bed and listened, hearing nothing, not even Coriander. Julian had given her a heavy dose of medication last night before he left, enough to put a normal person in a coma. She had slept. But now it was morning and she had to get up. That's what morning meant: get up. Night meant go to bed, even if you didn't sleep. She felt most of the time as if she were a train on a track, coming, going, turning, stopping, but never feeling anything. Those were the good times. The bad times were when she could feel. Feeling meant fear.

She got out of bed and dressed slowly, taking time to concentrate on each article of clothing. That had been one of the signs of her illness, neglecting her personal hygiene.

She felt a certain sense of accomplishment each day when she went downstairs and no one seemed startled by her appearance. Nevertheless, the struggle to keep in touch with the world kept her exhausted.

Elise examined herself in the mirror, although she wasn't sure exactly what she was looking for. She smoothed her hair back, wondering if her braid was neat enough or whether Julian would tell her to fix it. Julian often told her when something was wrong, but he was never unkind. Not like her father.

She closed herself off from the morning, remembering the day her father brought her home from Oxnam. A hospital, that's what he had called it, but it wasn't a regular hospital. It was a hospital for lunatics. He sent her there after she'd destroyed Anna's baby, and two years later he brought her home to attend Anna's funeral.

Standing there beside the coffin, looking down at the beautiful, white face all framed in its golden hair, Elise had suddenly heard all the windows in the house fly open, and the air had blown through fresh and clean.

But then something had happened that Elise never forgot. "You killed Anna," her father had said to her. "As sure as if you had cut out her heart. When you murdered our child, you destroyed her will to live."

Elise had been powerless to speak. She knew she'd killed the child, but in her wildest dreams never imagined that in doing so she would be rid of Anna as well. Now Anna was dead, and she had killed her. Father said so. There would be no more golden-haired demons in her life. Now she would be able to come home and take care of him the way she'd always wanted to. Finally feeling safe, she'd made herself smile at the corpse. *Father will learn to love me again,* she'd thought. *He'll never send me away now that she's dead.*

But her father had not loved her. He had sent her back to the hospital as soon as the funeral was over. She'd cried, promised to be good, even cut off all of her own dark, dirty hair and put on one of her stepmother's golden wigs which she found hidden way up in the top of the closet. But it had all been for nothing. Instead of softening his heart, instead of making him love her, she'd simply driven her father into a black rage. He had ripped the wig from her head and called her the worst kinds of names. She had no doubt that had it not been for Julian, her own father would have killed her.

Julian had taken time off from his studies at the conservatory to drive her back to Oxnam. "Welcome back, Elise," Dr. Cutter had said.

Elise wondered if he could hear the rushing behind her. *Take care, take care,* said Coriander.

"Was it very difficult?" the doctor asked.

She nodded. Everything was difficult.

"Was I wrong in allowing you to go? So you could see for yourself that your stepmother was dead?"

She considered that for a minute. At least the doctor hadn't lied to her. Anna was indeed dead. "I saw," she said.

"Did it help?"

Elise felt confused. It helped because now that Anna was gone, she was safe. She had no reason to fear that her stepmother would send her away, not ever again. And yet here she was, back in a hospital. But why? "Because my father hates me," she said to herself, and was horrified to see that Dr. Cutter had heard. She jerked back.

"He doesn't hate you, Elise. He just doesn't understand."

Understand what? she wondered, and the hard laughter came up in her throat. She felt a stab of anger, then fear, as she watched Dr. Cutter shrink away. Don't go, she screamed, falling, but it was too late. She could see him running toward her, but it was too late.

* * *

Strange, she thought as she tried to straighten the bed covers. Strange how the important things in her life had all been measured by death. She held up her right hand to count on her fingers. First her mother's. Then the death of Anna's wicked baby. Her middle finger was reserved for Anna herself. And the ring finger? She closed her eyes, feeling the familiar wave of sickness. Ring finger was for her father.

When she was seventeen her father died. Julian had brought her home from Oxnam for the funeral, but afterward didn't send her back. Her doctor had told him that with proper medication she should be capable of taking care of herself. As long as she was not subjected to any kind of stress.

Stress and fear, Elise thought. Her worst enemies. The doctors had warned her time and again about what they could do to her. Stress caused words to change into all kinds of bizarre creatures, so that she could neither speak nor write. It drained all color from the world. It robbed her of the ability to distinguish between the important things in life and the absurd. That was why sometimes she laughed when she should be crying, why she spoke out when everyone around her was silent. And fear had the power to throw her into the pit, where she could neither see nor hear, where all memory ceased to exist.

Julian had promised the doctors that Elise would lead a quiet, solitary life with him, and they had agreed to let her try it on a temporary basis. So she had come home to New York City, to live with Julian in their father's house on East Sixty-fourth Street, the house where she'd been born, the only home she'd ever known. And from then on she had been content. Julian was away on tour a good deal of the time, and although Elise was lonely, she was less confused when left alone. There were two servants in residence, living on the fourth floor. They did most of the work—

things Elise would have found difficult, like shopping and paying bills—and they left her strictly alone.

For the most part she stayed inside the house, and on nice days worked in her tiny terraced garden with its high brick walls. She visited the clinic once a week, and the doctors were most pleased with her progress.

The only time she was truly happy, however, was when Julian was at home. Then she would curl up on the sofa, as she had as a child, and listen to him play. It didn't matter whether it was his own creation or someone else's work, he played everything as if it belonged only to him. She could understand why, at only twenty-five, he was considered a genius.

One night as she lay awake waiting for sleep, she heard Julian cry out, and as she often had before, went to give him comfort. It was always the same. First she would hold him in her arms and cradle him against her bosom, and then, after a long time, she would feel his hands moving under her nightdress to her breasts, his lips murmuring appreciation, seeking her small, hard nipples. Then she would call him her darling baby and he would suckle as if he believed her as she shivered, terrified with delight.

The night he cried out, though, something was different. Julian had just come back from a long trip he'd taken with another woman. But he had come back. Alone. Not like Papa. Julian had brought no golden-haired demon to torment her. That meant he did love her beyond all else, Elise thought. And when he finally spread her legs and found the place, she wept with joy, not knowing why he did what he did, not caring. Sex had no meaning to her except that Julian enjoyed it. And when he was doing it to her, he always told her he loved her. Nor did she care if he had other women, as long as he didn't bring them home to their father's house.

For the next twenty years Elise Ferrare lived with her brother just inside the limits of a place called Sanity, content to keep his house, and upon occasion—when he required it—to share his bed. For the next twenty years Elise was happy. Until the day Francesca, with her golden hair, came to send Elise back to Hell.

Elise walked to the window and looked out. Down below she could see Hildy and Christian standing at the edge of the lawn. She glanced down at her fingers. The fifth finger, and appropriately the smallest, was reserved to mark the death of Dr. Stahlberg. She'd never met the man, but it was because of him that Francesca had tried to kill herself and Julian had come to get her at the clinic.

She frowned. She had used up all the fingers of her right hand. Now she would have to begin again with her left. But with whom? *You know,* Coriander whispered. *You know who it has to be.*

"I do not," Elise said. *Yes, you do, Elise. Try to remember.* Elise was confused. Had she forgotten something important? She was always forgetting, so it would be nothing new. She sat down and tried to concentrate. Hearing Christian laugh in the distance, her breath caught in her throat and the fear began to roll up around her like mist from an ancient swamp. *You know what you have to do to stay with Julian,* Coriander said. *You did it before. Destroy the child and you will destroy the mother. Now take your pills. It's the only way you'll be strong enough to succeed.*

Elise pushed the fear away and did as she was told. She examined the color codes on each bottle carefully, to make sure she took exactly what she was supposed to take. She felt a small thrill each time she successfully accomplished her task, since there had been times in the past when she couldn't even distinguish between the colors. *Good work,* Coriander said. Elise was so proud of herself that she decided to go downstairs and make herself a cup of tea.

12

Hildy squinted her eyes to see where Christian was pointing. "See? I told you something was down there."

"What is it?" She could see flashes of movement on the narrow strip of sand below, but whatever it was remained hidden.

"I think it's a walrus." Christian was excited. "Let's go see. Maybe it's hurt."

"There's no walruses around here, silly," Hildy said. Nevertheless she was curious. She looked back toward the house and saw no sign of activity. "We aren't supposed to go down there," she said. "You know what Julian said. The water is filthy."

Christian nodded, considering whether this was something worth risking his father's rage. "But what if it's hurt?" he asked quietly.

Hildy looked down again, and this time saw a flutter of feathers. She frowned. Whatever was down below had been there since the day before yesterday. Christian had seen it on Monday afternoon. That meant it probably couldn't fly. She gave one last glance over her shoulder, then began to scramble down the steep bluff to the narrow beach below. "Be careful," she warned Christian, who was slipping and sliding right behind her. "If you get your

103

clothes dirty, he'll know we've been up to something, and you know what that means."

Christian slowed himself down.

As they approached the spot where they'd seen the movement, Hildy held up a cautioning hand. "Let's go very carefully," she said. "So we won't frighten it."

The two children inched their way through the brush and were almost to the site when, with a frantic beating of wings, a large sea gull rose up right in front of them. It flew a few feet in the air, then jerked back and fell straight down, as if it had flown into a glass wall. It made a few crackling sounds in its throat, then struggled to its feet and stood silently observing the two.

"What's the matter with it?" Christian whispered.

Hildy squatted down, trying to see. The gull was holding its wing at a peculiar angle. "I think it's caught on something."

"Maybe its wing is broken," Christian said.

"It didn't look like it," Hildy said. "It tried to fly, then all of a sudden it just crashed down. Let's see if we can get closer."

"But we'll scare it away."

Hildy snorted. "If it could fly away, we wouldn't have any problem now, would we?" She took a few more steps, but the gull gave a startled shriek, and with a frenzied flapping of wings took to the air again, only to be jerked back like a dog on a chain. This time it lay exhausted.

"It's got a fishing line tangled around its wing," Hildy said. "And the line is caught in the bushes."

"It must be hungry," Christian said. "What are we going to do?"

"We'll go up to the house and get some scissors. If we cut the line, it will be able to fly away."

"But what if the line gets caught on something else?"

"We have to do the best we can, Christian," Hildy said. "We can't worry about what happens later."

Christian nodded. "You get the scissors. I'm going to sneak into the kitchen and get some crackers for him to eat."

Hildy grabbed him by the shirt and held him back. "We have to be very careful that no one sees us, Christian, so go slow." Like most five-year-olds, Christian often fell down when he was in a hurry. Hildy looked back at the gull, still lying on the sand, its beak opening and closing like a fish's mouth, trying to suck in air. From where she stood, Hildy had a clear view of the wing keeping the bird trapped. "Christian," she said, suddenly horrified, "I think he has a fishing lure stuck in him."

Christian almost fell down. "Where? I don't see anything."

"In his wing. See? You can just see the end of it. It's orange."

Christian shivered. "I see it. It must hurt an awful lot."

"We can't just cut the line if he has a lure in him. He still won't be able to fly. Someone has to take it out."

"But how can we? Maybe one of us could hold him still and the other one could yank it out."

Hildy looked hard at her brother. She knew she couldn't hold a gull as big as this one, and if she couldn't, then surely Christian wouldn't be able to either. No, they had to have help, there was no doubt about it.

She considered asking Julian, and immediately discarded the idea. It was his rule that they never come down to the beach. Besides, something told her that Julian wouldn't care at all about a starving gull.

Mama would help, but Julian never let her go anywhere without him anymore.

Hildy didn't even consider Elise.

"How about Mr. Kaiser?" Christian asked suddenly. "I bet he'd know what to do."

"You're right, Christian. He would," Hildy said. "You sneak over and tell him what's happened. I'll keep a watch out for Julian." The sudden mention of their father made her pause. If he ever found out . . . Hildy shivered. Julian got furious over the merest hint of disobedience. She wondered if the wisest course might be to just leave the gull where it was and forget about it.

She glanced back at the bird, still lying where it had fallen. A flock of sea gulls wheeled overhead, swooping low over the jetty then heading free out toward the open ocean, and Hildy made her decision. Some things you just had to take risks for.

Kaiser was enjoying a productive morning at the typewriter, finishing the chapter on Ludvik Svoboda, when Mrs. Minstrell came to the door. "You have a visitor, Patrick," she said. "A small but very anxious one."

Before he had a chance to ask who it was, Christian Ferrare half fell into the room. He was breathless. "Mr. Kaiser, you have to come quick. Hildy and I need your help." He spoke so fast that Kaiser couldn't understand a word.

"Slow down, old boy," he said. "What's the panic?"

"It's a gull," Christian said, and told Kaiser about the bird.

"I'd be glad to help," Kaiser replied, "but there's one minor problem. I'm assuming that for some reason you don't want anyone in your house to know."

Christian nodded vigorously.

"Then how am I supposed to get down there without anyone seeing me? I like sea gulls but I don't like them well enough to get killed trying to climb over your fence."

Christian frowned. Neither he nor Hildy had considered that difficulty.

"There's an old rowboat down below," Mrs. Minstrell said from the doorway. "If it doesn't leak, maybe you could row 'round the end of the jetty."

"How old is old?" Kaiser asked.

"Very old. But your nephews used it last summer, and except for a few slow leaks, it seemed to be seaworthy."

Kaiser looked down at the boy. "What do you think, Christian? If I sink, will you call out the Coast Guard?"

"Whatever you say, Mr. Kaiser," Christian promised. "Just let's help the gull."

Kaiser nodded. "You go home and tell Hildy I'm coming. I'll bring the scissors and something to put on the bird's wound."

Christian nodded and was gone before Kaiser could say anything more.

"Why all the secrecy?" Mrs. Minstrell asked. "Why doesn't he ask his own father to help?"

Kaiser frowned. Even knowing as little as he did about the man, he hadn't had to ask Christian that question. He'd seen the answer last night in the cold, unsmiling eyes of Julian Ferrare.

When Mrs. Minstrell had mentioned a few slow leaks, she was being kind. Kaiser was only just beyond the breakers and the water was already sloshing over the tops of his sneakers. Fortunately the sea was calm, and he was able to stop rowing long enough to bail.

As he rounded the end of the jetty, he could see Hildy and Christian standing at the top of the cliff. He waved, and seeing him, the children started down the steep bank. Wisely, they had taken off their shoes and socks; by the time he was close enough to throw them a line, they were up to their knees in water. Just before the boat ran ashore, Kaiser jumped out, and together the three of them pulled it onto the sand.

It took Kaiser only a matter of minutes to free the sea gull. He simply reached down, held the bird firmly against his leg, and disengaged the hook. The bird was too exhausted to struggle. There had been no blood visible on the wing, but when Kaiser pulled the barbed end out of the gull's flesh, a sudden spurt stained the gray-white feathers a dark crimson. With his free hand Kaiser poured a half bottle of peroxide over the wound then felt carefully for breakage. The wing seemed to be intact.

"Did you bring something to feed him?" he asked, gently smoothing the gull's feathers.

Hildy nodded. She had never seen anyone take care of a wild animal before. And Mr. Kaiser had done it as if he really cared. "We brought some crackers," she said.

"Put them right there on the sand. This old guy may be too weak to fly away, at least for a while." Then he released the bird and stepped back.

The three sat down and watched in silence. The gull didn't move for a long time, seeming not to know that it was free. Finally it took a few hops over to the pile of crackers and ate them all. "Gulls are hardly ever too sick to eat," Kaiser said. "Not only that, but they eat just about anything."

Hildy and Christian were sitting on either side of him, and he felt the boy move closer. "You did that real well, Mr. Kaiser," Christian said. "He didn't struggle a bit."

"I think he was too tired," Kaiser replied.

"I think he knew you were trying to help," Hildy said. "I think he knew you were his friend. I just wish he would fly away so we'd know he was okay."

Almost as if it understood, the gull looked over with a suspicious eye, then with a squawk it gave a tentative hop, stopped, and looked around as if puzzled to find no corresponding pull on its wing, no pain. Testing, it fluttered its wings, but only enough to move onto one of the rocks in the jetty. Then, as if someone told it that it was free, the gull spread its wings full, swooped out over the water, and was quickly lost in the fog rolling in from the sea.

"He's as good as new," Christian said, clapping his hands. "Isn't he, Hildy?"

She nodded, smiling at the feeling of goodness flowing over her. She'd taken a huge risk in disobeying Julian, but it had been worth it. Even if she were caught right now, the sight of the gull flying free was something she wouldn't have traded for anything.

She looked over at Mr. Kaiser with real curiosity. He was a man, but he seemed so different from her father. Julian was powerful and strong, but there was no kindness in him. And when he got that dark look in his eyes, she was truly frightened. But there was nothing frightening about Mr. Kaiser. In fact, Hildy guessed that he was about the nicest grown-up she had ever known.

A sudden sound from above brought her down to earth with a crash. It was Julian's voice. Thinking they'd been found out, she froze, waiting for him to appear at the top of the bluff. But he never came. She listened, then realized he was calling her mother.

"We'd better get out of here," Kaiser said. "You kids help me push the boat out, then climb back up and when the coast is clear, head for the house."

The three scrambled back over the sand to the spot where they'd left the boat, and within minutes they had it launched. Kaiser jumped in, but before he was even able to set the oars in the oarlocks, he was up to his waist in saltwater.

"Mr. Kaiser," Hildy said, horrified. "You're sinking!"

Kaiser stood up, but before he could begin to bail, the boat filled with water and then slowly settled to the sandy bottom. He was left standing hip deep in the ice cold ocean. Cursing under his breath, he splashed ashore.

"What are we going to do now?" Hildy asked, looking anxiously toward the top of the bluff.

Kaiser frowned. He wasn't concerned for himself, but he didn't want the children to get into trouble. "Don't worry," he said. "You two follow me up to the top. When we're sure the coast is clear, I'll lag back and you head for the house. Then I'll just sneak through the garden and be on my way right out the front gate." He kept his voice light.

The three moved cautiously up the cliff, taking care not to make any noise. When they were almost up to the edge of the garden, Kaiser motioned for them to stop. He pulled himself up and looked to see if anyone was there. The place was deserted, so he signaled for Hildy and Christian to come ahead. They were crouched just below him, ready to run on his signal, when he suddenly drew back and sucked in his breath.

Julian Ferrare had appeared out of nowhere and was standing with his back to them, only inches away. Kaiser could have reached out and touched the back of his shoe.

"Francesca," Julian called to his wife, who was somewhere out of Kaiser's range of vision. "Will you stop fussing with those damned shrubs? Can't you see they're all dead? Besides, we have to talk."

13

"I'm leaving in the morning for London," Kaiser heard Julian say. "I'm bored to death, so I've decided to do Max Frankl a favor and attend his recital. I want you to come with me. Just you and me, my love. It would be like a second honeymoon."

Kaiser still couldn't see Francesca, but he heard her clearly. "You must be mad," she said.

"How long are you going to carry on this way?"

Her next words were full of venom. "You dare ask me that?"

Julian answered without hesitation. "I'll never let you go. You know that. So why are you making life so difficult for all of us?"

"Dear God, Julian." Francesca's voice was filled with such pain that Kaiser wished the two children hadn't been there to hear. He could feel them shivering beside him. "Have pity," she said.

"I feel no pity, Francesca," he replied with startling intensity. "Only love. Don't you understand? I will never let you go. I love you."

"Love? You don't know the meaning of the word." She paused, and her next words were a curse. "You are an obscenity, Julian. I wish you were dead."

There was no mistaking the depth of hatred she felt, and

Kaiser wondered what Julian could have done to deserve such loathing. He heard Julian sigh. "Very well, Francesca," he said. "Have it your way."

"My way?" she choked. "Dear Jesus, what a joke."

"You leave me no choice. As long as you continue to behave so unreasonably I will have to continue to take Hildy with me when I go away. It's my only insurance. I know you'll never leave without Hildy."

There was a long silence, and Kaiser prayed for the sake of the two beside him that the conversation was at an end. Neither one of them had made a sound. In fact they were both so quiet that Kaiser turned to see if they were all right. Hildy was crouched beside him, her face pressed almost into the dirt, and she made no attempt to see what was happening above. Christian was huddled up against him on the other side, his face hidden.

Francesca spoke again, her voice icy cold. "What would you do if I simply packed our things and took the children away? Filed for divorce. You couldn't stop me." There was a pause, and Kaiser had the impression that she was like a child who says something preposterous, then hopes for the best.

Julian did not sound at all upset by the question, his voice infinitely patient when he answered. "I've told you before, Francesca, but I'll tell you again—I'd simply have to tell the children the truth. And the rest of the world as well."

Francesca let out a strangled sound, like the cry of a wounded animal. It was all Kaiser could do to hold Hildy back when the little girl tried to scramble up the slope. Kaiser caught her by the edge of her jacket and pulled her back, holding her tight against him, praying that the two above hadn't heard.

It seemed they hadn't. Julian continued, "You are mine. I will stop at nothing to keep you. I love you."

"You don't love me," she said, her words barely audible. "If you did, you'd let me go."

Julian's voice changed to black iron. "I will never let you go, Francesca. Not one way or another. When we're together I'll watch you constantly, because I know that if you get the chance, you'll take my children and run to a place where I'll never be able to find you, where I can't tell them the truth. Well, that's a chance I will never take, Francesca, my love." There was a pause, as if he wanted to make sure she understood. "When I cannot be here, I'll take Hildy with me so that you will be waiting for me to return."

"If you're so sure I won't leave without Hildy, must you keep Elise here as my watchdog?"

"Elise is simply a companion. And a nanny, if you will, for Christian."

"She's here to make sure I see no one while you're away. And as for Christian, my poor son is terrified of her."

Kaiser felt Christian jump beside him. He took one arm from around Hildy and pulled Christian closer. He had no idea what would happen if they were discovered, except that it would be disastrous. Hildy and Christian must have known it, too, because they made no further attempt to move. They remained where they were, pressed up against him.

"I don't know what you're talking about, Francesca," Julian was saying. "Elise is here only to help. If you think anything else, you're hallucinating. As for Christian, you indulge him. He needs some firm discipline."

"He's a good child, Julian," she said coldly. "What he needs is a little love."

"He needs a firm hand, and since you refuse to see to it, I'll have to."

"I put you on warning, Julian," Francesca said quietly. "I seem to have no choice as to where I live, at least not for the moment. But don't push me. There may come a time when I decide that the truth is less damaging to my children than living with you. And then, may God damn your soul to hell!"

"I'm not worried, Francesca," Julian said smoothly. "I don't think anything would ever drive you to tell them the truth. You love them too much. It's your only weakness— the one thing I can count on."

There was another long silence before Julian spoke again. "Since you won't be traveling with us, I'd better let Elise know that Hildy will be the only one going with me."

"Why don't you do that?" Francesca said bitterly. "And while you're at it, you might tell dear Elise to keep her bloody pills to herself. I may be a slow learner, Julian, but I know when I'm being drugged."

"You're talking nonsense, Francesca."

"Am I? Well, if you really don't know what goes on here when you're away, why don't you ask Elise?"

"I will, but I don't know why you're so cruel to her when you know she needs all our understanding."

"I know what Elise needs, Julian, and it's far more than understanding. This house is no place for her."

Kaiser could hear the sound of her footsteps receding, then Julian's, but he didn't move for a while. He was immobilized by what he'd just overheard—not the words so much as the depth of hatred with which they were spoken. When he lifted his head to look, the garden was empty.

"I think the coast is clear," he whispered, but the children didn't move. Hildy was quivering, crying soundlessly into her sleeve. Christian was making no sound, as if he'd been stricken dumb. Kaiser stood up. "Come with me," he said quietly. "We'll talk."

Hildy began to cry openly now, the tears streaming down her cheeks. Kaiser picked Christian up, took Hildy by the hand, and together they climbed the rest of the way up the slope and into the garden. Kaiser set Christian gently on his feet. "We're going to my house," he said and without waiting for an answer, took them by the hands and led them around the side of the house, not caring anymore if they were seen. He still didn't know what was going on with the

Ferrares, but at this point he only cared that the children had heard far more than they should have.

They followed Kaiser into Mrs. Minstrell's kitchen without protest. She was in the middle of baking bread, but Kaiser didn't have to ask her to leave. She could tell by the children's stricken looks that something calamitous had happened. "I've got some ironing to do upstairs," she said, heading for the door. "There's a fresh batch of lemonade in the refrigerator if anyone's in the mood." With that, she was gone.

Kaiser turned to the children. "Sit," he said, pointing toward the kitchen table. "I'm going to call your parents and tell them where you are. Then we'll talk." He picked up the phone. "What's your number?" he asked Hildy. She told him and he dialed. Elise answered.

"Hi, Elise," he said as pleasantly as he could. "Patrick Kaiser here. I saw Hildy and Christian out on your front steps earlier so I invited them over to get Christian's fish. We didn't want anyone to worry."

Julian came on the line and Kaiser repeated what he'd just said. "I offered them a glass of lemonade. Oh? How nice. Where? I'll tell her. They'll be over within the hour." Kaiser hung up.

The two children were watching him in silence, Hildy's skin red and blotchy from her tears. "The coast is clear," he said lightly, trying to ease the tension. He poured them each a glass of lemonade, then sat down. "Well, would you like to talk or would you rather just forget about it?"

Hildy shook her head, unable to speak.

"Mama hates Julian," Christian said. "And Julian hates me."

Kaiser winced at his directness, but he knew that children often had a way of cutting through to the bone.

"Francesca wants a divorce and my father doesn't," Hildy said, beginning to cry again. "That's why she keeps trying to run away."

"Is that what happened that day on Esther Island?" Kaiser asked.

Hildy nodded. "But I don't know why, Mr. Kaiser. They used to be so happy. Before."

"Before your grandfather died?"

Hildy buried her face in her hands. "I don't understand what's happening to us. Why can't I just pinch myself and wake up?"

Kaiser didn't have any answers, and he cursed fate for having put them in the wrong place at the wrong time. "I don't know what's wrong, Hildy," he said gently. "All I know is that grown-ups sometimes really screw up their lives. The best you can do is wait out the storm and remember that it isn't you they're unhappy with, it's each other."

Hildy took a deep breath and looked across the table at him with the look of an old, old woman. "What do you suppose the secret is? The thing Mama doesn't want Julian to tell?"

Kaiser shrugged. He hadn't the faintest idea, but was glad they hadn't discussed it in any detail. "Both of your parents love you very much. That's what you have to remember." He wondered as he spoke why he had such a bad taste in his mouth.

"It's an awful mess," Hildy said, wiping her eyes.

Kaiser had to agree, and it made him furious because of the affection he felt for Hildy and Christian. They were innocent children caught up in the middle of a vicious battle which was none of their doing. But there was something else about the situation that bothered Kaiser. This was no simple domestic quarrel—it was blackmail, and God knew what else, and Kaiser had an awful gut feeling that the two children were in physical danger.

"It sure is a mess," he said. "But just remember one thing," he added in a tone that was almost fierce. "If you ever need help, just to talk, or something more, I'm your man."

"I like you, Mr. Kaiser," Christian said. "I really do."

"I like you, too, Christian," he said.

"Where is Julian going?" Hildy cut in.

"He said he was going back to London. You're going with him again, I understand." He tried to sound enthusiastic.

Hildy turned pale, but it was Christian who took the news hardest. "You can't go, Hildy. You heard what Mama said. Elise gives her pills. That's why she gets sick whenever you're away. I told you Elise was a witch."

"But Mama knows, Christian. She told Julian to make Elise stop. She won't get sick this time, and you two will be just fine."

Christian considered that for a minute, and it seemed to help. Two spots of color appeared on his cheeks. But Hildy was still ashen. "Is Julian really taking me with him so that my mother won't run away?" she asked Kaiser.

Kaiser didn't say anything for a minute. He put his hand to his scar, trying to decide what words would be best for Hildy to hear right now. He suspected that Christian hadn't understood a lot of what his parents had said in the garden. But he knew that Hildy hadn't missed a thing. She knew what their words meant, and worse, she'd recognized the sound of real hatred.

"I think he only said that, Hildy," Kaiser said finally. "People say things they don't mean when they're angry. Your father takes you with him because he's proud of you. Anyone can see that. And because he wants to give you a chance to learn all there is to learn about the world of music. I'm sure if he and your mother weren't fighting, he would still take you with him."

Hildy managed a weak smile, with that same little-old-woman look in her eyes. "Thanks, Mr. Kaiser," she said. "You really *are* a very nice man."

Nice, maybe, Kaiser thought, but I'm not sure how smart.

14

Elise went up the stairs knowing exactly what she had to do to get to her room. There was a rumbling in the back of her mind that always came when Julian said he was going away, and in spite of the cool dampness of the upstairs hall, she began to perspire. She knew she was in trouble—such terrible trouble that had she been at the sanitarium, she would have begged for a pack, that icy-wet cocoon that shocked and calmed all at the same time, the freezing wet sheets the nurses wrapped around her like a mummy's shroud to keep her safe.

Get your pills, Coriander said. *Quickly, or you'll fall.* She saw the dark hole ahead. Julian was leaving her, and without him there was no salvation. No one to hold back the fear. I want to tell you where I'm going, Julian, she thought, but she was unable to speak. She heard rushing wings behind her and she hurried to get there before the floor melted under her feet.

It was cold when she finally opened her eyes. Is it winter again, she wondered, or is it winter still? She was lying on her back in her bed. You are pathetic, she said to herself. You don't even know the time of year.

"'Lise." She heard Julian's voice. "Take these." She opened her eyes to see him standing by her bed. She opened her mouth and swallowed what he offered though she wasn't sure what it was.

"I thought you had gone," she whispered.

"Not yet," he said.

Not yet. That meant soon. All color and dimension drained from the room, leaving Julian flat, a black-and-white outline in a black-and-white sketch. "When?" she whispered.

"Tomorrow morning. We need to get Hildy's things together. Do you think you can manage?"

She wanted to tell him that it was impossible when everything was so flat.

"'Lise," he said, sitting down beside her. "You've got to remember to take your medication." He frowned, and she heard an unfamiliar edge to his voice. "All of it, 'Lise." He sounded like a stranger. "You haven't been giving any to Francesca, have you? When I've been away?"

Elise slammed her eyelids shut, choking back the fear that had risen in her throat, thick and vile-tasting.

"I don't want you to give any pills to Francesca, Elise. Do you understand?"

She nodded. It was all she could do.

"And you are not to keep people from visiting. Francesca needs company. It will help to make her happy again."

The fear in her throat swelled up and flowed into her mouth, making her gag. Julian was forbidding her to use her only means of defense. Now Francesca would surely send her away as soon as Julian left.

"'Lise?" Julian was looking at her. She tried to hide. "Sweetness," he said, and all at once he seemed like the old Julian, gentle, loving. "You have to help me. You have to be kind to Francesca. Make her like you. So she won't want to leave us. You understand, don't you?"

She didn't understand anything. Not anything at all. But she nodded.

"I brought you here because I hoped it would help. I

hoped you would become a companion and friend to my wife. I want her to tell you her secrets, what she plans to do each and every day. You have to help me, 'Lise." He held her close. "You're the only one I can trust."

"I love you, Julian," she said.

"I know you do. That's why I know you won't fail me."

Elise didn't sleep all night. In spite of a double dose of medication she lay awake, waiting for the word from Francesca that would send her back to the sanitarium. But the word never came. Elise shouldn't have been surprised. To send her away quickly would have been a kindness of sorts. Now she would have to wait for the blow to fall.

Don't be a fool, Coriander said. *There is no time for waiting. You must act before she does or all will be lost.*

But I don't know what to do, Elise said.

You will, Coriander said. *When the time is right you'll know*.

When Elise finally came downstairs the next morning, Julian and Hildy had gone. Francesca was at the table, sipping her tea. "Good morning, Elise," she said.

"Good morning," Elise responded. She crossed to the cupboard and took out a can of tomato juice. "Can I get you something?" she asked politely. It was required in the real world that they treat each other with courtesy.

"No, thank you. I've just made myself some tea."

Elise was feeling surprisingly calm, in spite of the fact that Julian had left her. She'd taken her full complement of medicine, as he had instructed, and she felt almost courageous. She looked out from under her lids. Through the thin veil of reality she could see her sister-in-law sitting there, patiently waiting. How will I protect myself now? she wondered. How will I keep her from sending me away now that Julian has forbidden me to give her the only thing that makes her sleep?

She picked up the opener and punched two careful holes in the top of the can. She watched her hand pour the juice into a glass. She took a sip; it had no taste. She wondered if perhaps it had been poisoned, then discarded that notion. Francesca would never kill her. She didn't have to. All Francesca had to do was call the sanitarium and she would be gone.

Elise glanced down at the can opener on the counter and wondered why it seemed so special to her. She tried to think. It had something to do with Francesca and Julian. She picked it up and held it, feeling the coolness, remembering the sharpness of its metal point, and then she remembered the day eleven years ago when Francesca had come for the first time and had sent her away.

It was her thirty-seventh birthday, but Elise had forgotten all about it. She'd been carrying a stack of towels to the linen closet when she heard the front door slam.

"'Lise!" Julian had called.

She had dropped the towels and run to the head of the stairs. Julian, Julian, Julian, her heart sang. He's home. My darling only best friend lover brother all things. She hadn't seen him in over a month. But then the measure of time meant little to her. Maybe it had really been longer. No matter. He was home, back in their father's house, and Elise was safe once more.

She flew down the staircase and into his open arms, feeling every dimension of life, seeing all of its color, hearing all the beautiful music it had to offer. "You're home at last!" she cried.

He hugged her. "I'm home," he said. "And I have a surprise for you."

She pushed herself out of his arms and stood looking up at him, her face radiant, expectant. Julian never forgot to bring her a present when he came home.

He turned away from her, and for the first time Elise became conscious of an alien presence in the house. She felt a terrible coldness that folded itself around her like a shroud. But why? This shouldn't be. Julian was home. Julian was warmth. Julian was sanity. Instinctively she held out her hands to him for help, but he'd turned away from her, walking toward whoever had come with him.

"'Lise," he said, "I want you to meet my wife. This is my beloved Francesca."

Elise looked across the hallway and found herself face to face with her worst nightmare. Another golden-hair! Another Anna! A beautiful, golden-haired, silken woman had come to steal her beloved Julian from her. Someone who would surely send her away.

Julian was making movements with his mouth, but Elise couldn't tell what he was saying. The floors had begun to melt where her own sweat was touching them. It was running off her in great waves, splashing everywhere.

She sank to her knees and tried to hide, but it was no use. She had gone unpunished for too long, and now she must begin again this awful business of perpetual atonement for crimes she never remembered having committed.

Later on in the day, as she sat alone in the kitchen— waiting for Julian to take her to the sanitarium, the place she hadn't been in twenty years—her vision cleared long enough for her to see her hand carving a careful track in her arm with the bottle opener. She knew it was the track on which the train would come to take her away from Julian, the train that belonged to Francesca. It was slow work because each time she cleaned out the track, more blood seeped in and she was forced to go over and over the same area with the sharp point of the bottle opener.

"I'll be outside with Christian if you need me," Francesca was saying.

Elise knew what she had to do. In spite of what Julian had said, she was going to have to give her sister-in-law some of her pills. She had never disobeyed Julian before, but now she had no choice. She wasn't strong enough to fight her. She had to have help.

"And Elise," Francesca said, "I don't know if Julian said anything to you or not, but just in case he didn't, I will." Her face was cold, punishing. "Keep your pills to yourself. It is you who need them, not I." Then she went out the back door.

Elise slid behind her keyhole and watched through the window as her sister-in-law went out onto the terrace and sat down next to the boy. Elise covered her face and wept. "What am I to do?" she cried, trembling all over. "Now she surely will send me away."

It was then that her father's words came to her like lines from a long-forgotten play. "You killed Anna," he had said. "As sure as if you had cut out her heart. When you murdered our child, you destroyed her will to live." Elise stopped trembling and listened, tipping her head to one side like a newborn infant, hearing sound for the first time. Of course. That was the answer. It had been there the entire time, and she'd just been too blind to see. Now all that remained was to decide how to do it.

15

Kaiser hung up the phone and took a deep breath. Toby had
assured him that in the week he'd been away the accoun-
tants had accomplished great things. Property division had
been settled to her satisfaction, except for selling the condo
in St. Martin. They were supposed to split the proceeds,
but now Toby had decided she wanted to keep it. She
thought they ought to talk about it. When was he coming
back to New York? Having no intention of flying back to the
city just to fight with Toby, he told her he'd be leaving the
island as soon as *Seabird* was ready to sail.

Sometimes life can be a real bitch, he thought for the
second time that morning. Earlier he had stood by the
window and watched an ashen-faced Hildy say good-bye to
her mother and brother. She'd smiled and hugged them
both, but there had been a terrible straightness about the
set of her thin shoulders, and he'd cursed the Ferrares for
causing their children such undeserved pain.

He called the boatyard but there was no answer. He
wasn't surprised. He would have to walk down himself and
see if he could light a fire under some native behinds, he
thought.

Putting on his windbreaker, he stepped out into a raw
November mist. He glanced next door, wondering grimly
how little Christian was adjusting without Hildy, then

headed toward the harbor. He'd only gone a short distance when he realized he wasn't the only one braving the cold. Just ahead he recognized the figures of Francesca and Christian walking briskly toward the center of town.

There was something about the set of her shoulders and the precision with which she moved that made him think of a soldier about to do battle. He quickened his pace until he was almost behind them, then slowed down. At the same time, Christian turned and saw him.

"Mr. Kaiser," he shouted, and let go of his mother's hand to run back toward him. "Guess where we're going?"

"I can't imagine," Kaiser said. "Somewhere nice, I hope." He was about to greet Francesca when she silenced him with an icy stare.

"Why do you follow us?" she asked with undisguised hostility.

Under normal circumstances Kaiser would have been taken aback by such a bizarre question, but considering her past behavior, he simply smiled and said, "Because we both happen to be going in the same direction, I suppose."

She made a tiny movement with her mouth, then appeared to relax a bit. "I apologize, Mr. Kaiser," she said. "I seem to forget that other people's lives do not necessarily revolve around ours." Then she smiled, but it was such a strange smile that Kaiser for a moment could only stare. It was as if someone else had come out from behind her eyes, someone desperate for a friend. Then the smile faded, leaving only vagueness.

"Guess where we're going?" Christian broke in.

"Where?"

"Mama is going to let me fish off the pier."

"That sounds like one of the best ideas I've heard in a long time," Kaiser said.

"Want to come?"

Kaiser glanced at Francesca, but she was looking away. He was sure that he wasn't welcome, but decided he didn't care. It was Christian he was concerned about. "I'll walk along," he said. "At least as far as the boatyard. I have to check on *Seabird*."

The three began to walk, Francesca slightly in front, as if she were alone. "You aren't going away, are you?" Christian sounded alarmed.

"Not for a while," Kaiser said. "Not until my boat is back in condition."

"Then will you leave?"

Kaiser nodded. "I have to sail her back to the mainland before the fifteenth of this month. She can't stay out here all winter."

Francesca hadn't seemed at all interested in their conversation, but at the mention of the mainland she turned with such abruptness that Christian bumped into her and fell down.

Kaiser lifted him by the shoulders and set him gently on his feet. Francesca bent down and without speaking brushed the dirt from the little boy's knee. They walked the next block in silence and were almost to the dockyard when Francesca finally spoke. "When are you leaving the island?" she said, then seemed to wish she hadn't asked.

"I hope by the beginning of next week. Why? Is there something I can help you with?"

She considered for a moment, then shook her head. "I'm afraid not," she said. "Come, Christian. Let's see if we can rent a fishing pole."

"You should have asked me," Kaiser said. "My brother's house is full of them."

"You're very kind, Mr. Kaiser," she said in her soft accent, "but we've imposed too much already." She took Christian by the hand and turned toward the shack that served as an office of sorts.

"Wait a minute," Kaiser said. "I think I have a rod or two on *Seabird*."

Without waiting for her to reply, he headed down the

walkway toward the slip where his boat lay anchored. The fishing boats that had been there earlier were gone, and Kaiser knew they were out at sea. Still, the empty slips served as a silent reminder that he had to get his own boat back to Noank soon.

It took him only a minute to find a pole suitable for Christian. He was surprised to find that while he was below deck, Francesca had come aboard and was standing in the bow, staring intently out across the harbor. She seemed to have forgotten that he and Christian were there.

Kaiser handed two dollars to the boy and pointed toward the office. "Go get some bait from Hank," he said, "and come right back."

Christian was off without a backward glance.

"How long does it take to cross to the mainland?" Francesca asked, still staring out to sea.

"With a steady wind and reasonably calm seas, about eight hours."

She turned, but still he couldn't see her face. "How many people will this boat accommodate?"

"Six comfortably. More, if you don't mind close quarters. Why do you ask?"

She answered too quickly. "Just curious," she said.

"Are you planning a trip to the mainland?" he asked.

She shook her head. "I'm afraid not."

"Why not?"

She laughed, but without humor. "What would I want to go to the mainland for? There's nothing there for me." She seemed about to say more, then changed her mind and turned once again to stare at some unseen horizon.

Kaiser was tempted for a minute to tell her what he and the children had overheard in the garden, then decided against it. Francesca Ferrare had problems, the worst of which was that her husband was blackmailing her, for reasons that remained to be seen. The fact was that she didn't seem to trust anyone or anything at this point.

Maybe if he didn't push, he thought, she would come to realize that he was concerned about her situation, not only because he cared about her children, but also because blackmail was a filthy business. And also because he was touched by the terrible look of despair he'd seen more than once in her face.

But all that would take time, and time was something he didn't have right now. Not unless he took *Seabird* to Connecticut and then came back to the island. But what for? he asked himself suddenly. What was he possibly hoping to accomplish if he did come back? He knew that Francesca Ferrare wanted to leave her husband, wanted to take her two children and go somewhere Julian would never find her. Was he actually considering he might help her escape? The notion was so preposterous that he almost laughed out loud. Slow down, old boy, he said to himself. Before you do another thing you better know exactly where you're headed. And why.

He turned away from her and looked up the walkway. "Here comes Christian," he said. "Do you want me to get him started?"

"Would you?" she asked, and he could hear the strain in her voice.

"Be glad to." He swung off the boat to meet the boy, who was running down the walkway with an empty bucket and a container of squid. "Follow me," he said to Christian. "Let's see if you can catch an eel."

"What about Mama?"

"She'll be along." He took the boy by the hand and together they walked to the edge of the pier, where the eels swam unconcerned.

When Francesca finally joined them, she was in perfect control. "Thank you," she said to Kaiser, then turned to watch her son. "Are you getting any bites?" she asked, sitting down beside him.

"Not yet," he replied, "but I just started. This takes time, you know."

She nodded and said no more, watching intently where Christian's line disappeared into the water.

"Would you like a cup of coffee?" Kaiser asked. "I'm going to check on Hank's work schedule, then I thought I'd walk up to Downy Flake and get some."

She looked up, and for the first time he saw Francesca Ferrare as she might have looked once upon a time. "But what if he catches something?" she asked, almost breathless. "What do I do?"

Kaiser laughed. "I think Christian can handle it."

Christian took his eyes off his line long enough to throw his mother a withering glance. "I'm not a baby, Mama. Mr. Kaiser taught me all about this stuff."

She smiled and put her arm around her son. "Of course you aren't a baby, Christian," she said. "I'm just a dumb old mother. And a girl besides." She looked over at Kaiser, repressing a smile, and Kaiser couldn't believe how beautiful she was. *What is it*, he wondered, *that is tearing such mighty chunks out of you? What secret can possibly be so damaging?*

"I'll go get coffee," he said, and turned away before he might say something to ruin her mood.

He was gone only ten minutes, and when he returned, Christian had one eel safely dehooked and in the bucket and was back at his post, eager to catch another.

Francesca had moved a little to one side, but her face was still tranquil, and as Kaiser approached she smiled. "Ugly, isn't it?" she said in her soft accent. "I'll be eternally grateful that I didn't have to touch it."

Kaiser handed her a cup of coffee. "It's black," he said. "I wasn't sure how you like it."

"Black is fine, thank you." She took the cup and sipped. "If I had known how cold it was going to be down here near the water," she said, "I might have had second thoughts about letting Christian come."

"I'm glad you didn't," Kaiser said.

She didn't answer right away, and he was afraid for a minute that she was going to fall back into one of her black humors, but instead she smiled. "I guess I'm glad I didn't either," she said. "I tend to forget how many small pleasures God has provided, even for the most pathetic of His creatures."

Kaiser sat down beside her, but didn't speak.

"Where do you come from?" she asked, as casually as if they had just been introduced.

"Originally from Connecticut. After that, you name it, I've lived there."

"Are you married?"

"I was."

Her voice was soft. "Widowed?"

"No. Divorced."

"Oh," she said with a faint frown. "Somehow I wouldn't have guessed that."

"Why not?"

"You don't seem the type to have failed at anything."

He smiled. "Does divorce always have to be a sign of failure?" Then he held up his hand. "Don't answer that. It was a stupid question. And in my case particularly so. My marriage was a miserable failure. That's the only part about it that really bothers me."

"Is that why you came out here to the island?"

He nodded. "To hide myself away and lick my wounds."

"Your wife left you then."

"She left me. To marry Henry Crandall, walking oatmeal cookie."

She smiled. "I take it you don't care for Mr. Crandall."

Kaiser stopped to think. "To tell you the truth," he said, "I'm not sure. Henry Crandall would make the perfect spy because he has the kind of face and figure that no one would ever be able to remember for more than five minutes."

She laughed then, a real laugh that made her tip her head back, and Kaiser was enchanted. "You ought to do that more often," he said.

"What?"

"Laugh."

"It's been a long time since I've had anything to laugh about," she said quietly.

"Death of someone close is always hard to take," he said.

She turned away. "Sometimes, Mr. Kaiser, it isn't the dying that's the problem. Sometimes it's the living." Then she looked back at him, and the old expression had reappeared, but as Kaiser looked across the distance between them, it seemed less formidable.

A splash in the water caused them both to glance over at Christian, who was fighting to land his second catch of the morning. "He loves this fishing business," Francesca said. "Poor child. Lord knows he has little enough in this life to love, but he never complains. At least not to me." There was a sudden edge to her voice. "He thinks I'll go insane if he does. Quite a burden for a five-year-old, wouldn't you say?"

"And would you?"

"Would I what?"

"Go insane?"

Her smile was bittersweet. "If you had asked me that question two months ago, I would have laughed at the absurdity of such a thought. Now I realize what a thin line there is between sanity and madness, and how many of us live on the wrong side of the asylum wall."

Kaiser turned to see her expression, and as he did, caught sight of a sudden movement just past her shoulder. It was a small, jerking movement that brought his breath sharply into his throat. "Christian!" he shouted, but it was too late. In the same instant, Kaiser saw the pole arc out over the water, and in the next, as smoothly as if he were doing a swan dive, Christian followed it into more than ten feet of ice-cold water.

"Christian!" Francesca shrieked. "Dear God, he can't swim!" And before Kaiser could stop her, she jumped off the edge of the wharf after her son.

Kaiser tore off his windbreaker and hit the water a short distance from where he'd seen the child disappear. He saw Francesca dive and he did the same, but the water was murky and he could see nothing.

He came up for breath then dove again, trying to feel the water around him. Nothing. He surfaced and sucked in some air. There was no sign of either Francesca or the boy. He felt a sudden wave of panic and dove again, feeling his way until he knew he couldn't last any longer without a fresh breath. As he twisted his body sharply toward the surface, he suddenly sensed something beside him. He reached out, grabbed Christian by the arm, and dragged him up. The boy was limp, but Kaiser could see now that he was breathing.

Kaiser was exhausted by the time he reached the wooden ladder that led up to the walkway. He had Christian securely under his arm, but when he tried to push him up, he realized that he wasn't going to be able to do it alone. He looked for Francesca, but she was nowhere to be seen. "Help! Somebody!" he yelled. "For Christ's sake, help!"

Hank's face appeared above. "What the hell are you doing down there?" he said, annoyed.

"What does it look like, you jerk? Pull him up." He pushed Christian's limp body up the ladder and Hank grabbed him, lifting him to safety. "Take him in where it's warm," Kaiser said. "I have to find his mother." He turned and was about to dive again when he heard a pitiful, choking sound beside him.

She was only inches away, clinging to a piling, gasping for breath, her eyes wide, her face pale. "Is he dead?" she whispered.

"No, he's all right," Kaiser replied.

He went up the ladder first, then turned and pulled her up. Together they stumbled toward the shack where Hank had carried Christian, but just before they reached the door Francesca stopped. She turned and looked at Kaiser. "If he should die," she said with terrible urgency, "help Hildy. Promise me you'll help Hildy."

"He won't die," Kaiser said.

"But if he does . . ."

Kaiser didn't know what to say.

She grabbed him hard by the arm, her nails digging into his skin. "I'm begging you, Mr. Kaiser. Hildy must not stay alone with her father."

"But where do you plan to be?"

"You asked me earlier if I thought I would go insane. If Christian dies, the answer to your question is yes." Kaiser could see her breaking to pieces in front of his eyes, and he knew without a doubt that she meant what she said.

"Will you promise?" She began to shake uncontrollably.

Kaiser hesitated, but only for a minute. The questions he had asked himself earlier were suddenly answered. He cared about Francesca Ferrare and her children. He had no idea what her terrible secret was, but he had a violent aversion to blackmail and an even more violent aversion to a man who would use his two innocent children to keep his wife in line. He decided then and there that he would do whatever he could to help her. "I promise," he said. "For whatever it's worth, I'll do what I can."

"I believe you," she replied, and turned to open the door. But her hand was shaking so badly that she couldn't turn the knob.

Kaiser moved past her and opened it.

Christian was sitting on the edge of Hank's desk in front of a wood-burning stove, wrapped in an old army blanket. "Hi, Mr. Kaiser," he said through chattering teeth. "Hi, Mama. I hope you're not mad at me."

Francesca went to her son and held him.

"You're all wet," Christian said.

Kaiser couldn't see her expression, but the terrible quaking had stopped. "You gave us quite a scare, my little Christian," she said. "If you plan to take any more dives like that, we'd better teach you how to swim."

Kaiser stood by the door, listening. There was no trace of hysteria in her voice now, nor would anyone have suspected that just minutes ago she was close to total collapse.

"You saved my life," Christian said to Kaiser. "Just like you saved the gull. Wait till I tell Hildy."

"What gull?" Francesca asked.

"It's a long story," Kaiser said. "First let's get you home and into some dry clothes." He turned to Hank, who was sitting in silence on the other side of the stove, leafing through a sporting goods catalogue. "Can you give us a lift?"

Hank frowned. "I guess so, but it's going to raise hell with my schedule."

Kaiser nodded. "I guess that means you won't be working on *Seabird* today."

"*Seabird*? Hell, no," Hank snapped. "That isn't scheduled till Friday. Now it's probably going to be Saturday at the earliest. Maybe even Monday."

"Depending on the weather," Kaiser said.

"You know it," Hank said. "Tell you what. My pickup's around back. Why don't you just take it. Bring it back after you get into some dry clothes. You're making a real mess in here."

"That's very nice of you," Kaiser said. "We won't be long."

"Take your time," Hank said. "I ain't going nowheres."

I'm sure of that, Kaiser thought. "Come along, people. Let's get home before we all catch pneumonia."

"Catch of the day," Hank said with an unexpected spark of humor.

Jesus, Kaiser thought. I don't need all this. He pushed Christian and Francesca through the door, but not before Hank informed him that the truck could use some gas.

16

Hank had neglected to mention that the pickup truck had only one forward gear, so they lurched along for several minutes before Kaiser discovered that it was impossible to shift.

Francesca had been ashen and sober when they first got into the truck, but after a few seconds all three of them were shaking with laughter. "Where did you learn to drive?" she asked as they bucked around the corner onto Main Street and stalled.

Kaiser didn't bother to answer. He turned the key in the ignition and the engine caught, backfired twice, and stalled again.

Francesca threw her hands over her face. "I hope no one recognizes us," she said, laughing.

Kaiser couldn't agree more as he started the engine for the third time and almost smashed into the car ahead. "Thank God we don't have far to go," he said.

When they pulled up in front of the Ferrare house, Francesca was still laughing. "That was wonderful, wasn't it, Christian?" she said. "I don't think I ever had a more enjoyable ride home." She opened the door and slid out, lifting Christian in her arms.

On impulse Kaiser said, "Would you like to have dinner with me this evening?"

He expected her to say no, but after a brief pause she said, "We'd love to. Wouldn't we, Christian?"

"You mean I'm invited too?"

"Of course you are," Francesca said. "I'm never going to leave you alone again."

"I'll pick you both up at six-thirty sharp."

Christian sneezed, and Francesca pulled the blanket closer around him. "I'd better get you inside and into a warm tub," she said. She headed up the walk without any further word, but at the front door she turned. "You didn't just save Christian's life today," she said simply. "You saved us both." Then she carried her son inside.

Elise stood in the upstairs window and watched as the red pickup truck disgorged its passengers. She was breathless to find that she didn't feel the usual panic at the sight of Francesca or the boy. On the contrary, she felt calm and dry. Not a drop of perspiration dampened her brow. Not even Coriander seemed alarmed. That was because she had found a way to get rid of them.

She watched Francesca talking to someone in the truck, then her sister-in-law turned and came into the house, carrying the child wrapped up in a blanket. Elise knew she would have to be very, very careful. Sometimes Francesca could read her thoughts, so she would have to jumble her mind whenever Francesca was near.

Are you strong enough for this? Coriander asked suddenly, and Elise sucked in her breath. She wasn't sure. All she knew was that if she wasn't, Francesca would send her back to the sanitarium and she would lose Julian again, as she had eleven years ago. She left her room and went to the head of the stairs. Francesca had come into the hallway, still carrying the boy. "Did you have a pleasant morning?" Elise called down the stairwell. Was her voice too loud? she wondered. Did it betray her hatred of them?

"Christian had an accident," Francesca said, coming up the stairs. "He nearly drowned."

Elise felt an electrifying surge of excitement. *Calm yourself,* Coriander said. *He isn't dead. There is no cause for rejoicing.*

Elise suddenly became aware that Francesca was staring at her, and she was frightened. Had Francesca read her thoughts? "Is something the matter?" she asked through dry lips, hoping she sounded pleasant.

"You smiled," Francesca said coldly. "When I told you that Christian had almost drowned . . . you smiled." She paused and looked hard at Elise. "Or didn't you realize?" she asked quietly.

Elise felt the rumbling in the back of her mind, but she pushed it away. She forced herself to remember that she had no time to be frightened or confused. She knew what she had to do. "I was smiling because he didn't drown," she said. "Don't you see, Francesca? Isn't that cause for celebration?"

Her sister-in-law didn't answer. She simply continued to bore into Elise's mind with her eyes. *She's trying to read your thoughts,* Coriander said. Elise nodded and dropped her line of vision to follow the pattern of the carpet along the hallway.

Francesca turned away without another word and carried Christian into his bedroom.

Elise leaned against the wall, weak. She had never before faced the enemy head on. All her life when confronted, she had hidden like a spineless coward behind her keyhole, or been carried away to the pit. Always before she had allowed them to send her away without a fight. "Never again, Francesca," she said aloud. "You will never send me away again, no matter what I have to do to stop you."

* * *

True to his word, at precisely six-thirty Kaiser arrived at the door and rang the bell. Elise answered at once. She opened the door wide and smiled a timid smile. "Good evening, Mr. Kaiser," she said. "Won't you come in?"

Kaiser stepped into the hall, surprised by the uncharacteristic display of cordiality. He smiled at her. "You're looking well this evening, Elise," he said, and realized that it was true. She did look well. In fact she looked most attractive, and much younger than her years.

Although Elise had always given the impression of being neat and clean, her hair, face, and skin had seemed to blend and fade into one, a running together of paleness, as if time and circumstance had washed all the browns and tans and pinks away, leaving only gray. But not tonight. Tonight there was a flush to her cheeks, and Kaiser thought he even detected a hint of lipstick. She had on a plain lavender dress that had nothing to do with current styles, but it picked up the color in her eyes, giving her a soft, almost fragile look.

Elise crossed the hallway to the foot of the stairs. "Francesca," she called, "Mr. Kaiser has arrived." Then she turned back. "I understand we have much to thank you for, Mr. Kaiser," she said quietly. "Poor little Christian had quite a fright."

Kaiser was astonished. Was this the same woman who had terrorized Christian, calling him wicked? Trying to cut off his hair? Elise Ferrare was not only looking better, she seemed to be trying hard to be gracious.

"Is something wrong?" she asked, a faint frown appearing between her eyebrows. "Have I said something wrong?"

"Not a thing," Kaiser said. "You must forgive me for staring. It's just that you look lovely this evening."

For a moment she looked blank. Then she smiled. "Thank you. It's not often I hear such kind words."

At that moment Christian came hopping down the stairs, followed by his mother.

"I hope you have a pleasant evening," Elise said, so quietly that Kaiser almost didn't hear. "You all deserve one after your morning."

Francesca stopped with a look of genuine surprise. "Why, thank you, Elise," she replied.

"I'll leave the lights on in the living room," Elise said, and without another word turned and went up the stairs.

Francesca took Christian by the hand. "This has been an extraordinary day," she said to Kaiser. "Simply extraordinary."

The cobbled streets were almost deserted as they walked up the steps to the restaurant. Inside, the dining room was quiet; not even the echoes of noisy summer crowds lingered. Kaiser decided that there wasn't another place in the world he'd rather be right now. Nantucket in the off-season was the jewel in the crown.

He gave no further thought to Elise's transformation, for Francesca seemed different, too, and her appearance captivated him. The strained look on her face had vanished, and she was like a young girl on a first date. She wore a cloudy blue sweater, so soft that it seemed to melt around the curves of her body. For the first time Kaiser became acutely conscious that she had beautiful breasts.

From the beginning he'd been aware of her rare beauty, appreciating it as one would appreciate an extraordinary work of art—objectively and at an appropriate distance—but tonight she was a radiant, incredibly desirable woman, and he had a sudden, overwhelming urge to touch her. He drew in a breath, deciding not to dwell on it. He wanted to help her, but a physical relationship was out of the question. Francesca Ferrare was gorgeous, but she was also married, and Kaiser made it a habit never to tangle with married women. Except to help them escape from their husbands, he thought sarcastically.

He suddenly realized that no one at the table had spoken a word. He took a breath and said, "Elise certainly seemed pleasant tonight, didn't she?"

Francesca raised her eyebrows. "I've never known her to be so helpful."

"She brought me some cookies and hot chocolate this afternoon," Christian said, looking hard at Kaiser. "Elise doesn't ever give me anything."

"Let's not talk about Elise," Francesca said. "Let's talk about you, Mr. Kaiser."

"There's not much to talk about," he replied.

She leaned across the table and touched his arm lightly. "You're too modest. We've all heard of you. Even I have."

I want you, he thought suddenly. Married or not, I want to make love to you. In fact it had been a long time since Kaiser had wanted a woman with so much intensity. "Call me Patrick," he heard himself say, and he winced. It sounded like a line from a B movie.

She smiled. "I'd like that," she said, and he found himself wondering if she could possibly be flirting with him.

"I have to go to the bathroom," Christian said.

"Would you like me to take you?" Kaiser asked.

Christian jumped down from his chair. "I can go alone, can't I, Mama?"

"You may. But you come right back."

He disappeared, leaving Kaiser at a sudden loss for words. He had had no difficulty talking to her before, but now he was tongue-tied. You ass, he said to himself.

"Christian loves you, you know," she said. "He's never had a father. Certainly not a caring one. I hope you don't mind."

"How could I mind? It's an ultimate compliment."

"I have a feeling it has something to do with a sea gull. Christian told me to ask you about it. He said if you thought it was all right, you'd tell."

Kaiser looked across at her and decided that it would do

no harm to tell her about the gull. He began to relate the story, omitting the fact that they'd overheard her conversation with Julian.

"My poor children," she said. "Afraid to ask me to help them even in the simplest things. How much have they suffered because of me?" She shook her head. "I have much to answer for, don't I?"

"That depends."

"On what?"

"On your reasons. You must have taken your father's death very hard."

She didn't answer, but for an instant Kaiser had the feeling she didn't know what he was talking about, that her despair had nothing to do with the death of Dr. Stahlberg. "I think I've missed something," he said, almost to himself.

She looked straight into his face, and he caught a glimpse of the old haunted expression. Then it was gone, but it left her looking beaten.

"I'd like to help you," Kaiser said. "I told you that before, and I meant it."

She shook her head. "People can't be expected to help other people without explanations, and explanations are something I can't afford."

"What if I offered to help without any explanations? What if I simply offer to do anything I can, no strings?"

"I wouldn't ever ask you to do that," she said quietly. "I wish I could, but I can't."

"You know I'm leaving the island as soon as my boat is ready. I've been here almost a week, and I can't stay much longer."

She nodded, toying with a piece of lettuce on her plate. "How soon do you think you'll be leaving?" she asked with a casualness that Kaiser knew was forced. She was clearly interested in his departure date—this wasn't the first time she'd asked about it. Why? he wondered.

"In a day or two," he said. "If all goes well."

"Today is Wednesday. Hildy won't be back until Sunday," she said, then seemed startled to find that she had spoken aloud. She smiled. "She'll be sorry not to see you."

At that moment Christian returned to the table and began telling them about the hand dryer in the men's room. From that point on the conversation jumped and jolted from one topic to another as Christian led them through the intricacies of his own five-year-old thought processes. Kaiser never had another opportunity to speak to Francesca alone.

The evening passed too quickly, and so when Francesca asked if he would like to stop in for a nightcap, he accepted without hesitation.

Elise was nowhere to be seen when they arrived at the Ferrare house, and Francesca excused herself to put Christian to bed. "Make yourself a drink," she said, pointing toward the living room. "I'll be right down."

The lights were on across the hall, so Kaiser had no trouble finding his way. He mixed himself a drink and was about to make one for Francesca when something made him stop. He had the sudden eerie feeling that he was not alone. He looked around the room, but all was still except for the ticking of the French porcelain clock on the mantel.

He picked up his glass and crossed to the fireplace, where hot coals still glowed from the evening's fire. He still couldn't shake the feeling that someone else was in the room. Then he saw her. She was standing by the window, almost hidden by the drapery. She could have been a marble statue for all her movement. She didn't even appear to be breathing. He found it more than odd that she'd been standing there the whole time and hadn't spoken a word. He wondered suddenly if she had even seen him.

"Excuse me," he said. "I didn't realize that anyone was in here."

* * *

Elise heard him speak before she saw him, but told herself not to be frightened. She was determined never to be frightened again. She had heard them all come in. She'd been waiting. Putting her hand into the pocket of her smock, she felt the cold comforting warmth of polished metal. It gave her a sense of strength and courage.

She hadn't planned on Mr. Kaiser coming in for a drink, but it really didn't matter. In fact it might help. As long as she took care of things before Julian came home on Sunday, she would never be sent away again. That gave her three days.

She turned away from the window. *Smile*, Coriander told her. "Good evening, Mr. Kaiser," she said, doing what Coriander said as precisely as she could. Coriander was so much better about these things than she. "I was just getting ready to go to bed," she said, crossing to the door. "Did you have a pleasant dinner?" *Perfection*, Coriander said. *No one would ever guess that you do not live in their world*.

"Very nice," Kaiser said. "I'm just waiting for your sister-in-law. She's putting Christian to bed."

"Of course," Elise said, smiling timidly. She hesitated by the door, and Kaiser got the peculiar impression that for a minute she wasn't sure where she was going. "Yes, of course," she said, as if to someone else. "I'm going to bed. Good night, Mr. Kaiser. I hope you won't be such a stranger to us in the future." Then she left the room.

Kaiser sipped his drink, thinking that Elise Ferrare was one of the most peculiar people he had ever met. After their first few meetings he'd become convinced that she was mentally disturbed, but earlier tonight she'd seemed like a different person—unsure of herself, true, but perfectly sane. Now he was thinking that his first impression had been closer to the truth.

He wondered whether Elise had ever been in a mental institution, and decided to ask Francesca about it, but she looked so tired when she came into the room, that he changed his mind. "I'd better go," he said. "You look as if you could use a good night's sleep."

"It's been a long day," she admitted, sitting down in front of the fire, "but please stay. I won't sleep even if I do go to bed. I rarely sleep anymore."

He sat down across from her and tried to read her expression. She did look exhausted, but for some reason the lines of pain around her mouth seemed to be less noticeable.

"Did Christian get off to sleep?" he asked.

"Like a rock." She frowned. "But do you know what he made me promise before he went to sleep?"

"What?"

"Not to eat or drink anything Elise might give me."

Kaiser wasn't sure how to respond. "Christian is afraid of Elise," he said at last.

She narrowed her eyes. "How do you know that?"

"He told me the day I took him fishing."

"Why is he afraid? She has never harmed him." Then she shook her head. "Never mind," she said softly. "I know why."

Kaiser waited.

"Elise is a diagnosed schizophrenic. She has been in an institution for as long as I have known her. Until two months ago, that is. Her doctors have assured us, however, that she is harmless. A danger to no one, not even herself, and quite capable of leading a relatively normal life, provided she keeps calm and takes the proper medication." She took a deep breath. "But Christian doesn't know about schizophrenia. Nor do I for that matter, except to say that it is a tragedy. Difficult for an adult to understand, impossible for a child."

"Why is she living here now?"

"Julian brought her here. To be my companion," she said, making no attempt to hide her bitterness. "He brought her here after I . . . after I tried to kill myself.

But you can see for yourself she is no companion to me. In fact I think she views me as the enemy."

For a moment Kaiser was caught off balance. Her reference to her suicide attempt was almost casual. "Why did you try to kill yourself?" he asked quietly, and again had the peculiar feeling that although she'd just made reference to it herself, she didn't know what he was talking about.

Then she smiled, but it wasn't really a smile. It was simply an upturning of the corners of her mouth. "I guess I was just tired of it all," she said. "Besides, it does me no good to talk about it." She dismissed the subject with a wave of her hand. "We were talking about Elise. Not a happy subject, but preferable to some others."

"Why do you let Elise stay with you?"

"I have no choice. Only Julian can make the decision to send her away. Besides, where would she go? Back to the sanitarium? I don't think they'd take her. Their beds are reserved for people much sicker than Elise is. And she wants so desperately to live with Julian. Have I the right to add to the hell she already lives with every minute of her life?" She looked away. "I know what it's like to live in Hell. What difference that hers happens to be in another place?"

"In any case," Kaiser said softly, "I would be very careful of Christian."

"I have no intention of letting my sister-in-law terrorize my son." She shook her head. "Poor Elise. She was giving me her pills whenever Julian was away. The first two times I really thought I was going mad, but when it happened a third time . . ." She frowned. "Though why she did it is still a mystery to me. In any case, I think that somehow Christian knew."

"I wouldn't be surprised."

She shrugged. "I will never understand Elise. You saw what she was like tonight. She was trying so hard to please, that it made me want to weep, and yet . . ." She took a slow sip of her drink, considering. "At least with her here I don't have to be alone with my husband." She said the last with such venom that Kaiser was startled. "Don't look so shocked," she said. "It's no secret that I hate him."

"Then I suppose my next question is obvious. Why do you stay married to him?"

She turned her face away. "Because of my children," she said. "If it weren't for them . . ." She brought her teeth together with such force that Kaiser heard them click. He knew that Francesca was shielding Hildy and Christian from something, and whatever it was, she was prepared to spend the rest of her life with a man she loathed. Unless she could escape with them. Kaiser wanted to tell her again that he would help her, but he decided against it. The next step had to be hers.

He stood up and put his empty glass on the sideboard. "It's late," he said. "I'd better be going."

She didn't answer, but sat stone still in the chair, as if she had no strength left even to say good night.

He turned at the door, not wanting to leave without some assurance that he would see her again. "If you and Christian haven't had enough, I'd be happy to take you fishing again tomorrow."

She stood up and crossed the room to stand close beside him. He could sense her shaking, and he was filled with an overwhelming urge to pull her against him. Instead he looked down at her upturned face to see tears in her eyes. "Don't cry," he said softly. "Nothing is worth your tears."

"On the contrary, dear friend, my tears are worth nothing." She turned away. "They make me sick," she said fiercely. Then she turned back abruptly. "Christian and I will be happy to go with you tomorrow. What time?"

"Nine."

"Nine it is."

Kaiser left then, feeling as if he had been in the middle of some kind of war, without any idea who was doing the fighting.

17

Elise walked down the hall to a rhythm only she could hear and opened the door to her room. Everything looked the same, and yet she knew it wasn't. She reached into her pocket, took out the silver letter opener and looked at it, amazed to see how beautiful it was. She'd never noticed before. She traced the pattern with the tip of her finger, remembering the day Julian had given it to her. That terrible day more than thirty years ago. It wasn't a pleasant memory, but she decided to think about it. It would be a good test to see just how much pain she could stand.

It was right after their father died that Julian had given her the gift. "But it isn't even my birthday," Elise said, holding the box at arm's length, playing the game she loved so dearly.

"You don't need a birthday to give something special to your favorite lady." It was Julian's usual answer.

Elise sat down on the edge of her bed and ripped the paper off the box. "What can it be?" She was excited. She never tired of receiving beautifully wrapped boxes, and was much less concerned with the contents. In fact most of the time she didn't even know exactly what it was Julian had given her. The thrill was all in the receiving. It meant that she was loved.

Opening the box, she found an exquisite silver something set with tiny emeralds. "It's lovely," she said, still flushed from the pleasure of opening the box.

"Do you know what it is?" Julian asked.

She shook her head. "What is it?" she whispered.

"A letter opener."

She held it in her hand, feeling its cold warmth. "What is it for?"

"To open letters with, my darling," he laughed.

She was puzzled. "But I never receive any letters."

"But you will," he said.

She felt the ancient dread begin to edge its way across the plains of her mind. "Why will I?" The words were round, like small O's.

"Because I'm going to write to you. From the island."

"What island?" She wasn't sure she'd asked the question, wasn't sure she would hear the answer.

"I'm going to spend some time at Grandmother Ferrare's house in Nantucket."

Coriander told her to smile. She did. At least she thought she did. "Well, I've been alone before," she said. "And I've survived." *Just barely*, Coriander said.

"That's my girl."

"How long will you be gone?" It was a whisper.

There was an almost imperceptible pause before he answered, but she heard it. "I don't know," he said.

She felt her hand fly to her throat. "Am I to go with you?" It was a ragged prayer. Waves were crashing on the beach behind her eyes.

Julian sat down beside her and held her close, until her heartbeat began to slow. "I cannot take you, 'Lise," he said softly.

"Why not?" She began to cry. "I won't be any trouble. I won't embarrass you, I promise."

"I cannot take you, dearest sister, because I'm not going alone. Juliette is coming with me."

He's taking Juliette, Coriander said. But Elise didn't know who Juliette was. "Who is she?" Elise whispered into his shoulder.

"She is the most wonderful woman alive. When you meet her, you'll love her, I know. She is the woman I intend to marry." Julian said the words, but Elise didn't hear him. She was already far away, falling, and no matter how hard he tried, Julian couldn't catch her.

But Julian hadn't married Juliette. When he had finally come back months later, he'd come alone. And he never mentioned marriage again. Not for twenty blissful years. Not until Francesca.

Elise turned the letter opener over in her hand, noticing the intricate detail of each delicate scroll. Then she dropped it back in the pocket of her smock. She listened hard to see what trouble she had stirred up by remembering Juliette, but to her great relief, her voices were quiet.

She undid her braid and began to brush her hair. It would probably be a long time before Mr. Kaiser left and Francesca was alone, but Elise didn't mind. She wasn't at all tired. She finished brushing her hair, then sat down on the edge of her bed to wait.

It was well past midnight when she heard Francesca coming up the stairs and down the hall to Christian's bedroom. She wasn't in there long before Elise heard the door open then close softly, and the sound of Francesca's footsteps moving away.

She waited, gathering her courage. *It's time*, Coriander said. *If you wait any longer she'll be asleep.*

Elise slipped out into the hall. She walked quietly but with firm purpose. Just outside Christian's room she stopped. Her hand opened and closed around the hasp of the letter opener in her pocket, and she felt such a surge of impatience that she nearly shouted. Just in time her hand flew up to cover her mouth.

She took several deep breaths, then turned away from the boy's door and walked back up the hall. She knocked softly on Francesca's door.

"Who is it?"

"Elise." She modulated her voice so that it sounded just right.

The door opened and Francesca stood beside her.

"May I speak to you?" Elise said, and allowed one tear to slide down her cheek.

Francesca looked uncertain, then opened the door. "Come in, Elise," she said.

Elise sat in the straight-back chair beside Francesca's dressing table and carefully folded her hands in her lap. "I have come to beg your forgiveness," she said, and found that her tears were flowing as naturally as if she really meant what she was saying.

Francesca sat down on the edge of the bed. "You have no reason to ask for that."

Elise didn't dare look at her. Instead she kept her eyes on her hands. "But I do. I gave you my pills."

"I know that, Elise. But I also know that you aren't always responsible for what you do."

Elise shrugged and closed her eyes. She'd rehearsed her speech, but had to use every bit of concentration to make the words come out right. "I was afraid you would send me away," she said in a whisper. "I know you don't like me."

She heard Francesca take a deep breath. "I don't understand you, Elise."

Elise nodded. "Julian is the only one who has ever understood." She felt her courage beginning to slip away. She was telling too much of the truth. "I would like us to be friends," she said with great effort. "It's what Julian wants.

Just tell me what I must do to make you and Christian like me." She could feel Francesca's eyes boring into her skull.

"I'd *never* send you away from your brother," Francesca said. "As far as I'm concerned, you may live with him for the rest of your life."

Elise was startled. She hadn't expected that reply. She looked over at Francesca, confused. Then she heard the rumbling begin. *She's a liar*, Coriander told her. *She doesn't mean a word of what she says. Just like Anna. Don't be fooled.* Elise felt reassured. Of course he was right. "That's all I want, Francesca," she whispered. "To live with Julian forever."

Francesca stood up. "Then it's all settled," she said. "You needn't worry, Elise. I'll never be the one to send you away."

Elise sucked in her breath. She had to ask the crucial question. "Will you help me to make Christian like me?" she said, breathless. "It would make Julian so happy." She held her breath waiting for Francesca's reply. Her whole plan depended on the answer. She made herself look up. She knew she was shaking, but couldn't control it. "Please, Francesca."

"I don't really think it matters to Julian," Francesca said coldly. "He doesn't like Christian himself. But if it means so much to you, I'll do what I can."

"Christian is Julian's son. And yours," Elise said, gaining control with great effort. "He's the key."

"The key to what?"

Elise's hand flew to her throat. She hadn't meant to say that. *Stupid*, Coriander said. *Foolish girl. You've given it away.* "The key to happiness," Elise said quickly, and when she dared to look up, she was thrilled to see that Francesca didn't look at all alarmed. In fact Francesca seemed to have forgotten that she was even there.

* * *

Kaiser slept very little during the night. Just before dawn he finally fell into a dreamless sleep. It was the sound of the front door knocker that wakened him. "The Ferrares are downstairs," Mrs. Minstrell said from the doorway.

Kaiser sat straight up in bed. "What time is it?"

"Nine-thirty."

"Jesus," Kaiser said under his breath, then told Mrs. Minstrell to say that he'd be right down.

He showered, dressed quickly, and went downstairs.

Francesca was sitting by the window in the living room with Christian close beside her. When he came into the room, she rushed to greet him as if he were a dear friend who had been away a long, long time. Kaiser was non-plussed. Here was a side of Francesca he had never seen before. "I'm so sorry we woke you," she said, as breathless as if she'd been running. "But we couldn't wait to be on our way on such a glorious morning, could we, Christian?" She smiled a brilliant smile, and in spite of his confoundment, Kaiser found himself fighting the impulse to embrace her.

She took him by the hand like an impatient child. "Let's go, shall we? I promised Christian we'd stop at Downy Flake for jelly doughnuts."

"Just let me get my jacket," Kaiser said, laughing. Her enthusiasm was contagious, but the questions in the back of his mind bothered him. What had happened to change her mood this time? He grabbed his coat from the front closet and shrugged. What the hell, he said to himself. You don't understand her and you probably never will, but there's nothing that says you can't enjoy it while it lasts.

He watched her walk hand in hand with Christian down the middle of the road, and had the curious impression that she was acting out a part. Up until now, she'd shown a variety of moods ranging from cold indifference to anger to utter despair. But this was the first time he'd seen an unguarded warmth in her, a warmth that seemed to be directed at him. But why? It was almost as if she were testing him, that she wanted desperately to trust him but wasn't sure how.

When they arrived at the boatyard Hank was hard at work on *Seabird*, to Kaiser's surprise. "Now this *is* unbelievable," Kaiser said to him. "How much longer do you think it will take to finish?"

"Be done this afternoon, if I don't get interrupted," Hank said.

"Fantastic," Kaiser said, and turned to Francesca, only to find her pale and shaking. "What's the matter?" he asked. But even as he did, Kaiser had an idea about what she was thinking: Hildy wouldn't be back by the time his boat was ready to sail.

She turned and began to walk down the pier.

"Francesca," he said, grabbing her before she could get away, spinning her around to face him. "Speak to me. Tell me what you're thinking."

She shook her head and covered her face with her hands.

"Mama?" Christian whispered, close beside her. "Are you getting sick again?"

She dropped her hands and straightened up. "No, sweetheart," she said. "I'm not sick." She turned to Kaiser. "I'm sorry," she said. "This was a bad idea. I think we'd better go home."

"Christian," Kaiser said, handing the child a dollar. "Go disturb Hank and buy some bait." Then he took Francesca by the arm, led her up the walkway, and sat her down on a wooden bench. "Listen to me," he said. "Don't you think I can see that you were perfectly happy until you found out my boat is almost ready to sail?" He lowered his voice. "Don't you trust me enough to tell me what's on your mind?"

Kaiser couldn't see her face, but he could tell she was truly devastated. "It's just that it's so soon. I wasn't expecting it."

"That's not good enough, Francesca," he said. "I know it's

not because you can't bear the thought of me leaving. In fact you probably don't care at all about me."

"That's not true," she said. "You're the only friend I have."

"Maybe, maybe not," he said, frowning. "That's still not good enough."

Francesca got up and walked to the edge of the dock. He saw her square her shoulders, then exhale. "Do you know what it's like to wish to be dead?" she asked. "I don't mean a fleeting thought in a moment of adversity, I mean a living, growing desire that never leaves your conscious mind?" She turned back and faced Kaiser, her eyes the color of a winter sky. "If it weren't for Christian and Hildy," she said without any emotion whatever, "I would kill myself."

A chill touched him. Francesca Ferrare wasn't exaggerating. She was stating a simple fact, and he believed her. "But why?" he said, spreading his hands before him in a gesture of noncomprehension.

She shook her head. "The why is unimportant. But someday," she said quietly, "when they're both old enough not to need me anymore, when I know they can take care of themselves and are safe, I'll do it."

Kaiser went to her, put his arms around her, held her against him. "I know there's nothing I can do," he said into her hair. "But Jesus Christ, I'm so very sorry. I wish it weren't so. At the very least I wish I understood why." He was filled then with a sudden rage, with a desire to destroy whatever had caused her such utter hopelessness. "Who did this to you?" he asked.

She backed away and stood looking at him for a minute, then smiled sadly and shook her head. "That's part of my pain, dear friend," she said. "I can never tell." Then she turned away and began to walk up the dock to meet her son, leaving Kaiser with the terrible feeling that somehow he had failed her.

18

Elise checked the table setting for the tenth time. Everything had to be perfect. The colored balloons hung like pieces of exotic fruit high above the center of the table, and she adjusted the streamers that Christian would pull to release a shower of candy and nuts. *You have outdone yourself*, Coriander said.

Elise stood back and smiled. Christian and Francesca would be coming back from their fishing trip very soon, and look what she had done for them. The neatly trimmed sandwiches were all prepared and waiting beside the bowls of cherry gelatin, and the icy lemonade in its crystal pitcher formed little beads of moisture on the outside of the glass. There were small gingerbread cakes for dessert with tiny whipped-cream flowers on top.

Elise hadn't baked like this for years, not since she shared a home with Julian, but it had all come back to her. Coriander had helped, but most of her strength had come from her own magic. She'd been very careful to use exactly the right spells, some of which she had almost forgotten.

"Three more days before Julian comes home," she said aloud. "You only have three more days to destroy the child." She felt a rumbling in the back of her mind, but paid no attention. There was one last bit of magic she needed to make the day go perfectly, but she couldn't quite remember what it was. It had something to do with an article of clothing. *Your blue dress*, Coriander said. Of course, Elise thought. My blue dress. And she flew up the stairs to change.

Elise had been wearing her blue dress the night Julian came back from Nantucket all those years ago. He'd been gone more than two months, living hidden away with his precious Juliette, writing to Elise only occasionally to let her know he was still alive. And to tell her how desperately in love he was and how anxious to be married.

Then one day he called to say he was coming home. Elise didn't sleep at all that night. She was too busy preparing spells to ward off catastrophe. It seemed that all of her life the worst things happened only when she was caught off guard, only when she had failed to work her magic. Like when Anna had come. And then Anna's wicked child. This time when Julian came home to her, she would not be unprepared.

She turned all the knives around in the kitchen drawer, and turned the cups all upside down in the cupboard. She buried five copper pennies in the soft earth beside the front steps and cleaned out Julian's initials, which she'd carved in the top stair, using iodine to make them pure.

She took particular pains in her garden—that part of the world that belonged only to her. She knew every plant intimately, knowing somehow that their roots were her own. Coriander never came with her to that place. It was the only spot in the world where she was truly alone. She scattered clumps of her own hair along the path to keep out the evil she feared might come with Julian, and when she was sure that everything was safe, returned to the house.

Inside she touched the wooden frames of all the windows and doors and clicked her heels five times in each threshold, and after she'd made certain that all was secure, went upstairs to dress for Julian's homecoming.

She had a terrible time deciding what to wear. Coriander wanted her to put on her pink wool, but pink frightened her. Instead she chose the dark blue, the dress she'd worn to her father's funeral. She felt almost peaceful when she wore it, almost sane. When Julian came home alone that night to tell her that his beloved Juliette had left him and run away, Elise knew that her dark blue dress was full of power.

For the first time in many months he made love to her. Afterward Elise lay awake, secure in the knowledge that if she could just remember all of her magic spells, she would never be sent away again.

"Please stay, Mr. Kaiser," Elise said anxiously. "It's to be a happy party, and everyone seems so much happier when you're here."

There was an awkward silence while Kaiser tried to make some sense of this latest madness. Elise had met them at the door, all dressed up in blue silk, eager for them to come in and see her surprise. She led them to the dining room door and opened it wide.

Inside, the table was laid with every kind of confection, enough food to feed a dozen people or more, but that wasn't what took Kaiser's breath away. It was the nightmare quality of the room itself. Garish-colored streamers and paper flowers crisscrossed in every direction without any apparent plan, like giant spiders' webs, and enormous bunches of balloons hung here and there with the same total disregard for order.

"It's a party," Christian shouted, clapping his hands, oblivious to the bizarre quality of the scene. "But who is it for?"

"It's for you, Christian," Elise said. "Because we're all so grateful that you weren't hurt yesterday. Do you like it?"

"Please stay," Francesca broke in, turning to Kaiser. "Elise has gone to so much trouble." She turned to her sister-in-law. "This is a wonderful surprise, Elise," she said gently. "Especially for Christian. It's been a long time since he's had a party."

Elise said nothing, but Kaiser saw the color rise in her cheeks. "I hope he likes it," she said. She turned to Christian. "Come, child. Let me show you something." She was shaking, but she took him by the hand and led him to the table. "Pull this," she said, pointing to one streamer.

Christian shot an anxious glance at his mother, but Francesca smiled and nodded. "Go ahead, Christian," she said.

The little boy tugged at the streamer, and from above came a shower of candy and nuts, some striking him on the head. Christian looked as if he didn't know whether to laugh or cry.

"Now," Elise said, smiling broadly, "we can have our party."

The food was edible, but Kaiser couldn't rid himself of the feeling that he was at the Mad Hatter's tea party. Elise said very little, nor did she do anything out of the ordinary, yet Kaiser had the eerie sensation that she wasn't really with them. There was an almost imperceptible pause before she spoke, as if she weren't sure what should come next.

"I didn't realize you were such a wonderful cook," Francesca said to Elise.

Pause.

"I'm not really."

"But you're too modest. Wherever did you learn?"

Pause.

"When I was very young."

"Who taught you?" Francesca asked, still smiling.

Pause.

"Anna." At that point Elise stood up abruptly and poured more lemonade into Christian's glass, spilling some onto the table. Kaiser noticed that her hand was shaking badly.

"Would you like me to show you how to make the flowers on the gingerbread cakes?" she said to Christian. The little boy looked over at his mother, still uncertain about his aunt, but his mother nodded. "I think you'd find it lots of fun," she said. "I'm sure Hildy would love to learn, too, sometime."

Christian hesitated.

"We'll be right here, Christian," Francesca said softly. "If you need me, just call."

That seemed to reassure the child, and he followed after his aunt.

"What do you make of all this?" Kaiser said when they were alone.

Francesca shook her head.

He gestured at the room. "Does this look as strange to you as it does to me?"

She nodded. "Poor Elise." Then she told him about her sister-in-law's strange late-night visit. "She seems so desperate to please."

"Do you know why?"

"She says it's because she wants to make Julian happy, and I don't doubt that she does. What she doesn't seem to realize is that Julian has no use for his son." She sighed. "In any case, whatever mental problems she has, one thing is certain: she'll do anything in the world to stay with Julian. He's more than her life—he's her only reason to fight for sanity."

"Does he know how much she depends on him?"

"Julian doesn't care about other people," she said coldly. "He uses Elise to suit his needs. Housekeeper, companion, whatever. As long as he has a need for her, she'll stay. When she doesn't fit any longer, he'll send her away. Either to some institution or to live alone. He doesn't care. Do you know that in all the eleven years of our marriage, he never visited Elise once?"

"When do you expect him home?" Kaiser asked.

"Sunday." She shivered in spite of the fact that the room was uncomfortably warm, then stood up, crossed to the window, and opened it wide. "I need some air," she said.

He was about to go to her when the phone rang. She left the room to answer, then returned without speaking, indicating with a motion that it was for Kaiser.

It was Mrs. Minstrell. Hank had just called to say that *Seabird* was ready. "Hank also said that if you have any intention of sailing to the mainland," Mrs. Minstrell said, "you'd better get going. They're predicting a spell of bad weather to move in by the end of the week."

Kaiser hung up the phone. He wasn't ready to leave yet, but knew he had to. If Francesca wouldn't trust him, he'd have to leave without her. He started back toward the dining room, but Francesca stopped him in the doorway.

"You're leaving," she said flatly.

He nodded.

"When?"

"Tomorrow morning."

"You can't wait any longer?" Her face was pale.

"They're expecting bad weather."

She nodded. "Then there's nothing to be done."

"What do you mean?"

She looked away.

He walked to her and put his finger gently to her chin, making her look at him. He couldn't believe the hopelessness he saw in her eyes. "Francesca," he said softly, "I know you want to leave your husband. And I know that he won't let you. He's holding something over your head. In most civilized countries it's called blackmail."

She looked as if he'd slapped her across the face. "How do you know that?" she gasped.

"I heard you talking—that day in the garden when I helped Hildy and Christian with the gull."

"Did they hear?" She looked physically ill, and tears had come into her eyes.

"No," he lied. "They heard nothing."

She covered her face with her hands. "Oh, dear God," she whispered. "Has this nightmare no end?"

"It may if you let me help."

She shook her head forcefully. "How can I ask you? What can I possibly offer in return? Nothing. Not even an explanation."

"I'm not asking for anything in return. I'm asking you to let me help you."

"But why?" she whispered. "Why would you want to get involved in this . . . this cesspool?"

"Because I love you," he said quietly. He hadn't even considered saying such a thing, but now that he had, it seemed the most natural thing in the world. He did love her. Simply. Without condition. Not knowing her secret. Not needing to. "I love you," he said again. It made everything else seem inconsequential.

She looked at him, incredulous. "How could you love me? You don't know. I don't deserve to be loved. I'm a disgrace."

"You're not a disgrace, Francesca. You are the most utterly lovable woman I have ever met. And if you will let me, I will help you. No strings whatsoever."

She brushed a tear from her eye and stood staring at him hard, as if she were trying to see through his face into his soul. "You really mean it?" she whispered finally.

"Cross my heart and hope to die," he said, performing the ritual. "I'll wait for Hildy to come home, and as soon as she does, I'll take you wherever you think you'll be safe."

All at once she smiled; the most glorious smile, and it was

all the reward he would ever need. "I can give you nothing, Patrick Kaiser," she said softly. "But I will never, ever forget."

His breath caught in his throat, but he forced himself to stay calm. "Now, if you think you can concentrate, how do you plan to get Hildy and Christian out of here without Julian knowing?"

Francesca had come alive, and in a spontaneous gesture of gratitude and trust grabbed his hand and held it to her lips. "I don't know yet," she whispered. "But don't worry. I'll figure it out."

19

Elise read each word carefully and without difficulty. She rarely had problems reading when she remembered to take her medication. It was only when she forgot, that the words came alive on the page, twisting themselves into goats and loaves of bread and wisps of smoke which drifted off to disappear into space.

The boy sat still beside her and listened without interruption. He had said it was one of his favorite stories, and although Elise had no trouble reading the words, none of it made any sense to her. "But Eeyore wasn't listening," she read. "He was taking the balloon out and putting it back again, as happy as could be. . . ." She closed the book, not because she knew the story had ended, but because there were no more words on the page.

The child got up and stood silently observing her. Can he read my thoughts? she asked Coriander, but Coriander was quiet.

"Thank you for reading me the story, Elise," he was saying. "And now it's time for me to go to bed."

"Good night," she said.

"Good night." He hesitated, then to Elise's real horror, he tiptoed up and kissed her on the cheek. "Thank you for the party too," he said, and ran from the room.

But Elise didn't see him. The skin on her cheek was

melting where his lips had touched her, and the rumbling and roaring flooded her mind. This time she was unable to push it back. She held herself tight, trying to understand what was happening. She'd made tremendous strides today. The child had not hidden from her. He had allowed her to show him how to make gingerbread flowers, to be alone with him, to take his hand and read him a story. All that was critical if her plan were to succeed.

But the waves of black were coming now, washing the colors from the room. Help me, Coriander, she begged. What's happening? And then she heard his voice above the roar. *You're allowing yourself to become confused, Elise. You're forgetting that the only way you can protect yourself is to destroy the child. The way you destroyed Anna's. Think, think.*

She held herself tight and rocked back and forth, drawing pictures in her mind. *You must be strong,* Coriander said, *or Francesca will send you away and you will never see Julian again. You have only two more days. If Julian comes back, he won't let you destroy Francesca. He knows what you did to Anna and he will never allow it to happen again.*

At the sound of his words Elise felt the waves subside, the rumbling fade like thunder echoing across a distant hill. After a time she was able to stand up. The children's book fell to the floor and she pushed it under the chair with the tip of her shoe. "You won't confuse me," she said aloud. "I know who the enemy is, and none of your tricks will work."

She crossed to the desk and picked up the calendar. On it she had circled the number of the day Julian was to return home. She squinted and forced herself to think. Only two days left. She clenched her teeth until they hurt. *It must be tomorrow,* Coriander said softly. *If you are going to save yourself, it must be tomorrow.*

Elise nodded and began to get ready for bed.

* * *

Kaiser woke the next morning with a dull headache, and he knew why. He'd spent most of the night arguing with himself over Francesca Ferrare.

He had offered to spirit her away with her two children, to a destination that she refused to reveal to him until they were well under way. He'd offered in spite of the fact that he knew she had something to hide, a secret so unbearable that she'd tried to kill herself and her children to keep it, a secret she obviously thought was worse than death. What crime was she guilty of? He couldn't imagine. But at this point it didn't matter to him.

He went into the bathroom to brush his teeth. Every argument he could conjure to persuade himself that what he was planning was madness came back to him. But again he concluded that he had no choice. He stopped brushing his teeth and looked at himself hard in the mirror. He'd offered to help Francesca because he knew that she was desperate, and he was in love with her. Simple as that.

He took a mouthful of water and rinsed, spitting vehemently into the sink. "You're crazy, Kaiser," he said. "You are in love with a woman who's giving you a second glance only because you own a boat."

He crossed to the bedroom window and looked out. The Ferrare house was quiet, the shades still drawn, no sign of life. Kaiser remembered his first night on the island, when he had heard the pathetic sobbing. Mrs. Minstrell had been right when she said it could have been any one of them. They all seemed to have plenty of reason to cry.

He was about to turn away when out of the corner of his eye he saw the front door open and Christian step out, followed by Elise. Kaiser frowned as the two turned west, heading up toward the old beach road. He watched until they were almost out of sight, no more than two specks blown along by the wind. "What the hell . . ." he said aloud. "I better find out what's going on."

Francesca opened the door before Kaiser had a chance to

knock. She was almost trembling with anticipation. "Come in," she said in an anxious whisper. She grabbed his hand and pulled him inside. "I've gone over and over it in my mind," she said, "and I really think it has a chance to work. Oh, dear God, if only it does." She closed her eyes, then opened them wide. "You haven't changed your mind." She went suddenly pale.

"I haven't changed my mind." He looked past her shoulder, toward the doorway. "Where was Elise going with Christian?"

She looked puzzled. "What? Christian's still asleep."

"He isn't still asleep," Kaiser said. "I just saw him leaving the house. With Elise."

"You must have been mistaken," she said, turning toward the stairs. "Christian!" she called. "Elise!"

There was no answer. Francesca started up the stairs, then turned abruptly. "She's taken him somewhere," she said, her voice sharp. "But where? And why?" She didn't wait for his answer. Instead she went to the door, threw it open, and called. There was no reply. "I shouldn't be frightened," she said. "Elise would never harm Christian." She looked hard at Kaiser, and her next words were a gasp. "So why am I terrified?"

Quickly he took her by the hand, and together they ran up the road toward the beach.

The wind was blowing cold from the sea, but Elise didn't notice.

"Look at this one," Christian said, holding out a tiny scallop shell for her inspection.

Elise looked down at what he held in his hand and nodded, but didn't touch it. She barely saw it. She kept her hand in her pocket, feeling the cold warmth of the letter opener, and she listened for Coriander to tell her what to do. But there was no sound.

She watched the boy as he stooped to pick up another shell, but she didn't move. She listened. Her world had been strangely quiet all morning, as if it were waiting to see what she would do, and the silence made her nervous. Even a little frightened. Her doctor had told her many times that the sounds she heard in her mind were symptoms of her illness, that if she were sane, she wouldn't hear them anymore.

Can this be sanity? she wondered suddenly. This deafening, terrible silence? She prayed that it was not. If the roaring and rumbling of her world had been terrifying, this was so much worse. This was absolute desolation. She felt a sudden overwhelming urge to scream.

All at once, she heard Coriander. *Francesca is working her power, Elise,* he said, floating above the alien silence. *She is trying to confuse you. Don't think about the soundlessness. Pay attention to what you are about.*

"Here's a weird one," the boy said, running toward her.

She looked down at the small hand and felt her own fingers open and close around the letter opener.

Christian turned away and was bending to put his shell in the bucket. *Now!* Coriander screamed in a terrible voice that she had never heard before, and her brain exploded then with a hundred familiar sounds. Every voice she had ever lived with shrieked out the command. *Now! Do it now!*

She took two steps toward the child, and he looked up, startled, as if she had called out to him. She could see his eyes grow round, and he tried to stand up, but the earth caught fire around him. She tried to hurry before the ground melted under her feet, but it was too late. She didn't even have the strength to pull the letter opener out of her pocket. As she fell, the last thing she saw through the smoke and flame was Francesca, running toward them over the top of the dunes.

* * *

When she was a child, Elise used to think that someday when she grew up she'd be able to walk on every road in the world. There would be no path too small to be noticed, no highway too broad to be crossed, and she would go from town to town, wandering without care until she was too exhausted to go any farther. That must be where I've been, she thought, because I'm too exhausted to go any farther. She tried to open her eyes, but it seemed as if the lid muscles had been stretched beyond their limits and would never open again. Is it winter yet, she wondered, or is it winter still?

She lay on her back, listening for something to tell her where she was, who she was, or even if she was, but there was no sound until she heard the voice she knew was Julian's. With great effort she squinted through the keyhole in her eye, to see him looking down at her. But where was she? Had Francesca sent her back to the sanitarium? Her teeth began to chatter even though she was burning up. *Be calm*, Coriander said, floating toward her from a long way off. *It will come in time. It always does.*

"Elise," Julian was saying, "you've given us all quite a scare. What happened?"

Memory grew wings and flew into her brain. She was filled with horror. Christian was not dead. Julian had returned, and now Francesca would surely send her away. She had failed to save herself, but worse, she didn't know why. What spell had she forgotten to cast, what magic words had she left unspoken? "I'm sorry," she whispered brokenly. "I have failed."

Then, as she lay there beaten and ashamed, a horror worse than any yet occurred to her. Did Julian know that she had tried to kill Christian? Had the child seen her weapon? Had Francesca seen? Now I really am afraid, she thought, and all the ancient terror she'd tried so desperately to conquer cut at her like a knife, hacking off parts of her brain. She began to cry.

"It's all right," Julian said. "It's all right, 'Lise. You are safe in your own bed. I won't let anything happen to you."

With every fiber of control left to her, she made the words: "Are you sending me away?"

"Of course not, 'Lise," he said, and his voice seemed gentle and loving. "Why would I do such a thing? You've done nothing wrong. Except to frighten everyone half to death with your fainting. Dr. Bryson told you to avoid stress of any kind, that it brings on these episodes. So what upset you so?"

He doesn't know, Coriander whispered. *And neither does Francesca. Or the child. You're not beaten yet. You will live to fight another day.*

Elise opened her eyes to a world full of color and shape and form. And Julian. She sucked in the sweet air and smiled. "I love you, Julian," she said.

20

Hildy lay on her back on the floor behind the stairs, watching the prisms of crystal that hung from the candelabra above her head, listening to the faintest tinkling they made whenever a door opened somewhere else in the house. She'd been there almost an hour, waiting for Christian to wake up, and had decided not to tell him what had happened on her trip—partly because she wasn't sure herself what it meant, partly because it made her feel ashamed.

Julian had kissed her on the mouth. In the middle of the night he'd come into her room and kissed her on the mouth. Her father had never kissed her before. Not ever. And it had confused her, frightened her. And then the phone had rung. It had been Mama, telling Julian to come home right away. Elise had taken a bad fall. She was having one of her episodes and Mama wasn't sure if she should call a doctor. Hildy had heard Julian say to do nothing. The last thing he wanted was for the locals to find out that Elise was schizophrenic. Absolutely no doctor, Julian had said. Just put her to bed. Try to get her to take her pills. He would come at once.

They had taken the next plane home. Hildy had said a special prayer of thanks to God, because she didn't want to be alone with her father ever again. She shivered and made a promise to herself never to think about it anymore.

She propped herself up on one elbow and listened. Something had changed in the house while they were gone, something that had nothing to do with Elise's collapse. It had to do with Mama. She'd met them at the door last night and hugged her so hard that it hurt. But that wasn't the strangest thing. The strangest thing had happened after Julian had gone upstairs to see Elise. Her mother had taken her by both shoulders and held her at arm's length, looking at her as if she were trying to read her mind.

"What's wrong, Mama?" Hildy had asked, alarmed, wondering if her mother somehow knew that Julian had frightened her.

Her mother smiled then, a bright, sweet smile like the kind she remembered. "Nothing is wrong, my darling," she'd said. "I'm just so happy to have you safely home."

"I'm happy to be here," Hildy replied, close to tears. She brushed them away. "What happened to Elise?"

Her mother's face had gone pale. "Is something wrong with you, Hildy? Has something happened to upset you?"

"Nothing happened, Mama." Hildy buried her face against her mother's breast. "I'm just happy to be home, that's all." How could she ever tell her mother how ashamed she felt? What if it was all only her imagination? She squeezed her eyes shut tight, thinking only that she was home now, and safe.

Francesca pushed her away gently, and Hildy could see from the look on her face that she was concerned. "Has Julian done something to upset you?" she asked, her voice hard.

Hildy shook her head vigorously. "Everything was fine, Mama," she said. "Just fine."

Her mother started to say something else, then to Hildy's relief changed her mind. "It doesn't matter," she said, almost to herself. "You aren't ever going with him again."

Hildy stared at her mother and was about to ask what she meant when Julian called from upstairs, and the conversation ended.

Now she sat up with a jerk and listened. She heard footsteps coming down the back stairs, and knew it was Christian. She got to her feet as quietly as she could and crept to the corner, holding her breath. Just as her brother reached the bottom step, she leaped out from behind the door. "I declare war!" she shouted, and tapped him on top of the head. She turned and with a whoop ran through the kitchen and out the back door.

Like shadow upon shadow they ran to the very edge of the cliff, spreading their arms out as if they would fly away. "Stop!" Christian screamed. "I tagged you."

"Did not," Hildy called over her shoulder.

"Did so, Hildy. You're cheating."

"I am not," Hildy said, stopping to let Christian catch up with her. "You never touched me."

"Did so."

"Did not."

"I quit, cheater." Christian flopped down on his knees in the dry grass.

"Oh, all right, silly." Hildy sank down beside him, pulling him close. "Of course you tagged me. I was only teasing."

All at once Christian realized that Hildy really was there. She wasn't supposed to be home until tomorrow. "Oh, Hildy," he said, throwing his arms around her neck. "I'm so glad you're back."

"Me too," she said. "Now tell me quick, before Mama calls: Why does she seem so different?"

Christian frowned and shook his head. "I don't know. First I almost drowned, and then Elise started being so nice. She had a party for me and read me stories. She didn't seem at all like a witch, Hildy."

"I told you she wasn't."

"Well anyway, yesterday she took me to the beach to collect shells, and then all of a sudden she growled like a bear and fell down. Mr. Kaiser and Mama had to carry her home. They had to drag her, like this." He stood up and showed his sister.

"That must have been awful."

"It was. It took them forever to get her home. She's pretty heavy. At least that's what Mr. Kaiser said."

Hildy nodded. "What about Mama?" Christian looked puzzled. "Christian, think. What's happened to make Mama seem so excited about something?"

The boy shook his head. "It was right after Elise showed me how to make whipped-cream flowers. Mama was talking to Mr. Kaiser, and when I came out to show her my cookies, she was all stirred up, like she was in a hurry to do something." He paused. "Maybe Mr. Kaiser gave her a present."

Hildy shook her head. "I don't think so. I don't think any old present would make Mama so excited."

"Let's ask him."

"Let's ask Mama first. If she won't tell us, then we'll ask him. He's our friend. He'll tell us the truth." Hildy got up and brushed off her skirt. "Did you practice your lessons, Christian?" she asked, suddenly remembering.

Christian grew ashen.

"You didn't. Oh, Christian, how could you forget? You know what Julian said before we left."

Christian's eyes filled with tears. "We were so busy, Hildy, and nobody ever reminded me." He stood up slowly. "I wish Julian had never come back," he said with sudden force.

"Christian," Hildy said, "that's a terrible thing to say."

"I don't care. I mean it. We were all happy while he was gone. Even Elise. Now he's back and you just wait and see. It's going to be awful again."

Hildy thought about it. "Maybe not," she said hopefully.

"Maybe Mama will be strong enough to make things like they used to be."

Christian brightened noticeably. "Maybe. She's a lot better, Hildy. She didn't cry the whole time you were gone. And she didn't act sick either."

They heard their mother call, and they turned back toward the house, but not before they made their special X in the grass and spit on it for good luck. "Maybe something good is going to happen," Hildy said.

"It already has," her brother said, reaching up to take her hand. "You came home."

Hildy looked down at the blond head beside her, and squeezed her brother's hand. She decided that what had happened in London was all in her imagination. She'd just made a mountain out of a molehill, and tonight when she said her prayers, she would ask God to forgive her for being such a ninny.

By late afternoon Elise felt well enough to take some tea, and to her surprise, Francesca brought it herself. Elise studied her sister-in-law through her keyhole, trying to detect any change in her attitude, but Francesca seemed perfectly calm. In fact she seemed almost cheerful.

She knows, Coriander said. *She knows what you tried to do, and that you failed. That is why she's smiling.*

No, she doesn't, Elise snapped. Francesca doesn't know anything about it at all. If she did, she would have told Julian.

"How are you feeling, Elise?" Francesca asked, pouring her a cup of tea. "Can I get you anything else?"

You see, Elise said to Coriander. She doesn't have any idea what I tried to do. "No, thank you, Francesca," she said politely, even managing a weak smile. "This will do quite nicely."

"Well, if there's anything else . . ."

Elise shook her head. *Ask about the boy,* Coriander said. *Did he see you with the weapon?* "I hope Christian wasn't too frightened yesterday," she said.

"We were all concerned, Elise," Francesca said. "You had a terrible fall."

Elise leaned back on her pillow and closed her eyes. You have no idea, sister-in-law, she thought. No idea at all. "I'm very tired," she said.

"I'm sure. Why don't you try to sleep?"

Elise nodded, but didn't open her eyes. Instead she watched through the keyhole until Francesca had left the room. Then she sat bolt upright, full of new courage and determination. Tonight, she told Coriander. Tonight I will finish this business once and for all. *But Julian is home,* Coriander said. I know, she said shuddering. But I cannot wait any longer. I'm getting weaker while Francesca gets stronger with each passing day. It must be done tonight. Julian or no Julian.

Time passed. It always did, Elise knew, and she waited. Julian was the last to go to bed. He came into her room long after the house was quiet and sat down beside her on the bed. "Are you all right?" he asked.

She nodded, feeling the cold warmth of the letter opener on the mattress beside her.

"Have you taken your medication?"

She nodded, still not daring to speak for fear he would sense her excitement.

He kissed her cheek. That was all she needed. A simple kiss on the cheek. Julian hadn't had sex with her in years. Not since Francesca. But Elise didn't care. Julian could have sex with whomever he pleased. The act meant nothing to her. It never had, except to serve as proof that he loved her. And now he had kissed her on the cheek. It was enough. "Good night then, little 'Lise," he said. "Sleep well."

She reached out and squeezed his hand. Tomorrow we will be safe, she said in her mind. You'll see. And you'll thank me. "Good night, Julian," she said aloud. "I love you."

The hallway was deserted, and all the doors were closed. Through the narrow window at the end of the hall came a faint ribbon of moonlight, casting long shadows where in the broad light of day there were none. Normally the darkness would have frightened Elise, but now she hardly noticed. She moved barefoot down the corridor and stopped before each room to listen. She felt as if her ears could hear the slightest sound, and yet all was quiet. Little wisps of dust stirred around her feet then settled down to wait.

Here I am, she said to Coriander, and felt her fingers curve around the warm blade she carried, still safe in the pocket of her robe. She slid along the wall like a shadow, smiling. She felt safe in the dark, and was glad she wouldn't have to look at the boy when she killed him. Looking at him on the beach yesterday had been the thing that had thrown her into the pit.

She stopped just outside Julian's room. There was no sound, but she ran her fingers lightly over the door frame as if to check. Then she moved on. She had a sudden urge to run past Francesca's door, but forced herself to stop and listen. *Take care*, Coriander said. Elise listened, but all was still. She paused only a moment outside of Hildy's room. Of all the occupants in the house, she knew that Hildy would be the most soundly asleep. Hildy never woke even during the worst thunderstorms. Elise had a sudden, terrible thought. Sometimes when Christian was frightened at night he crept in and slept with his sister. *What if . . .* she listened, but no sound came to her.

Suddenly she saw her own bare feet sticking out from below the hem of her robe. *Where are your slippers, Elise?* she asked angrily, and started to turn back. But Coriander urged her on, whispering so that only she could hear. *Forget your slippers and get on with it.*

She moved on. Christian's room was behind the last door on the left, at the darkest end of the hallway, and Elise had to feel for the doorknob. But she wasn't concerned. She curved her hand around the knob and turned. The door swung inward effortlessly and Elise slipped into the room, closing the door softly behind her.

She listened, but there was no sound. *It's been a long trip,* Coriander said, *but you are almost home. Be brave.*

She could feel the carpet moving beneath her feet as she crossed the room to the bed. It was just light enough for her to make out the outline of the boy lying still beneath the covers. The sight brought her breath sharp like a dagger into her throat. For a single instant she couldn't remember why she was here, and was filled with panic. *Think!* Coriander screamed. *Think!*

All at once it came to her, and she brought the blade straight up over her head to come arcing down, plunging through the covers and deep into the boy's body.

At once her legs collapsed from under her and she dropped to her knees beside the bed. Her world erupted in a thunder of applause. *You have done it!* Coriander shouted. *The boy is dead, and when Francesca finds out, she will die too. We are safe.*

Elise lay on the carpet and pulled her knees to her chest, hugging herself tight, fighting for breath. Somewhere she heard doors banging as if they had broken free in a violent wind. She tried to get up but couldn't move. *Get out of here,* Coriander begged. *If they find you, all will be lost.*

She struggled to her knees, holding herself together with all her strength. Help me, Coriander, she begged.

I can't. You must do it yourself.

Elise reached out and grabbed the side of the bed, pulling herself to her feet. She was making sounds with her mouth but they had no meaning. How long have I been here, she wondered. *Too long*, Coriander said. Then all at once the door flew open and a shaft of light bolted across the floor.

Elise shrank back and saw Julian cross to the bed. She heard him speak but couldn't understand the words. He turned toward her, holding the letter opener in his hand. "What have you done, Elise? What have you done?"

She tried to tell him but she couldn't.

Julian grabbed her by the shoulders and began to shake her. "Where is Christian?" he hissed. "And the others? What have you done with them?"

Unable to understand, Elise pointed to the bed. "He is there," she whispered. "I have killed him."

Julian's face was black with rage as he threw back the covers. His voice was pitiless. It reminded her of someone else, but she didn't know who. "You are insane, Elise," he said. "There is no one in this bed. You have killed a shadow, nothing more. They are gone. All of them. Francesca, Hildy, and Christian."

Elise stared at him, stunned. What does he mean, they are gone? she asked Coriander, but he didn't answer. She held her hand out to Julian in a silent plea for help, but he didn't move. He stood looking at her as if she were a rock or a tree. "Please, Julian," she whispered. "I don't understand." And as she slid to the floor she remembered who it was he sounded like. "I'm sorry, Father," she said, and the waves roared over her head and sucked her down into familiar blackness.

21

The wind came cold but steady out of the northeast, and within minutes the *Seabird* was well beyond the breakwater. It was just past eleven, and Kaiser watched in silence as the few lights still visible along the coast faded to black. He listened, feeling the waves, but the seas were blessedly calm. From the cabin below he could see the faint glow of light where Francesca was settling her children down to sleep.

He'd hated to get Mrs. Minstrell involved in this mess, but without a moment's hesitation she had promised to do as he asked. If anyone were to inquire about his whereabouts, she would say that he'd flown back to New York yesterday, and say nothing whatever about *Seabird*.

For a few minutes he tried to forget about everything but the undisturbed rhythm of the ocean. He didn't want to think about the frightened, ashen faces of Hildy and Christian, holding tight to their mother's hand as they scrambled aboard his boat an hour earlier, nor did he want to remember the sound of Hildy's voice when she asked if she'd ever see her father again.

He looked up at the stars and felt a cold chill at the back of his neck that had nothing to do with the weather. "I hope I'm not sorry," he said out loud.

"You won't be, I promise you."

He turned to see Francesca standing a few feet away. "Are they asleep?" he asked.

"Not yet. But soon. They're two very tired children."

"And frightened?"

She shrugged. "I suppose so. But there are many more frightening things in the world than this. They'll survive," she said, the words harsh.

"You're certain that you're doing the only thing you can? No doubts?"

She shook her head. "In all my life I have never been so sure." She sat down next to him and pulled her jacket tight around her.

"Cold?"

She nodded. "But it doesn't matter. The only thing I care about now is that we're almost free." She looked at him with turquoise eyes filled with tears. "I owe it to you, you know. I will never forget what you have done." She leaned toward him, and for a moment he thought she was going to kiss him. His breath caught in his throat, but she stopped, her face inches from his. "I have to know one thing," she said with such intensity that he could see the muscles tighten along her jaw. "Is there any way Julian can catch us?"

"I don't see how," Kaiser said. "If the wind holds, we should be to Montauk by mid-morning. Besides, Julian has no idea where you are. He may suspect that I've helped you, but he doesn't know I have a boat. And Mrs. Minstrell is going to tell him that I flew out yesterday. If nothing else, we have time on our side." He touched the side of her cheek. "I don't think Julian will ever find you, unless you want to be found."

Immediately he saw the tension leave her body, and as it did, her face softened. She looked as she might have looked years earlier, before her life with Julian Ferrare had become such an obvious nightmare. "Thank you, Patrick

Kaiser," she said. Then she leaned over and kissed him full on the mouth.

His desire overcame him, and he pulled her against him, kissing her eyes, her cheeks, her hair. My God, how much I love you, he thought. It amazed him.

"Do you want to make love to me?" she whispered.

"Yes."

She unbuttoned her coat with one hand, the other still at the back of his head. "Touch me," she said. She moved his hand up across the flat of her stomach to the curve of her breast. It was as soft and firm as he'd imagined, but warmer.

"I want you, Francesca," he said.

"I know. And you may have me." She spoke gently, but there was something behind her words that brought Kaiser up short.

He leaned back and looked at her. "Why?" he asked sharply.

She opened her eyes. "Why what?"

"Why may I have you?" She looked puzzled. "Answer me," he said. "Is this supposed to be payment in full for services rendered?" He couldn't see her face, but heard the sharp intake of her breath.

"Would that be so terrible?" she asked softly.

"Shit," he said, and leaned back, closing his eyes.

"I'm sorry. The last thing I wanted was to offend you."

"You haven't offended me," he said quietly.

"Then what is it?"

"I have this peculiar hang-up. I have no desire to make love to someone who doesn't want me back. Besides that, it's a hell of a way to say thanks."

"Can't it be enough? For now?" There was a pleading note in her voice that Kaiser didn't understand.

"Not by a long shot," he replied. He felt her staring at him, but didn't look at her. "You'd better go below and get some sleep. I'll take the first watch, then you can take over.

When we get to Montauk you'll have to tell me where we go from there."

She looked as if she were going to say more, then turned away to look out across the black water. For the first time since they had come aboard, Kaiser became keenly aware of the cold.

He stood up and checked the auto pilot. The wind was steady and they were right on course. "You'd better get some sleep," he said again. "I'll wake you in about five hours."

She stood up and went below without speaking.

Hildy lay on her back in the berth she was sharing with Christian and listened to the faint sounds of the grown-ups talking above the rhythmic whooshing of the water as the boat passed through the waves. Her brother was fast asleep beside her, but she couldn't even close her eyes. She and Christian and her mother had sneaked out of the house like thieves in the night, while Julian sat unaware, lost in his music. Whenever he listened to his own recordings, it was as if he were in a deep trance. He heard nothing else, and they all knew it. But Mama had told them they must be absolutely silent as they left or Julian would hear them and make them stay. Hildy would never forget the look on her mother's face. "If he catches us," she'd said, "I will die," and both children had known without question that their mother meant what she said.

Mr. Kaiser had met them just outside the house, and together they had taken footpaths down to the harbor, avoiding the road.

Hildy was frightened for all kinds of reasons. She didn't want her mother to suffer, and more than that, she'd come to the conclusion that imagination or not, she didn't ever want to be alone with her father again. But most of all it terrified her to think about what Julian would do if he ever caught them. She shivered under her blanket and forced her eyes to close.

Mama said there was nothing to be afraid of now, that they were going to a place where they would be safe and happy forever. She told Hildy not to cry, that everything would be fine, so Hildy hadn't. She could see the tension in her mother's face, so she forced the tears to stay hidden.

But when Hildy finally slept, it wasn't for long, and when she woke, there were tears on her cheeks.

Kaiser had just made the decision not to wake Francesca, when she appeared beside him. "You'd better get some sleep," she said, and without another word she turned away to stare into the darkness.

Kaiser didn't argue. It was obvious that she wanted to be alone, and he was exhausted. He made a last check around the boat, then went below. He fell asleep almost as soon as his head hit the pillow, but came awake with a start to find someone shaking him frantically. He opened his eyes to see a terrified Francesca standing over him. She had abandoned all control.

"He's found us!" she cried. "Dear God, Patrick, he's found us!"

Kaiser was on his feet and up on deck in an instant.

"There!" she said, pointing back in the direction of their wake.

Kaiser squinted. In the first gray light of dawn he could see a powerboat coming up behind them under full throttle.

Francesca hurled herself against him. "Start the motor!" she shrieked. "Do something! Oh, Jesus, don't just stand there! Don't let him catch us, for the love of God!" She was close to hysteria.

He grabbed her by the shoulders and shook her hard. "Make sense," he said sharply. "We can't outrun that boat.

It has five times the power we have. Besides, we don't know that it's Julian."

Francesca's disintegration was complete. She collapsed against him. "It's Julian. Oh, dear God, Patrick, I know it is."

"Well, even if it is, there's no way we need to allow him on board."

He could feel her fear. "But he'll follow us. Don't you see? No matter where we dock, he'll be there waiting. And he'll make me come back." She said the last with a low moan, as if the thought were more than she could stand.

The powerboat had come up alongside and a man on the deck was shouting something, motioning for them to slow down. "That isn't Julian," Kaiser said.

Francesca looked numb. "It's a trick," she said, limp now. She leaned against him as if she hadn't the strength to stand alone. "He's below deck. I know it. He's going to make me come back."

"I have to see what he wants, Francesca," Kaiser said quietly. "I have no choice. We can't outrun him, and it's only a matter of time before we have to drop anchor." He pushed her away gently, and she slipped to her knees on the deck.

Kaiser eased back on the sheets, slowing their forward motion. At the same time their pursuer cut his engines and shouted across the way. "You lost your dinghy back there a ways." He pointed. "We thought you might need it."

Kaiser looked out over the stern to the place where *Seabird*'s lifeboat had been. Sure enough it was gone. "I'll be damned," he said, shaking his head. "I don't know how it happened, but thanks a lot," he shouted. "I'll throw you a rope and you can tie it on, if you will."

"No problem," the man called back. The transfer went without a hitch, and within minutes *Seabird* was headed west again under full sail.

Through all of it Francesca never moved. She knelt

huddled against the rail, her arms folded across her chest, her eyes closed tight. Kaiser crossed the deck and lifted her up, holding her close to try to stop her terrible trembling.

"I'm sorry," she said at last. "I'm so sorry."

"There's nothing to be sorry for," he said. "You were frightened."

"I was an hysterical fool," she said. "But I was so sure it was Julian."

"I told you before," Kaiser said, and tipped her head back so she could see his face. "Time is on our side. Julian has no idea where to look for you. I don't know where we're heading, but I ought to tell you that we'll be a lot harder to find if we sail along the coast."

"Head for Greenport," she said. "Do you know where it is?"

He nodded.

"Julian is bound to suspect that you helped me, in spite of what Mrs. Minstrell tells him." She shivered. "And if he ever finds out that you helped me . . ."

"If our paths ever cross again, I'll keep that in mind," he said, smiling.

"Don't take it so lightly," she said, her face pale. "Julian Ferrare is a madman. That makes him very dangerous, because there isn't any way to fight someone who doesn't believe in rules."

"I'm not worried, Francesca. And you shouldn't be either." He touched the side of her cheek. "Julian Ferrare is in your past, not in your future."

She looked up at him with the same curious expression he'd seen earlier, and again he found himself wondering what it meant. Then she tiptoed up and kissed him so softly that it was like the touch of a butterfly's wing. "I'm happy to be here with you, Patrick," she said. "And I'm sorry I lost control. It won't happen again."

He looked down at her in silence. As far as he was concerned, there was nothing to say. He wanted her with a passion he'd forgotten existed, but he had no intention of forcing the issue. He pointed toward the west. "In a few hours we should be able to see the Montauk light," he said. "Then we can go ashore to get supplies."

Francesca decided to stay aboard *Seabird* with the children while Kaiser walked down the road to the store in Montauk. It was Sunday, but he managed to buy coffee and milk, eggs and bread, and enough assorted supplies to get them through the day.

Francesca wanted to sail west to Shelter Island, anchor in the bay on the east side for the night, then sail into Greenport at dawn. She still hadn't told him their final destination, but he didn't mind. If the secrecy made her feel more secure, he decided, then so be it. He couldn't forget the look of terror he'd seen in her eyes when she thought Julian had caught her. It went way beyond fear, and he wondered what Julian Ferrare had done to deserve it.

He estimated that even if the weather held, it would take them a couple of hours to get to the bay, so he wasted no time getting back to the boat.

"Hi, Mr. Kaiser," Christian called from the stern, where he had set up a fishing line.

"Hi, Christian. And pay attention to what you're doing, okay? I don't want to go swimming today, if you don't mind. Where's Hildy?"

"She's still in bed."

Kaiser jumped down to the deck and went below. Francesca was sitting alone in the main cabin. "How about some coffee?" he said.

"I'll make it."

He began to unload the groceries. "Where's Hildy?"

"Still sleeping." She drew some water and put it in the pot. She sighed, then spoke quietly. "That's a lie. She's not sleeping. She's wide awake and frightened to death. And there's nothing I can tell her to make it any easier. She's old enough to need an explanation, and I have none to give her."

"Want me to talk to her?"

She turned to him with an air of quiet resignation. "That's kind of you, but I don't know what you can say that will help."

Kaiser shrugged. "I guess I could tell her that sometimes we do things for people we love simply because we love them. Sometimes we have to make do without explanations." He knew she was staring at him, but he didn't look at her. "You make the coffee. I'll see what I can do." He left the galley without waiting for her to say more.

Hildy was in her bunk. "Still asleep?" he asked, but she didn't open her eyes. He sat down. "Want me to go away?"

She said nothing.

"Things aren't going the way you had hoped, are they?" he said.

She shook her head, and he knew that she was trying hard not to cry.

"Are you scared?"

"I don't know what I am," she said into her pillow.

"I know you're scared, Hildy," Kaiser said, "because running away is pretty scary stuff."

Hildy sat up with a jerk and buried her face against his chest. "I don't understand anything," she said.

"Listen, sweetheart," he said, trying to find some way to ease her pain, "this isn't a whole lot different from getting a divorce, and people do that all the time. Your mother is taking you away to live with her."

"But people who get divorced don't have to hide."

"Sometimes they do. And we three know there's a secret that your mother is terribly afraid of. That's why she's hiding, and that's why you can't ask questions. She loves you and she loves Christian. She's doing the only thing she knows how to protect you."

"But what could be so terrible?"

Kaiser shook his head. "I don't even try to figure it out. But I know your mother is good, and she's suffered a lot, so I'm helping her. And you have to help her too. You have to trust her, Hildy. Sometimes it's the only thing we can do."

Hildy was quiet against him for a minute, then she turned her face up, her eyes wide with fright. "What if Julian finds us?"

Kaiser frowned. What in God's name had Julian Ferrare done to inspire so little love, so much fear? "Well, first of all, I don't think he'll ever find you. And second of all, if he does, he'll have to deal with me first."

"Are you going to be with us?" She sounded relieved.

"For a while at least." He picked up a small notebook that was lying on the shelf beside the bunk. He scribbled something in it, then handed it to Hildy. "And when I'm not, this is where you can find me. No matter what." Then he handed her a tissue. "Blow," he said.

"I love you, Mr. Kaiser," she said.

"I love you, too, Hildy. Now get up and bundle into something warm and I'll show you how to set the sails."

Before she left the cabin, Hildy picked up the notebook and turned to the page where Kaiser had written his address. Right below it she made the following list:

GOOD THINGS TO REMEMBER

1. I can still play the piano.
2. Christian won't have to.
3. Mama will be happy.
4. Mr. Kaiser is our friend.
5. I won't ever have to be alone with Julian again.

Then she tore the page out, folded it carefully, and put it in the very bottom of her treasure box, where she would be sure never to lose it.

22

The smell was overpowering, and she gagged, recognizing it at once. It was Hospital Smell. She opened her eyes and looked through her keyhole, but the only thing she could see was the picture of a dog hanging on the wall.

She was wet-cold, the kind of cold that comes from only one thing: a pack. She could move her toes and fingers, but the rest of her was wrapped between layers and layers of icy wet sheets, wound tight around her like the all too familiar mummy's shroud. *Welcome back,* Coriander said.

A woman appeared beside the bed. "Welcome back, Miss Ferrare," she said. "We were just wondering how long it was going to take before you came to."

Where am I? she asked Coriander at the same time her mouth said the words: "Where am I?"

"You're at the Nantucket Cottage Hospital," the woman replied.

Elise formed her next words carefully. "How long?"

"Since last night. Your brother brought you in. Now you rest. I'm going to get the doctor."

Elise waited, trying not to move, knowing from past experience that movement would cause nothing but pain. She tried to remember how she came to be here and what had gone on before, but memory had gone to hide in some secret place.

"Good morning," he said.

Is it? she wondered, but said nothing.

"How are you feeling?"

"I'm not sure," she said, wishing Coriander would come out of hiding to tell her what to say.

"Do you know where you are?"

She nodded.

"Where?"

"In the hospital."

"Good," he said. "Would you feel up to having a visitor?"

She tried to imagine who would want to visit her, but something kept her from answering. It was as if her mind, like her body, was wrapped in some kind of protective ice-wet cocoon to keep it from remembering, to keep it from destroying itself.

The doctor was waiting for some kind of answer, so she nodded. Help me, Coriander, she begged.

"If you wait just a minute," the doctor was saying, "we'll get you out of the pack. Then you may see your brother."

Brother. The word echoed through the empty halls of her mind, and all at once she remembered. Her brain quivered as if sliced by a knife, and she heard someone speak. "Julian," her own voice whispered. "Julian Ferrare." It seemed as if she had just repeated the answer to a prayer.

She kept her eyes closed tight until she heard him speak. That way she wouldn't be fooled if it really wasn't Julian.

"'Lise," he said, taking her hand. "Are you all right?"

It sounded like Julian, but she still didn't dare look at him. She was too weak, too close to the edge.

He lifted her hand to his lips and kissed the tips of her fingers. "Poor little 'Lise," he said. "It's Julian. Are you all right?" He didn't wait for her to answer. "I had to bring you here. You were like a zombie. I couldn't get any response at all." His voice took on a slight edge. "I didn't want anyone to know about you, Elise. I hate people knowing my business, but this time it couldn't be helped. How do you feel?"

"All right," she said. *Open your eyes,* Coriander said,

coming out of hiding. *How will you know it's Julian if you don't open your eyes?* Coriander's reappearance gave her strength, and she opened her eyes a crack, keeping a safe distance behind her keyhole. A distinguished-looking, silver-haired man stood beside the bed. "Julian?" she whispered. "Is it really you?"

"Of course it is," he said. "Who else would it be?"

She shook her head. "Forgive me," she said. "It's so hard."

"I know. But now you must concentrate."

She waited.

"Do you remember what happened last night?"

She shrugged. "I'm not sure." What she did remember was a ghastly nightmare. It couldn't possibly have been real.

"Do you remember going into Christian's room?" His voice was quiet, but something alien moved behind his dark eyes.

Elise nodded and tried to swallow, but her throat was too dry.

"And do you remember what you tried to do to Christian?"

She nodded. "I had to do it, Julian," she whispered through parched lips. "It was the only way to save us. Please understand. Please don't be angry."

"I understand very little of what you do, Elise. I'm not angry," he said. But she heard something in his voice that she couldn't identify. "I know you aren't responsible. Besides, what you tried to do to Christian is of little consequence right now. Something else has happened that matters far more to me."

She felt his hand tighten around her fingers. "You didn't stab Christian, Elise. And do you know why?"

She shook her head, knowing how miserable she was, how ugly.

There was a long silence before Julian spoke again, and Elise was grateful for it. It gave her time to gather her courage so that when she heard what he had to say, she wouldn't be thrown back into the pit.

"It wasn't Christian you stabbed because Christian wasn't in the house." Now his voice was black and menacing.

Elise closed her eyes tight. She knew her worst enemies were fear and stress. They were sisters, always running hand in hand. And yet how could she hope to escape them, considering the sound of Julian's voice?

"Hildy and Francesca weren't in the house either." She heard him pause, then he took his hand away. "Do you know where they went?" His words were cold, accusing.

Elise tried to say no, but the word wouldn't come out.

"Think, Elise. Where might they have gone?"

"I don't know, Julian," she finally managed to whimper. "But surely they'll come back. Francesca would never leave you. She would send me away first."

Julian's voice was black iron. "Why do you always assume that you are the central character in everything that ever happens? You have nothing to do with this. Do you understand? Nothing."

Elise began to quake, and the rumbling rolled up around her like a dense fog. She knew she was lost, but in that last instant Julian's voice softened. "I'm sorry, 'Lise," he said, taking her hand once again. "You know nothing about their leaving, do you?"

She shook her head. "Please don't be angry with me, Julian," she begged.

He took her in his arms and began to rock her back and forth. She stayed motionless for a long time, and when he finally lay her back on her pillow, she was almost asleep. "Rest, little 'Lise," he said. "I can wait. They're going to discharge you this afternoon. Then perhaps you can help me find them. For now, rest."

Rest, Coriander said. *There is need for rest even in Hell.*

* * *

That evening Elise sat across from Julian at the dinner table and watched him eat. They were still on the island, but she knew they would be going home soon. Back to their father's house in New York City. Back to the only home she had ever known, where she had not been for eleven years. *They are gone,* Coriander said. *All three of them. And now Julian will let you live with him forever.*

But what if they come back? she asked.

They won't unless you tell him about Patrick Kaiser, Coriander said.

"How are you feeling?" Julian asked, looking up from his plate to see her smiling.

"Wonderful."

"Do you feel strong enough to talk?"

"About what?" *Be careful,* Coriander cautioned.

"About where Francesca might have gone last night?"

She turned that around in her mind and looked at it from all directions, testing it for hidden meanings. "What is it you want me to tell you?"

"Francesca could never have left the island alone." His voice was distant, dispassionate. "I checked first thing this morning. The people at the steamship wharf had been warned not to allow her to board without my consent, and they didn't. There were no planes on or off the island between ten last night and seven this morning. So either she left with someone who had a boat, or she is hiding somewhere on the island." Elise could feel him taking measure of her, watching for a reaction.

Be calm, Coriander said.

"Can you think of anything that might help me find them?"

Elise closed her eyes. She held the key in her mind. All she had to do was turn it in the lock and Julian would have his answer. Patrick Kaiser. He was a famous person, easily traced, and through him Julian would find Francesca and the children. She opened her eyes wide. "I know nothing, Julian," she said, shaking her head. "Nothing at all."

"What about Kaiser?"

She felt his black eyes boring into her face, but she wasn't frightened. Julian had never had the ability to read her mind. "I think he left the island a few days ago," she said calmly.

"That's what the Minstrell woman told me. I wasn't certain that I should believe her, but I'm sure I can trust you." Julian poured himself a cup of coffee, but his eyes never left her face. "I *can* trust you, can't I, dear 'Lise?"

She nodded, but now the fear was rising in her throat. She had never lied to Julian before. Not ever.

"Would you like some coffee?" he asked.

"No, thank you, Julian. You know how much trouble I have sleeping as it is." She hoped he didn't notice that she was shaking.

"Of course." He began to think aloud. "Francesca has no friends on the island. Not anymore. Certainly no one who would hide her. So she must have left. But how?" He fell silent, stirring his coffee, and Elise could see the muscles working along the side of his jaw, feel the rage building inside him.

"Can't we just go back to New York and live as we did before?" she whispered. She knew that she was pleading, but Julian didn't seem to have heard. There was a long silence, and Elise finally spoke again. "If you do find them," she said, wondering how she dared ask, "what will you do?"

He looked across the table at her with an expression that would have chilled anyone else to the bone. "I will destroy her," he said.

Elise smiled. She wasn't sure what he meant, but it made her feel better. If Julian did find Francesca, he said he would destroy her. That would leave only Christian, and without Francesca, Christian would have no power to do harm, so Elise had little to fear.

As for Hildy, Elise was unconcerned. She knew she had nothing to fear from Hildy, with her soft, dark, curling hair. She never had and she never would.

23

It had been only fourteen hours since they left Nantucket but to Kaiser it seemed more like forty. The weather had turned cold and gray, and a heavy swell from the east sent Hildy and Christian below deck to escape the constant spray. Dressed in foul-weather gear, Kaiser and Francesca stayed on deck, speaking very little. Kaiser had made several attempts at conversation, but gave it up when he realized that Francesca wasn't paying attention. She sat in the stern, out of the wind, looking out to sea, and yet every now and then he would turn to find her staring at him.

Francesca's silence gave him time to think, to sort out his feelings. He had given no thought to the future. He wasn't even sure there was a future where Francesca was concerned. What he had done, he'd done because he loved her. He didn't know what her secret was or where Julian fit into it, but he'd promised not to ask and he wasn't going to. It had been a tremendous act of faith when Francesca accepted his offer of help, and he would never betray her trust by pressing her. The next step, if there was to be one, would have to be hers.

The wind was steady, and they reached Shelter Island just before dusk. Kaiser dropped the sails and headed around the east side of the island under power. "This is it," he said as he dropped anchor. "We'll stay here for the night." He turned and walked back to the stern to find her waiting for him, her distress obvious.

"I've hurt you, haven't I?" she said, twisting her hands in her scarf.

"Why do you say that?"

"I saw it in your face last night."

"Wounded male pride. Happens all the time." He smiled and touched her cheek. "Not to worry," he said. He could see that the old signs of despair were gone from her face, but now there was a new dimension to her expression: confusion, and a strange sense of urgency. "What's the matter?" he asked.

She turned away. "I'm not sure," she said, her voice quavering. "I'm such a mess."

He laughed. "You're not a mess, Francesca. You are the most unmessy woman I've ever known."

She didn't smile. "I want to kiss you," she said.

He took a quick breath, thrown off balance, and then before he knew what was happening her arms came up around his neck and she was kissing him with an intensity that shocked him.

"Jesus," he whispered against her lips. He wasn't going to try to understand what this was about. All he knew or cared about at that moment was the passion of her kiss, an almost violent passion he couldn't resist. His arms went around her and he could feel her whole body tremble as she pressed against him as close as clothing would permit.

"I know it isn't fair," she whispered, "and I know it makes no sense to you, but tonight I want you to make love to me. I need you."

He forced himself to push her away so he could see her expression, but her eyes were unreadable.

"I owe you my life," she said, tears coming in a rush, "but this has nothing to do with gratitude." She began to touch his face with quick little movements. "Just once before I die, I want to make love because I *want* to, not because I have to. I want to be myself, not what someone else demands I be. I want to be what I should have been, not what I have become. Is that too much to ask?"

He pulled her close and held her until she was calm. He stopped thinking, questioning, analyzing, no longer concerned with the whys of her passion. All he knew or cared was that it was real. She wanted him. The rest he would worry about later.

After supper they played cards in the main cabin with Hildy and Christian, and Francesca was transformed into a child, carefree and full of enthusiasm. She talked to Kaiser with easy affection, as if they had spent their lives discussing things, and her mood was contagious. Hildy lost the pinched, fearful look she'd worn since they left Nantucket, and as she watched her mother enjoying herself without constraint, Kaiser could see the tension leave her thin body. He told some outrageous stories and they all laughed.

Francesca let the children stay with her until Christian was nearly asleep, and Kaiser watched her tuck them into their berth with a tenderness so profound that he again found himself wondering how she could have tried to kill them, and why. No questions, he reminded himself.

He left them, went back to the galley, and poured himself a cup of coffee. Outside, the night was cold, but below deck it was warm. Kaiser was using one of the settees in the main cabin for a bed, and as he sat down on it he realized he was exhausted. He closed his eyes, and when he opened them, Francesca was sitting beside him. "I fell asleep," he said.

She nodded, and he became conscious of the pressure of her hand against his. He looked at her, studying her profile, and felt an ache in his throat that he hadn't felt in years.

She stood and held out her hand, her face flushed with a soft, expectant glow. Kaiser took it and walked with her to the fore cabin, amazed that he even had presence of mind left to close the door behind them.

She undressed at once, without any self-consciousness, as if they had been intimate forever, then stood before him naked. Kaiser forgot everything but the closeness of her, so suddenly accessible, so genuinely eager. He had no awareness of undressing himself, but when they finally lay naked beside each other on the narrow bunk, nothing mattered but the incredible softness of her breasts, the sweet taste of her flesh as he covered every inch of her with his lips. He felt her touch him, first with a tender, almost timid caress, then with a growing urgency that begged him to take her. And he did. But just as his senses exploded with the ultimate pleasure, he thought he heard her whisper two words. *Forgive me*. But then again, it was probably just the wind.

He woke in the night to find her sleeping quietly beside him, warm against the curve of his body, and he thought that in all his life he'd never felt such a need to be part of another human life—that he had finally found his soul mate.

But when he woke again in the first light of dawn to find her watching him, he had the sudden terrible feeling that she wasn't his at all. He pulled her close and kissed her, wanting reassurance.

Francesca returned his embrace with all the passion of their first lovemaking, and as he sank again into the softness of her body, he cursed himself for being a self-doubting idiot.

Kaiser was alive with plans as he walked up the street toward the supermarket. They had tied up at the town dock in Greenport just after dawn and he'd gone ashore at nine o'clock, as soon as he was sure the stores would be open.

Hildy, Christian, and Francesca had stayed aboard for fear someone might recognize them.

"A long shot," Kaiser had said, but Francesca had grown pale at the thought.

"I've come too far," she'd replied, her voice tight and brittle, "to be brought back because some well-meaning soul happens to be at the wrong place at the wrong time."

Months later, when he thought back, he decided that there must have been some sign of warning, some omen that a man wiser than he would have recognized. He'd gone ashore alone, full of feelings of warmth and well-being. He had filled his grocery cart with enough food for days, just as Francesca had instructed. He'd even stopped to buy a newspaper, to see if Julian had notified the authorities about his missing family. He hadn't.

It was raining when he got back to the boat, and he could hear a distant roll of thunder, uncommon for the time of year. "Hey, you guys," he called, "give me a hand before these bags get soaked."

He set the groceries on the deck and called again, but there was no answer. Must be some terrific card game, he thought as he went down into the galley, but he knew before the words were formed in his mind that there was no card game. He stood stone still, feeling the silence gather around him, and knew they were gone. He picked up the folded note she'd left on the table.

"Dearest Kaiser," she had written in her peculiar, slanted handwriting, "please don't try to find me. You are too visible, and if I stay with you, Julian will surely find me. That I cannot allow to happen at any cost. My deepest regret is that I could never tell you why."

Kaiser sat down slowly, suddenly feeling old, really and truly old. He sat for a long time without moving, conscious only of the sound of the rain on the deck and the gentle rocking of the boat. And then, like the slow roll of distant thunder, he felt the first small rumble of anger, an anger

that grew in intensity until he felt suffocated. Whatever
Francesca's reasons, whatever her plans, whatever her
fears, she had used him in a way that he found intolerable.
He'd been willing to help her, had asked for nothing in
return. But she'd allowed him to become vulnerable. He
hadn't asked her to make love with him. He had been
prepared to let her go, no questions asked. But she'd
crossed the distance between them, giving an intimacy that
should never have been to their relationship. For that he
would never forgive her.

But that night as he lay awake in his berth, he felt the
anger begin to crack and fall away, like protective armor
that had served its purpose but was no longer needed. "She
didn't set you up," he said to himself. "You did it to
yourself." He was left feeling only a deep sadness, and a
hope that Julian would never find her. And finally he looked
inside to see if he still loved her. And he did.

Elise Ferrare stood in the darkness just inside the front
door, waiting for the men to remove the shutters that kept
out the light. Their father's house had been closed since
June, when Francesca and the children left for Nantucket,
but for Elise it had been closed for eleven years. I am
home, she whispered to Coriander. Francesca is gone and I
am finally home.

Somewhere upstairs a door blew shut and she could hear
little wisps of dust as they stirred then settled back to rest
on the hallway floor. The whole house was full of tiny
soundless movement, as if it were not exactly sure who she
was. "It is I, Elise," she whispered. "I have finally come
home. And I will never leave you again."

She crossed to the music room and opened the door. In
the dim light she could make out only the outline of her
father's piano, but knew what it was. She threw her arms
around herself, answering the hundred gentle murmurings

of air that welcomed her. *It's been a long trip*, Coriander said.

She heard Julian call from the hallway. "I'm in here," she said. "In the music room."

"What are you doing here in the dark?" He switched on the light.

"I'm saying hello," she said, smiling.

"I'm pleased that you're happy to be back. I'm not." His voice was cold.

"You will be," she said, crossing to his side. "You'll see. It will be just as it used to be." She clapped her hands together. "I'm going to get new draperies for the windows, and maybe we can even get a kitten. And in the spring," she closed her eyes, "oh, Julian, in the spring I'm going to plant the most wonderful garden."

Julian didn't answer. Francesca had been missing for more than two weeks, but he was still in a black mood. This time, however, it didn't frighten her. She was home. In their father's house. Now it was hers and Julian's—alone. Her brother crossed to the piano and touched one key. "Badly out of tune," he said flatly.

"I'll call Mr. Consuelo first thing in the morning," she said, frowning, wondering if that was the right name. *Be calm*, Coriander said. *Don't get confused or you'll ruin everything*.

"I've hired an agency to find her," Julian said. "The best."

Elise heard the familiar rumbling begin. "But why, Julian?" she whispered, forming the words carefully. "We don't need Francesca to be happy."

Julian turned to stare at her, and there was no expression on his face when he spoke. "She must be found," he said.

"But why?" she asked, wanting to cry. She could feel the confusion tearing her thoughts into little pieces of confetti.

He didn't answer, but the merciless look on his face made Elise shiver.

24

It was amazing how quickly winter left the city. And how ugly. Kaiser ducked into a doorway and stood watching as a miserable March rain turned East Seventy-second Street into a river of slush. He pulled the collar of his trench coat up around his neck and ran for a cab that had pulled up to the curb, miraculously empty. Normally he would have walked the few blocks to Allison's apartment, but not in this weather.

"March sucks," the driver said sullenly as he pulled into heavy traffic on Fifth Avenue.

March does suck, Kaiser thought. I'm forty-four years old, I have a dinner engagement with a beautiful lady whom I should care about but don't, and March does suck.

He paid the driver and within minutes had been announced by the doorman, delivered to her floor in the elevator, and was ringing her door bell. "Good evening, Milly," he said to the housekeeper.

"Good evening, Mr. Kaiser. Dr. Pavane will be right out." She disappeared.

"Kaiser?" He heard her call from the bedroom. "Make us martinis, will you?"

Kaiser crossed the living room to the bar, pausing for a moment to look out at the lights far across the park. It was a spectacular view, he conceded grudgingly. About the only thing he liked about this city anymore.

"You're looking particularly sour tonight," Allison Pavane said, coming into the room, and Kaiser thought again how much the surroundings suited her: crisp, dramatic, and thoroughly modern.

"I'm feeling particularly sour," he replied, handing her a drink.

"Any particular reason?"

He shrugged. "Probably because March sucks."

"What an elegant way to describe it," she said. She sat down on the sofa and stretched her long, silken legs out in front of her. "You must have heard from Toby. What else would put you in such a foul mood?"

"As a matter of fact I haven't heard from Toby in a couple of weeks."

She raised her eyebrows. "Then what is it?"

"Like I said, March sucks." He sat down next to her on the sofa and looked at her over the top of his glass. She was a very attractive woman. Not stunning, but very nice to look at, with high cheekbones and deep, gray eyes that never seemed to miss a thing. Kaiser had heard comments that Allison Pavane was arrogant, but he knew she wasn't. She was simply sufficient unto herself. "How was your day?" he asked.

She looked thoughtful. "Disturbing would be an understatement. Hellish might be a better word. I operated on a little boy today."

"How old?"

"Almost three. Old enough not to be wetting his bed, wouldn't you agree?" Her voice was brittle.

"What happened to him?"

"His mother sat him on the stove."

"Jesus."

"You might say that. And while we're at it, where exactly

was Jesus, I'd like to know, when his pathetic little namesake Christian was getting his toilet training?"

Kaiser stopped sipping his drink. "Christian?"

"That's his name. Christian," she said, getting to her feet. "I'm going to call the hospital to see how he's doing, and then we aren't going to talk about it anymore." She crossed to the phone and dialed, but Kaiser didn't hear what she said. The name Christian had deafened him.

"Kaiser," she said, and he realized suddenly that she was talking to him. "Are you all right?"

"I'm fine."

"You look as if you'd seen a ghost."

He shrugged, forcing himself to be casual. "Must be bad gin." He glanced at his watch. "We'd better leave if we're going to make our eight o'clock reservations. It may take us time to get a cab."

She smiled and raised her eyebrows. "I have a car at my disposal, remember? I can't believe you've forgotten."

Kaiser stood up, hoping that movement would get rid of the sick feeling he had in the pit of his stomach. It wasn't the gin, he knew. It was that name. Christian. It had been four months since he'd even allowed himself to think the name Ferrare. He had thought he'd put it all behind him. Clearly he hadn't. The reference to a child named Christian had dredged up all the memories, and he was shocked to find that they were still so painful.

He took a deep breath and determined to bury it once and for all. It was no longer any of his concern.

He spent the rest of the evening trying to enjoy Allison's company, but it was a struggle. They had dinner at a new restaurant on Columbus Avenue, a meal that seemed to take forever as far as Kaiser was concerned, but when they finally got up to leave, he realized that it wasn't even ten o'clock. He said good night to her at her door, refusing the invitation to come in for a nightcap. He was tired, he told her. "Besides," he told himself as he unlocked the door to his own apartment, "March sucks."

It was still raining outside when Kaiser finally woke up, and almost morning. He reached over to close the window beside his bed, then lay back on the pillow, watching as drops of rain joined drops of rain to snake down the pane in crooked little streams. Since the day she left him, Kaiser had refused to consider her again. Not her name, not her face, not anything. He had not only closed a door, he'd convinced himself that it had never existed.

He rolled over and groaned. "Where in the hell are you?" he said suddenly. He knew he wasn't going to try to find her, but couldn't help but wonder if Julian had. "I hope not," he said. "I hope to hell he hasn't found you, Francesca."

At the sound of her name he sat up, and for the first time in months allowed himself to really think about her. He became aware that there was a deep sadness inside him, and realized it had been there all along. He'd simply been accepting it as a part of himself, a part of what is and cannot be changed. "I still love you, Francesca," he said. "Too bad for me." Then he swung out of bed, and while brushing his teeth, carefully packed his memory of her away in the furthest corner of his mind. He'd thought about her and it had hurt. He wasn't going to do it again.

In the airport, Kaiser decided he had just time enough for a quick cup of coffee before his flight left, a trip he was anticipating. For the past four months he'd lost himself in his research, and his book was almost finished. But there were still some critical points he needed to clarify, personal references that had to be absolutely accurate. Hoping to find the answers to his questions in London, he'd made appointments with two of his old colleagues, men who had been with him in Prague. Besides, he needed a change of scenery, and London had always been one of his favorite cities.

He sat down at the counter, ordered coffee, and scanned the front page of the morning paper. He was surprised to see that Pierson McGregor was still in London, and made a mental note to call him as soon as he got there. Pierson was someone else who might help fill in the gaps. He was just about to put the paper down and drink his coffee when a headline at the bottom of the page caught his eye: ACCLAIMED CONCERT PIANIST SHOT; WIFE CHARGED.

Within minutes Kaiser was in a cab headed back into the city. If what he'd just read was true, Francesca Ferrare was no longer in hiding. Early that morning she'd been arrested for the attempted murder of her husband, Julian Ferrare.

25

Hildy hadn't really stopped crying since yesterday, when Julian had found them. She'd hidden her tears, but inside she wept. Seeing him coming up the walk with the two other men, she ran upstairs to warn Mama, but had been too late. Mama fought and kicked and screamed, but there had been no one to help, and then Julian had hit Francesca so hard, right in the face, that she'd fallen down. Hildy had tried to lift her up, but Julian pulled her away.

"Come along, Hildy," he'd said as pleasantly as if he were taking her for a walk in the park. "Get your brother. It's time we went home."

"But what about Mama?" Hildy hadn't been able to stop the tears. Her mother still lay unconscious where she'd fallen.

"Francesca isn't going to live with us anymore," Julian had said. "She will stay here."

Then they had driven from Vermont to New York, back to the house on Sixty-fourth Street where they had once lived together. Hildy and Christian had gone to their rooms, and there they had stayed, huddled in corners, wondering what had become of their mother and what was to become of them.

Hildy was terrified. Mama will come, she kept telling herself. She won't leave me here alone with him. And she'd been right. Her mother had come last night with a gun and tried to kill Julian. But she had failed.

Now Hildy lay awake in her bed in her father's house. She'd never been afraid of the dark before, but she was now. Mama, she cried inside. I'm so scared. She could hear Christian's breathing beside her, wet and open-mouthed. He had sneaked into her bed and finally cried himself to sleep, but Hildy couldn't. She kept hearing her mother's sobs as they dragged her from the house, kept seeing the look on Julian's face when he told them that their mother had tried to kill him, that they would never see her again. "Mama," she whispered, "don't leave us here." She lay on her back and felt her eyes grow dry, but somewhere inside she still cried.

When morning finally came, Hildy helped Christian dress, then dressed herself, fingering the fabric of her skirt as if she'd never seen it before. She opened her treasure box and looked inside. Everything was there: the bit of lace, the piece of purple glass, the baby tooth. All the things she had collected her whole life. Only they weren't the same—they weren't any good anymore. "Here, Christian," she said, handing the box to her brother.

Christian's eyes were red and swollen, but a tentative smile appeared when he saw what Hildy was offering. "Your treasure box?" he said. Hildy nodded. "But Hildy, these are your best things."

She shrugged. "They're baby things," she said. "I don't want them anymore." She crossed the room and lay on the bed, listening to the sound of the rain moving through the city streets. Don't cry, she told herself. It will only make things worse.

Christian came over and climbed up beside her on the bed. "What will happen to us, Hildy?" he whispered, and she could see that he was about to cry again.

She sat up and hugged him. "We're going to be fine," she said, holding back her own tears.

"But what about Mama? What will they do to her?"

Hildy didn't know what to say. Both she and Christian had heard the gunshots the night that Julian had brought them home. They had watched in horror as their mother was subdued and dragged from the house, screaming obscenities at their father. They had both listened in silence as Julian told them coldly that they would never see her again. "Your mother is insane," he'd said in a voice that had sent chills through Hildy's body. "She has shot me and she has shot Elise. Now she must be put away where she cannot hurt anyone ever again."

Then an ambulance had come and Julian and Elise had gone off to the hospital, leaving Hildy and Christian alone with the servants. And with their fear.

"It's all my fault," Hildy whispered to Christian. "Julian would never have found us if it hadn't been for my stupid piano lessons. That was how his private detectives traced us. Julian said so himself." She felt as if she were going to get sick.

Christian was silent, shivering beside her.

Hildy sat up straight. "There's only one thing to do," she said. "We have to run away, so we can find Mama and help her."

Christian jumped off the bed. "Let's go."

Hildy yanked him back. "Wait a minute, Christian. We have to plan this carefully. Where can we go that Julian won't find us?"

Christian frowned and his eyes grew dark. "He'll get those private detectives to track us down, just like he did before. You know what he said—we should never try to run away again because there isn't a person his detectives can't trace, and there isn't a place they can't break into."

"Maybe so," Hildy said, considering. "But maybe we can get help . . ."

"Mr. Kaiser," Christian blurted.

"Of course," Hildy said. "We have to find him."

"But how? We don't even know where he lives."

Hildy jumped off the bed. "My treasure box." She opened it and took out the piece of paper. "This is where he lives," she said, "and that's where we're going. Right now. But first we have to get some money, and then we have to sneak out of here before Julian and Elise come back from the hospital."

Hildy knew where there was money. Lots of it. In the study on the third floor. Inside the cover of *Pride and Prejudice*, on one of the shelves in the bookcase. Mama had shown it to her once, long ago. She'd said, "If you or your brother ever need any money and I'm not here to help you, this is my secret hiding place."

Hildy had never thought about it again. She'd never had any reason to. Not until this morning.

She went to the door, pulling Christian after her. "Get your coat and boots on," she said, frantic now to be gone before Julian came back to stop them. "But don't let any of the servants see you. And Christian," she said, looking hard at her brother, "take whatever you want with you now, because no matter what happens, we're never coming back here. Not ever again."

With that the two went in separate directions through the house. Christian filled his backpack with those things he couldn't bear to leave behind, and Hildy went straight to the study, praying that the money her mother had shown her that day so long ago would still be there. It was.

At twelve minutes after eight in the morning Hildy and Christian Ferrare left the house and ran up Sixty-fourth Street in a frantic search for Patrick Kaiser.

26

"Would you like an egg?" the nurse asked.

Elise gasped. She couldn't remember a time when she hadn't hated eggs. She not only hated them, she was terrified of them. Clear, gelatinous slime that encircled a foul-tasting yellow glue, a glue that was in truth a living chicken. Once eaten, it would grow inside your stomach like a tumor, picking at your flesh until it had devoured you alive from the inside out. Only once, when she was seven years old, had anyone ever made Elise eat an egg, and she'd never forgotten it. Her father had taken hold of her cheeks with one hand and pressed until her mouth popped open. Then he'd jammed the piece of egg inside. She'd tried to cry out, but her father's fist had closed on her face, squeezing her flesh, re-forming it. You will be what I make of you, her father's fist had said, whether it hurts or not.

It had been one of the few times she'd welcomed the darkness.

Again the nurse asked if she would like an egg for breakfast. She shook her head. She didn't know yet where she was, but knew she didn't want an egg.

"How about some pancakes?"

Elise thought about pancakes. She wasn't sure what the word meant, but it didn't fill her with dread the way the word egg did. She nodded, and the nurse went away.

Elise lay back on the pillow, confused. How did she get here? And where was she? She hadn't been in the pit, so why couldn't she remember? Her head hurt and she touched it gingerly with her hand. Why am I wearing a hat? she wondered, beginning to feel the raw edge of fear that always rode on the back of confusion. *You were trying to save Julian's life,* Coriander said. *Don't you remember? Think.*

Somewhere down the hall someone was crying, and Elise wished he would stop. It made it so much harder to concentrate. And then, as if someone had switched on a movie projector and was playing it in reverse, she felt her mind wind back to yesterday.

She had wakened that morning heavy with dread, sure she'd heard her father calling her. It was several minutes before she remembered he was dead. And then she remembered why she was so frightened. After five months of searching, Julian's investigators had finally picked up Francesca's trail, and if all went the way he planned, she and the children would be back in the house before nightfall. Julian had said he would destroy Francesca if he ever found her, but Elise wasn't so sure. Francesca had great power.

Elise was as exhausted as if she hadn't been to sleep at all, but she realized she had work to do, that she had to get up. All her magic had to be in place if she were to stop Francesca from coming back. Fear lay like heavy mist everywhere in the room. She could see it, but didn't touch it. She moved around it, whispering her special words five times into every corner, frantic to find the one magic key that would keep Francesca out of her house.

Fear and stress are sisters, Coriander warned. *Be careful.*

Elise nodded and continued with her preparations.

Finished, she looked to see if everything was exact. *Have I forgotten anything?* she asked Coriander.

There was a low rumbling before he answered, *If you want to be sure, you'll have to use Anna's jewelry.*

Elise shrank back at the thought, her hand flying to her throat. Never, since Anna's death, had anyone been allowed to open that box, never had Anna's jewels been lifted from their velvet caskets. Father had forbidden it, so the box had remained on the shelf in that terrible room on the third floor. Julian was using that room for a study, but Elise knew it was really the place where Anna and her father had shared a bed. She also knew that mighty powers lived there, but she'd never before dared to wonder if they might be made to work for her.

There's only one way to find out, Coriander said. *You have no choice. But you must hurry. Julian will be back soon.*

Elise went down the hall slowly, then stopped at the foot of the stairs leading to the third floor. If she hadn't been so desperate, she never would have dared to do this. She looked down at her feet going up one step at a time, felt the carpet move under her as she inched her way toward the room where Anna's jewels lay. *I am frightened,* she told Coriander. *I am truly frightened.*

She put her hand on the knob and turned it. The door swung open, and to her horror, she found herself in Anna's old bedroom. She began to tremble. Perspiration soaked through her blouse in an instant. *Don't stop,* Coriander said. *Get the box and get out of here.*

Elise crossed to the bookcase, feeling the air move hard against her face, trying to push her away. With a quick rush her hand darted out and grabbed the jewelry box. Holding it close against her chest, she ran to the door and back out into the hall, the box pulsing wildly under her fingers. *Get to your room,* Coriander said. *You'll be safe there.*

She half fell back down the stairs, and once inside her

room collapsed on her bed, a hundred voices roaring in her ears. *Take some pills*, Coriander said. *Quickly*.

With her heart crashing against her ribs, she made her way to the bathroom. All color had drained from the world, and she couldn't tell what pills to take. *Take two of each*, Coriander said. Her hand was shaking so badly that she couldn't get them into her mouth, so she dropped them onto the countertop and licked them up with her tongue, swallowing without water. Then she sank into the corner to wait, to pray that the seas would grow calm.

She wasn't sure how long she huddled there, but all at once she heard earth voices. She listened. Julian was calling her. She struggled to her feet and went back into her bedroom. *The garnet necklace*, Coriander said. *Get it. It has the most power, and you haven't time for the rest.*

Elise opened the box and with trembling fingers picked up the garnet necklace. She'd never forgotten it. It had been Anna's favorite, and it was hot to the touch, glowing there in her hand.

"Elise," Julian called from below. "Come down here."

Trembling, she put the necklace around her neck and fastened it. Then she stepped out into the hall and crept to the top of the stairs. "Who's there?" she called.

"Come and see."

Elise reached out her hand to keep from falling, rocked by a sudden feeling that she was walking on the walls.

"Elise?" Julian's voice was impatient now.

She began to inch down the stairs, tread by tread, sliding one foot in front of the other. She stopped at the landing. I've done all my magic, she said to Coriander. It can't be Francesca. She started down again, feeling as though she were on an escalator going the wrong way. The steps seemed to be moving up as fast as she was going down.

"Look who's here," Julian said, coming into view.

She closed her fist hard over the necklace and it cut into her hand, but she didn't feel any pain. She stood suspended on the bottom step as Christian and Hildy came toward her, faces pale and tear-streaked. "And your mother?" she whispered.

Julian's voice was full of good humor. "Francesca isn't here," he said. "She didn't choose to live with us before. Now she is no longer welcome." He turned to the children, who were standing like frozen statues before him. "Go to your rooms," he said, "and get ready for dinner. And Hildy, my love, wear your rose silk. It's most becoming."

The two children moved like shadows up the stairs, leaving Elise gaping after them in disbelief.

"Well, little 'Lise," Julian said. "I told you I'd find them and bring them home. And I have."

Elise turned to her brother, still stunned. "But what about Francesca?"

Julian's face was devoid of expression, his voice a monotone. "I told you I would destroy her. I have. She has betrayed me. As far as I am concerned, she no longer exists." He turned away. "Have the servants see to dinner," he said. "And do take care of your hand, my dear. You seem to have cut it rather badly."

Elise felt her fingers come loose from the necklace, but as she stood looking down at the blood, she felt nothing except joy. Francesca was truly gone, and she would never come back. Elise sank down on the bottom step and for the first time in years felt warm, caught up in a drowsy, fur-lined pocket of air. *She is truly gone*, Coriander said. *But you must ensure that she never comes back.*

Elise paid no attention. Nothing could ruin this moment, not even Coriander's warning. Elise's world had turned soft and golden, like the coming of sunshine after years of rain.

That night at dinner Elise wore all of Anna's jewelry and didn't regret it, even though Julian told her that she looked like a circus horse. It was Anna's power that gave her the strength to push Francesca aside when she burst into the house and came after Julian with the gun. It was Anna's power that helped Elise to twist Francesca's arm, causing the bullet to strike Julian in the shoulder instead of the heart. It was Anna's power that kept Elise alive when Francesca, struggling to fire again, wounded Elise in the scalp just above the right ear.

"You saved my life, little 'Lise," Julian said after the police had taken Francesca away, broken and sobbing. Then he'd taken her into his arms and kissed her on the mouth.

Elise hadn't wanted to go to the hospital, but Julian had promised that it wasn't the sanitarium. It was a regular hospital, for the treatment of bodies, not minds. In fact he promised that she would never have to go to a mental institution again. It was Francesca who would go there now, he'd said, and Elise smiled in spite of her throbbing scalp. She wished she could be there when they welcomed Francesca to the wonderful world of ice-wet beds and blue electric terror.

27

Kaiser headed across town. He had to see Sam Massamino, the district attorney. Sam would know where Francesca was being held and whether or not bond had been set. He was also the one person Kaiser knew who would be able to get him in to see her, wherever she was. Unless . . . Kaiser thought back to the day on the wharf when Christian had almost drowned, the day she told him that if her son were to die, she would go insane. Be sane, he prayed to himself. Please, Francesca, be sane.

"Can you get me in to see her?" Kaiser asked Sam.

"Maybe. Is it that important to you?"

Kaiser nodded.

"She has a court-appointed attorney, Jake FitzPatrick. Let me check with him."

"A court-appointed attorney?" Kaiser was incredulous.

Sam nodded. "She has no money."

"But, my God, Sam, Ferrare is worth millions."

"Maybe so. But his wife isn't worth a dime. She's going to have a hell of a time coming up with bond money, if and when the judge agrees on an amount." He picked up the phone and dialed.

Kaiser sat back and considered what Sam had told him. There seemed to be no doubt that Francesca Ferrare had indeed shot Julian. And Elise as well. She'd been charged with attempted murder. No motive had been established, but Julian had given a formal statement. His wife was deranged, he said. This wasn't the first incidence of violence in which she'd been involved. She had tried to kill herself and their two children only eight months ago, then kidnapped them, refusing to let them contact their own father. Clearly she should be held without bond, pending psychiatric evaluation.

"Jake will let you see her. Reluctantly," Sam said, hanging up the phone. "And provided, of course, that she wants to see you. Apparently she hasn't wanted to see anyone."

"Where is she?"

"Bellevue."

Upon first seeing Francesca, Kaiser had the impression of viewing her in a carnival mirror designed to distort. Her slim figure had been reduced to emaciation, the once delicate bones of her cheeks standing out from her face, sharp and skeletal. Her eyes seemed glazed over, as if she were willing herself to be blind, and her golden hair hung dank and limp, plastered against the sides of her face.

He'd arranged to see her alone in one of the reception rooms, and when she was brought in he was stunned. She looked broken, like a china figurine that had been smashed to pieces then glued together by a careless hand.

In the first instant of recognition, she started toward him, then stopped. "I'm happy to see you," she whispered, dropping her gaze to stare at the floor.

"Are you?" he asked.

Her tears came quickly, but she made no sound. She nodded.

"You look like you've just been liberated from a concentration camp," he said softly. "What in the name of God has happened to you?"

She shook her head, unable to speak.

Kaiser crossed to where she stood trembling, and put his arms around her, holding her the way a parent holds a frightened child.

"Forgive me," she whispered into his shoulder. "Forgive me." The last was a broken echo.

"I forgive you, Francesca," he said. "I don't understand, but I forgive you."

She looked up at him. "After all I've done to you, why are you here? You have every reason to hate the sight of me."

Kaiser dropped his arms and took her hands, poor cold things that fluttered like frightened birds. "I love you, Francesca," he said. "That's why I'm here. It was reason enough before, and it still is. I don't care what your bloody secret is, or what terrible crimes you've committed. I love you and I still want to help you. Why do you find that so impossible to believe?"

"Because I don't deserve you." She put her hands up to his face, touching as if unable to see, but hoping to feel his expression. "Oh, Patrick," she said, "if only I had found you in another time, another place, how much I would have loved you."

Then she pulled her hands away and began to pace back and forth with quick, jerking movements, her hands twisting knots in the thin fabric of her skirt. "I don't know what to do," she said, almost to herself. "Dear God, what if I tell the truth and no one believes me? What if I destroy my children in the telling?"

"The first thing you have to do, Francesca, is sit down and tell me what happened. From the beginning. So I can try to get you out of here."

She continued her pacing as if she hadn't heard, locked in some silent battle.

"Francesca," he said sharply, "listen to me. If you really give a damn about those children, you'll tell me what happened. How in the name of hell can they be any worse off than they are right now?"

She stopped pacing and collapsed into a chair, all in a single motion, like a puppet whose strings had been cut. "I tried to kill Julian," she said. "But as in all other things, I failed."

"Why did you do it?"

"Because he found us. He took the children away."

"You could have gone to court to get them back," he said quietly. "You didn't have to try to kill him."

"I couldn't go to court." She was struggling for control. "Because Julian would have told them the truth."

"Which is?"

She ignored the question. "I have two choices," she said, seeming to think out loud. "I can keep silent and let Julian raise my children." Her whole body shuddered at the thought. "Or I can tell the truth and hope that by some miracle someone can help me."

Kaiser reached across the table and took her hands. "Try me," he said.

She lifted her head and looked right at him, and for the first time, naked and raw, he saw the true depth of her anguish. He had to force himself not to look away. "Listen then," she said. "And if when I'm finished you choose to leave without another word, I'll understand."

It was summer when she first met Julian Ferrare, the summer she turned eighteen, the summer that her mother died. She remembered the funeral in such detail that it seemed as if it were preserved on a film somewhere in the back of her mind. It hadn't rained that morning, and Francesca had felt outraged that the sun could dare to shine on a world that no longer had a place for her mother. She had felt naked and vulnerable, like a young sea creature stripped of its shell. Until then she'd lived like a princess, loved and nurtured by her mother and stepfather, kept protected from the ugliness of the world. Her mother had been reclusive, seldom leaving their house in the small Finnish town, rarely seen in public, and Francesca had accepted it as odd, perhaps, but not disturbing.

She worked hard to please her parents, especially when it came to her music. She played the piano beautifully, with a fine technique that came from faithful practice and a God-given talent. But even as much as she loved to play, her favorite pastime was to listen to her mother. "Why don't you play instead of me, Mama?" she would beg. "I love to listen to you."

But her mother would turn away. "I am the old rose," she would say. "I have accepted my falling petals. You, my darling, are the new-formed bud. You will have the success I could never have."

"But you have the gift, too, Mama. It's sinful not to use it."

"I have the gift," she would say. "But not the courage."

So Francesca would play, but she never really understood why her mother was so reluctant to share her talent with the world.

"What about your stepfather?" Kaiser said.

Francesca seemed startled to hear him speak. "I'm sorry," she said. "Am I rambling?"

Kaiser shook his head. "I'm the one who's sorry. Take all the time you need. I won't interrupt again."

Francesca took a breath and began again. "I loved my stepfather almost as much as I loved my mother. She married him when I was only a baby. He was older than Mama but there was a quality of quiet wisdom about him that made him seem ageless. He had a chronic heart condition even then, but it never mattered. It seemed to give him an understanding about life and death that made him the perfect doctor."

Gustav Stahlberg viewed his wife's reclusive habits with

enduring patience, she told Kaiser, even though at times it caused him great inconvenience, forcing him to leave his practice at all hours of the day to take Francesca where her mother dared not go. It was Dr. Stahlberg who helped the child adjust to her mother's odd life-style, and it was he who took full charge of the young Francesca after her mother's death. He saw it as his absolute duty to introduce her to the outside world, to help her accept life without her mother, to learn to be independent. And, on the evening of August seventeenth, after one of Francesca's public recitals in Helsinki, the old doctor brought his stepchild a surprise.

"My darling 'Cesca," he had said, coming to her dressing room door, "I have someone I want you to meet, someone who was most impressed by your performance. He thinks you have great potential." Her stepfather had moved aside and Francesca had been stunned to find herself face to face with Julian Ferrare, the brilliant American concert pianist. He told her he'd been curious about her when he learned that she had won the Prix Internationale, but now he was curious no longer. He was simply bewitched by both her talent and her beauty.

Francesca had been speechless. Julian Ferrare was the most handsome man she'd ever seen, with an almost electric air of vitality about him, and she had been enchanted, swept off her feet, dazzled.

But later what she remembered most clearly about their first meeting wasn't his striking good looks or his vibrant charm. Just before he left her dressing room he'd turned to kiss her hand and she'd seen a look in his eyes that chilled her to the bone. She was impaled where she stood, like a butterfly stuck on the end of a pin. She jerked her hand away, but he had seemed not to notice. He had taken her hand again and kissed it, and she'd been enchanted once more. She was a foolish schoolgirl to have been frightened, she chided herself, and laughed over it. But she never forgot.

Julian Ferrare courted her with irresistible style, and she was overcome by feelings of awe and admiration for his genius, thrilled by his attentions, speechless that such a great man seemed attracted to her; but still, there were times, when he thought she wasn't looking, that she caught him watching her with that strange, obsessive stare, and she would be frozen.

"In the past year," she said, "one of the only things that saved my sanity was the certain knowledge that I never loved him."

"What did your stepfather think of Julian?" Kaiser asked. He didn't want her to stop talking. He was afraid she might never begin again.

"I wasn't the only one who was aware of Julian's passionate obsession, but I was the only one frightened by it." Dr. Stahlberg had seen it as the answer to a prayer, and when, with his gentle but insistent encouragement, his stepdaughter and Julian Ferrare were married six months later, he relaxed. At last he would be able to mourn for his dead wife in peace; there was no longer a reason to hide his pain. He had found the perfect mate for his stepdaughter: a man who clearly adored her, a successful man who would give her everything she would ever need. And to frame a perfect picture, this man would share her love for music and teach her whatever she still had to learn.

Francesca remembered her stepfather's parting words to her: "I wish your mother could have seen you safely married, my little 'Cesca. She was so afraid of the world. She would be at peace now to see how comfortable you are in it. And how safe."

"How very wrong he was," Francesca said to Kaiser. "But in fairness, how could he have known? How could any sane person have imagined the truth?"

For the next twelve years Francesca lived with Julian Ferrare as obedient wife and loving mother, bearing him two children and thus completing the perfect family portrait. But gradually the girl she had once been vanished, leaving only Julian's wife, Hildy and Christian's mother. And looking back, she wondered how she could not have known that something was terribly wrong. Sometimes in the darkest part of the night she would wake in a sweat and wonder if she'd missed something along the way, some foreshadow that might have kept her from marrying Julian. But in the bright light of morning, with Hildy and Christian bouncing into her bed, she would push the doubts aside. She never allowed herself to indulge in what-ifs. It was unhealthy, and self-destructive. Instead she filled the empty places in her heart with love for her two young children.

Time passed quickly for Francesca, as it always does when children are growing, and except for the times when Julian was cruel to Christian, Francesca accepted her lot in life and made the best of it. She did her utmost to shield her young son, and she was successful, because while Julian never changed his attitude toward his children, he rarely came head to head with Francesca when it came to their upbringing.

"At first I thought it was because he loved me so," she said. "But it wasn't. It was simply because they were unimportant to him. He didn't give a damn." A tremor passed through her thin frame. "I cringe to think what life would have been like if he had."

"Was he never cruel to Hildy?" Kaiser asked.

"Cruel? If you mean in the same way he was cruel to Christian, the answer is no. Julian sees his children as extensions of himself, no more, no less. There is no love involved. According to Julian, if you see facets of your own personality that you admire, you polish them, you spend time perfecting them, and then you put them on display for all the world to see. Julian did that with his music, and when Hildy showed signs that she had inherited his genius, Julian cultivated her talent as if it were his own. He cared for Hildy as if she were one of his own hands." Kaiser heard a sudden tension in her voice, and he noticed that she'd clenched her fingers into tight fists. "Julian never cared for Hildy the way a father should care for a child. And now . . ."

At that point in the narrative she stopped. She sounded close to collapse, as if in physical pain, and tiny transparent beads of perspiration had appeared on her forehead. Wiping them away, she picked up the thread of her story.

"Last summer Julian thought it would be a wonderful change if we all spent some time at his grandmother's house on Nantucket Island. He was planning to be away a good deal, and he thought I might enjoy a change of scenery. At first I resisted his suggestion. Most of my friends and all of the children's friends were in New York. But Julian was adamant, and as usual I gave in because deep down, I was still afraid of him."

They moved to the island in the early part of June, and at first she was miserable, lonely, bored. But all that changed once they were settled in the house. Julian was gone most of the time, and except for the housekeeper and the staff, she and the children were alone. She felt herself begin to relax.

They took long walks everywhere, along the beaches, up the old dirt roads, through the town, and her imagination came to life. The island filled her with surprise and a curious wistfulness. She even took time out to play the piano again. She was happy, and so were her children.

The summer rolled by in golden squares of sunshine, but by the end of August Francesca realized with sadness that they would soon be leaving the island. Julian had already returned to the city, and one morning he called to say he'd made plans for her and the children to take the ferry back to the mainland at the end of the week.

She remembered the phone call with crystal clarity, the way one can remember a nightmare but seldom a pleasant dream. Hildy and Christian had gone to spend the day with friends, the housekeeper, Maude, was visiting her mother, and Francesca was alone. She wandered from room to room like a ghost, wondering why she felt so melancholy. It wasn't like her. She had always looked ahead to the fall, even as a child—the excitement of planning for school, the new dress, the shoes, and always a new pencil box.

But this year when summer was gone, something had gone with it. As she wandered through the empty rooms she realized that it was the dreaming she would miss. The city was real. There was no place there for her fantasies. This summer she'd allowed herself to do what she'd always been afraid to do before: to imagine what-if, and it had made her admit, if only to herself, how truly unhappy she was living with Julian Ferrare. She had always known she didn't love him, but now she was forced to admit that she didn't even like him, that she was much happier without him. Her summer solitude had proved it beyond any doubt.

She remembered counting to ten, telling herself that somehow she would pull it all together. She always did. But not yet. For some reason she wanted to cry. She needed to. But she was afraid that Maude might come back and see her, or that the children might come running in to find their mother in tears. So she went up to the third floor, where she knew she would be alone. No one ever went up to the third floor, except the housekeeper's Siamese cat, because the rooms were stifling in the summer. The windows had all been nailed shut years before, and one could always find armies of flies crawling endlessly along the panes of glass, looking for escape, never finding any.

Afterward Francesca wondered what would have happened had she gone downstairs instead.

The box was in a corner under the eaves, hidden behind stacks of old-fashioned folding lawn chairs, and she might not have noticed it had it not been for Maude's cat, who seemed determined to use it as a litter box. "I chased the cat away," Francesca said, "and thus began the nightmare that has no end." She looked up suddenly, as if in horrified disbelief that she was actually about to reveal the secret she'd been willing to kill to keep.

Kaiser reached across the table and touched her hand. "It's all right, Francesca," he said softly. "I love you. No matter what."

She did not answer at once. When she did she sounded beaten, as if she'd lost something she couldn't live without. "Why didn't I know you first? I would have made you so happy."

"You do make me happy. Now, tell me what happened."

She took a deep breath and began again. "The box was filled with bits and pieces collected more than thirty years before—old concert programs and sheets of music, clippings from newspapers and ticket stubs. And letters. Some were notes from Julian's agent, some were rambling, almost incoherent messages from Elise to her brother, begging him to leave the island and come home to her. Near the bottom of the box was a packet of letters tied in string, written by Julian to someone named Juliette Bertrand. All had been returned unopened."

Francesca remembered hesitating about reading the letters. "Perhaps the hand of some benevolent god," she said. "But I finally decided to read them, and do you know why?" Kaiser shook his head. "Because deep down I had a secret hope that in Julian's old love letters I might find some spark of human affection for another person, something that might make me able to love him, or at least like him. So I read them.

"At first I was intrigued. The tone of each letter shifted remarkably, enough to make you wonder how the same man could have written them all. One was pathetic, pleading, the next imperious, as if he were writing to a slave. Another was threatening, violently abusive. There were apologies for having mistreated her, excuses for having beaten her, accusations of infidelity, and in the same breath promises of eternal happiness, promises to seal their affair with marriage. Some letters were filled with the ravings of a madman, others the poetry of a genius. And yet all had the same closing theme: come back to me or I will find you and make you suffer.

"I was devastated. Julian had never been open about his feelings. I had hoped that by reading his letters I might find some vulnerability in him, some sign of unselfishness, some sign of an honest human emotion. But there was nothing redemptive in those letters, only ruthless, perverted passion, and an obsession with the woman that bordered on lunacy." Francesca stopped and sat staring at her hands, lying limp now on top of the table. "Do you want to know why she left him?"

Kaiser nodded. He didn't dare speak, didn't dare break her concentration.

"Because she found out that he had been sleeping with his own sister . . . poor, schizophrenic Elise." She looked over at Kaiser, and he could hear the revulsion in her voice. "Are you shocked?" She didn't wait for an answer. "I was," she said. "Not just shocked. Sickened." She made a sound that was supposed to be a laugh. "Simple me. I didn't know what it meant to be *really* sickened."

Francesca stood up and walked to the window. She was silent for a long time, but when she finally spoke, her voice was thick with loathing. "I have often wondered, since that day, what terrible thing I did in my life, or maybe in a past life, to deserve Julian Ferrare." She spit the name out as if it were an obscenity.

Kaiser kept silent. Some horrible truth was yet to come, and he could feel Francesca gathering what little strength she had left to reveal it.

"I tell you the truth now, Patrick," she said, her voice ragged, "only because I have no choice. I must try to save my children. Except for them, what I know would go with me to the grave." She took a deep breath, and all at once the trembling stopped. She became rigid, and her voice filled with a sudden, barely controlled fury. "I was going to put the letters back in the box, but I didn't. Something made me look further, an inbred desire to self-destruct perhaps. In any case, there was something else at the bottom. A stack of photographs. I picked them up. They were all of Juliette. Juliette and Julian. An obviously pregnant Juliette, I might add, who left her lover when she realized what kind of madman he was, when she could endure his perversity no longer. But she didn't flee in time. She still had to bear his bastard child."

She turned then, the expression on her face revealing the full depth of her horror and revulsion. She looked as if she were possessed of a terrible pain, a pain that had no physical source. She opened her mouth to speak, but when the words came out, Kaiser didn't really hear them. Then, with sickening awareness, he understood.

"Do you want to know who that bastard child is, Patrick?" she said. "That pathetic mistake? I am. Juliette Bertrand was my mother. And Julian Ferrare is my father."

Kaiser told the guard that he needed a few more minutes, then turned back to Francesca, who was sitting rigid at the table, her fingers gripping the edge as if it were a cliff she was about to fall off.

"Francesca," he said quietly, "I have to ask you one more thing. Did Julian know he was your father when he married you?"

"Of course he knew." Her voice was expressionless, as if she were reading the label on a can of soup. "After eighteen years he was still looking for Juliette, like a mangy cat that prowls endlessly back and forth in front of the cellar door, long after all the mice have been devoured. He was still looking for Juliette, but he found me instead."

"What did you do after you found the photographs?"

"I called my stepfather," she said, and her voice filled with self-reproach. "I couldn't believe what my eyes told me was true, so I called him and begged him to come." All at once she came to pieces. She began to cry, not hysterically, but with a slow welling up of sorrow that flowed as naturally as blood from a wound. "I should never have done that," she said. "I should have known better. All my life I had been warned about his heart. It had been my mother's greatest fear that her young, foolish child would excite him beyond his limits of endurance. And yet I did it. I told him something I should have known would kill him. But at that moment I truly believe I had lost my reason. I needed him to tell me what to do, to help me survive. So he came to me as he always had when I needed him, and I killed him." She looked up at Kaiser, begging for help. "I had to tell him, don't you see?" She made a pleading gesture with her hands. "I needed help. And I had to know what the risks would be for my poor, little children. Were they going to suffer some hideous fate as a result of such close inbreeding? Were they going to go insane, become babbling idiots?" She took a breath. "My stepfather was a doctor. He was the only one I could confide in."

"And did he put your mind at ease?"

She shook her head violently. "He died before he could say one word to help me." She swallowed hard. "Later I read every book I could find on the subject. According to the experts, defects caused by inbreeding are almost always detected at birth, or very soon after, so at least God has spared my children. And if I had been stronger, perhaps He would have spared my stepfather as well."

"You did the only thing you could," Kaiser said.

"I don't know," she said. "But when he died, I wanted to die too. But I couldn't leave my children behind."

"Is that when you decided to kill them too?" Kaiser asked quietly. "Is that when you jumped off the boat?"

"I never tried to kill myself," she said. Now she was speaking freely, as if she didn't care anymore, as if a dam had broken and its worst damage had already been done. "Nor did I try to kill my children. It was simply my first miserable attempt to escape. Julian had flown out to get us when he heard that my stepfather had died. That's when I confronted him with the truth. I told him I wanted an immediate divorce, that we would live with him not one second longer. And do you know what he did? He laughed. 'If you leave me, my dear Francesca,' he said, 'I will tell the whole world the truth. Imagine Hildy's surprise when she learns that her mother is also her sister. And that her father is her dear, old grandpapa. What fun when she has to explain to all of her friends. That is, if they haven't read all about it in the newspapers.'

"I knew then that Julian was insane. He would never let me go. I had only one hope: to escape. To go somewhere he would never find us. I had plenty of money. My stepfather had seen to that before I was even married. He had set up an account for me without Julian's knowledge. He'd said if I didn't ever need it, no harm would be done. But if I ever did . . ." She stopped and pressed her hand against her forehead as if she were trying to remember every detail. "We would simply disappear, I told myself, change our names. Julian would never find us, never be able to hurt my children.

"I made plans. Julian knew that I had always been afraid of the water and that the children couldn't swim, so once we were aboard the ferryboat, he relaxed. He actually went to sleep. It was simple to slip away. About fifteen minutes before we were to dock in Hyannis, I took the children to the back of the boat. I knew that at that point we were only about fifty yards from shore, and that outside the channel the water was shallow. I knew where the emergency ladder would be, rolled up right beside the railing. I threw it over the side and we climbed down. I had given each of the children one of those white life rings, but I underestimated the force of the current. We were swept away from the shore and were pulled out of the water by a fisherman who was in the channel, heading back to port. Poor man. I didn't want to be rescued. I just wanted to get away. I tried to scratch his eyes out, but he managed to get us all on board and call the Coast Guard.

"Julian was magnificent. The depth of his understanding for his deranged wife was admirable. Nor could I say a word in my own defense. What was I to say? That I was running away from my own father? So I played Julian's game of lunatic wife. But I didn't give up hope. And then you came along, Patrick." She began to shake.

"And now?" Kaiser said. "Doesn't Julian still want you back?"

She looked up at him, and the anguish in her eyes was devastating. "He doesn't want me anymore," she gasped. "He wants Hildy."

"Jesus. How do you know that?"

"Hildy told me. On their last trip to London Julian kissed her on the mouth. She wasn't even sure that he had done anything wrong. But I knew. I fear for Christian, but it isn't Christian who keeps me awake at night screaming. It's Hildy," she whispered. "My precious Hildy. It's what he might do to her." She closed her eyes. "I tell myself that this can't be true, that no one could be so depraved. But then I remember who it is I'm dealing with—Julian Ferrare, who is my own father. He is no stranger to incest. He has been intimate with his sister, he has had two children by his own daughter." She stopped, and all at once Kaiser could feel her fear as sharply as if it were his own. He took two steps, but before he could reach her she threw herself against him. "He's going to rape Hildy, Patrick!" she cried.

"No, he isn't, Francesca," Kaiser said, holding her against him. "Because we won't let him. I'm not sure how, but somehow we'll stop him. As soon as I leave I'm going to try to get a court order to have them removed from his custody. Today."

"Oh, Patrick," she sobbed against his chest, "if only you could do that. I just want them safe. I'll deal with the rest later."

He held her at arm's length so she could see his face, know that he was telling her the truth. "I promise you, Hildy and Christian will be out of that house by nightfall." He glanced at his watch. It was almost noon. "I'm going now. I have a lot of people to see." He kissed her on top of the head. "I'll be back."

At the door he stopped and looked back. "This really has been damnable for you, hasn't it?" he said quietly, and through her tears he saw the first hint of her old smile touch the corners of her mouth.

"Well, there's one good thing about it," she said, brushing away a tear. "When I die I know I'll go straight to Heaven. Because I've already been in Hell."

28

"I'm cold and I'm hungry," Christian said. "And I have a blister."

"You just ate two hot dogs."

"I know. But I'm still hungry. Besides, can't we go somewhere and sit down? We've been just walking and walking for hours."

Hildy looked down at her brother and sighed. She was cold, too, and they *had* been walking for hours. Around and around the same block, down Seventy-second Street, up Madison, and around again, hiding whenever they saw a police car, praying for Mr. Kaiser to come home before Julian found them. "We'll go around once more," Hildy said, taking her brother by the hand, "and if he's still not home, we'll go down to Forty-second Street to the library and I'll read you a story."

The two children ran around the corner and back onto Seventy-second Street. They had been trying all morning to see Mr. Kaiser, but no one was home. Hildy wasn't even allowing herself to think about what they would do if they didn't find him. They just had to, she thought.

They went into the foyer and for the tenth time, pushed the buzzer above Mr. Kaiser's name. There was no answer. Hildy could feel the tears welling up under her lids.

Christian was hunkering down in the corner, inspecting

his blister, and Hildy knew that if they didn't go somewhere to rest and get warm, he would probably start to cry. Not that she blamed him. She felt like crying herself. "Come on, Christian," she said. "Put your shoe back on. We'll go to the library."

"Do we have to walk?"

Hildy considered. She didn't want to spend a single penny more than she had to because deep down inside she was afraid it might be a long time before Mr. Kaiser came home. But Forty-second Street was a long way off. "We'll walk over to Fifth Avenue and take the bus," she said.

"What if it gets dark before we find him? Then what will we do?" Christian said as they hurried up the street.

"He'll be back," she said. But if he wasn't, she'd already decided where they would go—the only place where she knew there were people coming and going at all hours of the day and night: Kennedy International Airport. She'd been there dozens of times. They could even sleep there if they were careful, and no one would notice.

The inside of the library was warm and quiet. Hildy picked out a book and she and Christian went to the children's reading room and sat down. Within minutes they were both asleep.

It was noon by the time Elise and Julian were finally discharged from the hospital. Elise couldn't wait to get home. She was out of the cab almost before it stopped, and up the steps. Ever since waking up that morning she'd had the strongest feeling that Christian was gone. She touched Anna's necklace and it was hot. That meant the power was working. Elise felt a tinge of sadness that Hildy might be gone, too—Hildy, with her dark, soft hair. But if it meant that they were rid of Christian, then so be it. It was the price they would have to pay for safety. Just this morning Coriander had warned her not to let her guard down: *Even*

if Francesca seems to be gone, the boy has the power to
bring her back, no matter what Julian says. Remember,
Christian is still your enemy.

Elise stepped into the foyer and listened to the house
gathering itself around her. *They are gone,* Coriander said.

Are you sure? Elise whispered.

Listen, he said. *Can't you hear the emptiness?*

She stood still, listening past the sound of Julian's voice
and the servants' answers. Coriander was right. Beyond the
voices there was nothing. She heard one of the maids say
that just now, when she'd gone up to Hildy's room to get the
children for lunch, she'd discovered they were missing.

Elise's hand flew to her throat and grabbed the garnet
necklace, throbbing now like a living thing. Christian is
gone, she thought exultantly. Now I am truly safe.

"You find this amusing, Elise?" Julian asked, his voice
dark and angry.

She straightened her face. "What?" she asked.

"Christian and Hildy are gone."

"Gone?"

"It seems they left the house sometime this morning,
without telling anyone, and no one seems to know where
they've gone."

Elise looked away. It terrified her when Julian's eyes
grew black and still as death. *Stress and fear are sisters,*
Coriander said. *Stress and fear.*

"You wouldn't have any idea where they might have
gone, would you, sister dear?"

She shook her head and started for the stairs. She needed
her medication.

Julian followed up the stairs in silence, but just outside
Hildy's door he stopped.

Elise, scarcely daring to breathe, watched as he went
into the room. Please don't let him find anything that will
help bring the boy back, she prayed to the necklace, but
when she put her hand up to touch it, to her horror it was

ice cold. In that instant she was paralyzed with dread, and at the same moment Julian came out of Hildy's room, carrying a piece of paper.

"Would you know anything about this?" he asked, handing it to her. He was smiling.

She took the paper and tried to read, but the words were fishes swimming in the ocean. "What does it say?" she asked, hoping it wasn't a clue to their whereabouts.

"It says 'Good things to remember.'" Julian was still smiling, but it was a dreadful smile, and Elise felt the floor begin to move under her feet.

"And?" she asked, trembling.

"There is an address written here also." Still smiling. "I think I have another job for my very talented investigators."

Elise could no longer make words. Julian knew where they had gone, and he was going to bring them back. She wasn't safe at all. The boy was coming back, and it wouldn't be long before Francesca would be back too. Elise turned away and ran to her room, slamming the door just as the waves broke over her head.

Hildy was dreaming. She was living on the edge of the ocean all alone with her mother and Christian. Their house was tiny but immaculate, with flower boxes at the windows and a white picket fence all around. There was a small vegetable garden at the back door, and the ocean at the front. The sun was shining, and she and Christian were wading knee-deep in water, feeling for clams with their feet. But much to their amazement, the farther out they waded, the more shallow the water became, until all at once there was no more. The sea had sucked itself back, leaving the ocean bed dry and littered with hundreds of sea creatures. She and Christian ran in every direction, gathering clams to fill their buckets, picking up strange shells that had always before been hidden by the tides. Her bucket was almost full when she heard her mother call.

"Run, Hildy! Run!"

Hildy turned to see a mighty wall of water rushing toward her. She tried to run but her feet were cased in muck and she fell to her knees. "Mama!" she cried. "Save me!" And then someone was there, picking her up as easily as if she were a baby, running with her to safety. But she never saw who it was because at that moment Christian, still asleep beside her at the library table, wet his pants.

Hildy didn't want to spend a cent more than she had to, but Christian had to have dry underwear. She took him over to a discount store on Sixth Avenue, bought him the cheapest pair of undershorts she could, and stood outside the dressing room while he changed. Then she bought him a cookie, and together they took the bus back uptown to Mr. Kaiser's.

It was almost dark, and raining again, so they ran the last few steps to the front door. As Hildy pushed the buzzer, she felt a sudden rush of panic. Please be here, Mr. Kaiser, she prayed. Please be home. She pushed again.

"He isn't there," Christian said dully.

Hildy shook her head, feeling a terrible emptiness in the pit of her stomach that had nothing to do with how hungry she was. Her hand fell limp to her side.

And then a click, and his voice came like a miracle over the intercom. "Who is it?"

Hildy was ecstatic. "It's Hildy, Mr. Kaiser. Hildy Ferrare. And Christian. We have to talk to you."

"Come right up. Number 803."

Hildy and Christian almost knocked each other over in their rush to get to the elevator, but once inside, Hildy put her arms around her little brother. "We're safe, Christian," she said. "Mr. Kaiser will know what to do, I'm sure of it."

They got off on the eighth floor and went right to Number 803, but Hildy didn't push the bell. First she stopped to smooth down Christian's hair and wipe the crumbs off his mouth. "We don't want Mr. Kaiser to think we're beggars," she said. Then she straightened her own hair and pushed the button.

The door opened at once, but before she and Christian could step inside, two men came out and stood silently on either side of the startled children, the same men who had come to Vermont with Julian. Hildy looked from one to the other, confused, then back toward the open door. "Mr. Kaiser?" she said, feeling the slippery touch of real fear. But that was only the beginning of her nightmare, because the man who stepped into the hallway was not Mr. Kaiser, it was their father, Julian Ferrare.

29

"Go get Mrs. Ferrare," the attendant said. "She's leaving us."

Kaiser waited by the window, every once in a while glancing out at the rain pelting down. It was the kind of rain, he decided, that could drive someone into a terminal depression if he watched it long enough. He glanced at his watch. It was nearly five. He hoped they would bring Francesca in soon.

It hadn't been an easy task getting her released. And it had been impossible to persuade the judge to issue a court order placing Hildy and Christian in protective custody. Except for Francesca's unsupported statement that Julian was her father, the only crime that had actually been committed was hers. No physical or sexual abuse had taken place. "A kiss on the mouth," Judge Henry Denning had said, "cannot be considered a criminal act."

Kaiser had known Henry a long time, and knew him as a good man and a tough judge. But Judge Denning had refused to sign any order on the strength of Francesca Ferrare's word alone. She had, after all, tried to kill her husband. Julian, on the other hand, had broken no law, at least none where there was any solid evidence.

"If," Henry had said, "Mrs. Ferrare can prove familial relationship—one, that Julian Ferrare is indeed her father,

240

and two, that he was fully aware of the relationship at the time of their marriage—then she might have a case for defense. And at such time as she provides the proof, I will be happy to issue an order for his arrest. But all that takes time, Kaiser. No court in the country would have him arrested without some kind of evidence of wrongdoing. The sole word of the woman who tried to kill him is simply not enough."

Kaiser had spent almost three hours with Henry, appealing to him first as a jurist, but in the last resort as a friend. The judge had finally agreed to set bond for Francesca, releasing her into Kaiser's custody. But Hildy and Christian were a different matter.

"You are emotionally involved, my friend," Henry had said. "And from all that you have told me, this is an emotional issue. But as far as I can see, there has been no crime committed against those children. Not in the eyes of the law. No abuse, either physical or sexual."

"But I know the man, Henry," Kaiser had argued. "And I know that Francesca has every reason to be afraid of what he might do."

"That may be so, but it's not enough. I'll tell you what I will do though. I'll call Frank Mellady over at the Bureau of Child Welfare right now and have him pay a call on Julian Ferrare. He'll talk to him, talk to the children. If he decides they should be removed from the household, I'll sign an order. But not until I hear from Frank."

Kaiser waited while the judge called and briefly explained the situation. Hanging up, he told Kaiser what was said and that Frank Mellady was on his way to Julian Ferrare's house.

Kaiser was about to leave when the judge had stopped him. "Kaiser," he'd said, and all sign of friendship in his voice had vanished. "You and I go back a long way. But I warn you, don't let your emotional involvement with this woman cloud your judgment. I may be your friend, but I am first of all an officer of the court."

Kaiser heard the attendant say "You are free to go," and he was jerked back to the present. He turned to see Francesca standing by the desk. "Just sign here."

Her hand was shaking so badly that she could barely hold the pen, but somehow she managed to write her name. Kaiser crossed to her side and took her by the arm, just in time to keep her from falling over. "Let's get out of here." He led her out to the waiting cab.

She didn't speak until they were almost across town. Then she asked where they were going.

"To Julian's. Frank Mellady from the Child Welfare agency should be there by now." He glanced at his watch. "He's going to talk to Hildy and Christian, and then he's going to decide if the situation justifies further action." He took her hand. "He's going to let you see the children. At least for a few minutes."

She was silent, and he knew she was trying to prepare herself for the worst. Finally she said, "Is there a chance that Mr. Mellady will decide to leave them there? With Julian?"

"It's a possibility," Kaiser replied quietly. Then he told her about his talk with Henry Denning.

"Oh, dear Christ," she whispered. "It sounds like it's more than a possibility."

"We'll cross that bridge when we get to it. But I promise you one thing—we aren't going to leave Hildy and Christian there alone."

She began to tremble, and he pulled her close. He still wanted to ask about the box of letters she'd found, but decided to wait. He could feel that she was trying to pull herself together.

The cab was almost to Sixty-fourth Street when he spoke again. "You're going to have to prove what you say is true— about Julian being your father. You know that, don't you?"

She nodded.

"You can produce those letters and photographs?"

She nodded again. "They're still where I left them. I wanted to destroy them, but somehow I had enough reason left to think that maybe someday I might need them." She bit her lip. "If I ask you something, will you answer truthfully?"

"Yes."

"Does it make you feel sick? Being with me, I mean?"

The question startled him. "Why in hell would you ask such a thing?"

"Because it makes me feel sick," she said. "Ever since I found that box I've wanted to scrub my skin off wherever he'd touched me."

He took her hand. "I don't want you to think about such a thing ever again," he said sharply. "None of this was your doing. I know it, and it's high time you did too."

She leaned back against the seat, and he saw a hint of the same curious expression he'd seen on the boat so many months ago. "What is it?" he asked.

"Remember when I told you that once upon a time I wondered what terrible thing I had done to deserve Julian Ferrare?"

He nodded.

"Well, now I'm wondering what good thing I did to deserve you." She said it so softly that he almost didn't hear. Then she reached over and with breathtaking gentleness put both hands on the sides of his face. "I love you, Patrick Kaiser," she whispered. "No matter what happens, I want you to know that. This time you haven't just saved my life, you *are* my life." And she kissed him.

The cab came down Sixty-fourth Street and stopped. Kaiser helped her out and steadied her as she stood looking up at the house. "I won't have to go in, will I? I won't have to see Julian?" she whispered.

"No. We're simply here to talk to Frank Mellady, and so you can see the children."

He left Francesca on the sidewalk, went up the steps and rang the bell. No answer. He rang again.

"That's odd," he said. "Someone is supposed to be here."

"Someone *is* here," a man said, coming out from under the shelter of the front stoop. "Mr. Kaiser? I'm Frank Mellady. Child Welfare."

Kaiser walked back down the steps. "What's going on?" he asked.

Mellady shrugged. "There doesn't seem to be anyone here," he said. "I got here at five o'clock sharp, but no sign of life."

Kaiser turned to Francesca, who was staring at the house. "Do you have any idea where they might be?"

"He's taken them away," she said, and sat down hard on the step, as if blown over by a sudden wind. "I should have known he wouldn't stay in New York."

"Have you any idea where he might have gone?"

"I don't know. A million places. Julian Ferrare is a man of the world. He could be anywhere." And then all at once her head came up with a sharp snap. "Nantucket. He's gone to Nantucket to get those letters. To destroy them."

"And he's taken the children with him?" Mellady asked.

She nodded, struck dumb.

Mellady shrugged. "In that case, there's nothing I can do. Unless he comes back to New York. And even then I can't promise anything."

"Do we have any options?" Kaiser asked.

"You can see if Judge Denning knows someone in Massachusetts who could look into it, but I'm afraid there isn't much else you can do. Even if the judge here in New York signs a court order, Mr. Ferrare is out of our jurisdiction."

"You mean we can't call the police?" Francesca asked, her voice rising.

Mellady shook his head. "It's not a police matter. From what the judge told me, there is no evidence any abuse has ever taken place, only a suspicion that it may. And that's all academic now anyway because your husband has left the state. Legally. Now it's up to a judge in Massachusetts, if that's where they went, to decide if any action is warranted."

Francesca let out a low moan and covered her face with her hands.

"Thanks anyway," Kaiser said.

"I wish I could have helped, but . . ." Mellady threw up his hands. "Good luck," he added, then hurried up the street to find a cab.

Kaiser sat down beside Francesca, who was still sitting rigid on the step.

"He's going to destroy the letters," she said. "I'll have no proof of any of this." The rain was mixing with her tears, running down her cheeks, but she didn't seem to notice. "But worse than that, Kaiser, he has the children with him. With no one to protect them but . . . but Elise."

"Come on," Kaiser said, pulling her to her feet. "I have to find a phone. There's a bar on the corner. We'll call Mrs. Minstrell. If they're at the house, she'll know. And then we'll be on our way."

It only took Kaiser a few minutes to make the call. He put the phone back in the cradle. "Thanks," he said to the bartender. He threw enough money on the counter to pay for their drinks. "Let's go," he said to Francesca. "We have a plane to catch."

"Then they *are* there," she said, grabbing her coat.

Kaiser nodded. "Mrs. Minstrell said they arrived about an hour ago."

"What did you tell her?"

"As little as possible. There's nothing she can do. She has

no authority where your children are concerned. We're the
only ones who can get Hildy and Christian out of there, and
that's precisely what we're going to do. We're going to get
your children and the box of letters, and bring them back to
New York. Then we'll let the judge take care of it."

"I pray to God we're not too late," she said.

Together they ran up the street to find a cab, neither
saying it out loud, but both acutely aware of how very little
time they had.

Why are we here? Elise wondered. She stood on the
walk and looked up at the house. In the near dark she
thought she saw it smile at her. She shivered. Can houses
smile? she asked Coriander.

They can if they're amused, he said.

Why did Julian make us come back here?

He didn't, Coriander said. *The boy did. This is where his
power is strongest. This is the place where he can work his
spells to bring his mother back.*

"Come along, Elise," Julian said, and his voice was filled
with impatience. He herded the two silent children up the
stairs to the front door. He turned the key in the lock and
the three went in, but Elise couldn't. She stood on the
bottom step and tried to catch her breath, taking a series of
quick gulps. I can't go in, she said to Coriander. I'm too
afraid.

You must, he said.

"What are you doing out there?" Julian snapped, coming
to the door. "Come in and help me get this place in order."

"Yes, Julian," she said, and she went up the stairs,
carrying her fear like an extra piece of luggage.

Be strong, Coriander said. *You nearly beat them once
before in this house, remember?*

She made herself concentrate. Was Coriander right? Was
it here that she had nearly won? But when? And then she

remembered the ice-warm glow of the letter opener in her hand, the unparalleled thrill when she thought she had killed the boy.

You can do it again, Coriander said. *Get rid of the boy and we will never have to be afraid again.*

Elise reached up and touched Anna's necklace. It throbbed and hummed under her fingers, and she felt reassured. This time I won't fail, she said, and she marched in through the door and into the hall.

Hildy and Christian were standing together at the foot of the stairs, pale and puffy-eyed. But beyond the boy's dark eyes Elise could see his mind working, plotting. He's begun already, she said to Coriander.

I know. You have no time to waste.

"Where is Julian?" she asked.

Hildy pointed up the stairs, but she didn't speak.

Elise smiled in spite of herself. How much better she liked people when they were silent. There was so much less confusion. She crossed the hallway just as Julian came down the stairs carrying a box. She followed him into the living room. "What are you doing?" she asked.

"I'm going to start a fire to take the chill off, dear 'Lise. While we are waiting for the heat to come up." His mood had changed dramatically, and now he seemed to be in rare high spirits. "Do you suppose you can unpack what the servants sent along for our supper, while I seal my dear wife's fate once and for all?"

Elise stood still, watching him closely as he set the box down beside the fireplace. "First, the kindling," he said. "I wonder if there's some left out in the back entry?" He was humming, and she wondered what had happened to cause the sudden shift in his mood. Was it because Francesca was to be locked up forever? Or was it something else?

"It's going to be a wonderful change," he was saying, "to be away from the city for a while. The sea air will be just the thing to bring the color back into Hildy's cheeks."

"I'm sure," Elise said.

"These past months without her have made me realize how grown-up she has become, and how much I've missed her."

Elise didn't answer. She was still trying to understand why Julian's good mood was upsetting her so much, and why she'd suddenly heard all the windows and the doors in the house blow shut.

Don't be sidetracked, Coriander warned. *Remember the boy. He's the threat. You must handle one thing at a time. You haven't the strength to do more.*

"Are you going to stand there forever?" Julian asked. "While I'm looking for kindling, do you think you could get us something to eat? It's after eight."

"Right away, Julian," she said.

Supper that evening was an unsettling affair, even by Elise's standards. She watched the proceedings from a great distance, though she was sitting directly across from her brother. She listened to him speak, wondering still what joyous event had occurred to lift him to such obviously euphoric heights. He hadn't found any kindling, not in the entry, not out in the shed, but it hadn't seemed to dampen his spirits. "Plenty of time for a fire," he had said.

Normally when Julian was happy Elise was, too, but there was something in his present mood that she found frightening, as if he were slipping away from her. If she didn't do something quickly, she thought, he would soon be gone. She looked over at the boy.

He was sitting in silence, eyes cast down. Elise was somewhat relieved to see that he was swallowing his food with great difficulty. That meant he was uncomfortable.

He's not uncomfortable, Coriander said. *He is simply concerned with more important things. Like bringing his mother back.*

Elise cringed and forced her attention toward Hildy. "You aren't hungry?" she asked the girl, who had eaten nothing.

Hildy shook her head.

"She's exhausted, poor darling," Julian said, and put his arm around her. To Elise's shock, Hildy shrank back as if burned.

Elise glanced at her brother to see if he'd noticed, but he seemed unaffected. "It's been a long day," he said, still jovial. "We could all use a good night's sleep, don't you agree, dear 'Lise?"

Elise nodded, but she didn't mean it. There would be no sleep for her tonight. She had too many things to do.

We are in the eye of the storm, Coriander said. *And time is running out.*

Elise leaned back and closed her eyes, raking what pieces of thought she could find into a small, pitiful pile. Julian is going to leave me, she thought. I can feel it.

It's the boy's fault, Coriander said.

Are you sure? she asked.

What else could it be?

Elise thought about it, but could find no other explanation for her sudden fear. Coriander had to be right. The boy was working to bring Francesca back. That was why she felt so threatened. It had always been so. It always would be so.

She opened her eyes and looked straight into Christian's face. I won't fail this time, she told him with her mind. You have thwarted me long enough.

He looked back at her, his dark eyes brimming with tears, but Elise was unmoved. Trickster, she said. I won't be fooled again.

"Stop crying and go upstairs," Julian said to the boy. "Get into your bed and stay there. I don't want you bothering your sister tonight. You are not to sneak into her room."

"But it's no bother," Hildy said in the voice of a mouse.

"It's a baby's trick, encouraged by your demented mother," Julian said with venom. "But it's time for a change.

The first of many in that regard, I might add." He threw a dark look at his son, who seemed to shrivel up in his chair. "Go to bed!" Julian commanded.

Christian slid off his chair and headed toward the door, tears running down the sides of his face.

"I'll help you, Christian," Hildy said, getting up, but Julian reached out and blocked her way.

"He can do it by himself," he said, and the tone of his voice left no room for objection.

Christian hurried from the room without looking back.

"But he's only five," Hildy said, her voice quavering.

Elise threw a frightened glance at Julian, fearful of his reaction. Nothing enraged him more than to be questioned, and she was shocked to see that he was smiling. "You need not concern yourself with Christian any longer," he said to Hildy, reaching over, touching her arm. "I have plans for us, my darling, that don't include him."

What little color there had been in Hildy's face drained away. "What plans?" she whispered.

Julian put up a hand. "Not yet, my precious dove," he said. "I want you to be surprised."

"But what is to become of Christian?"

"Elise will take care of him. Won't you, Elise?"

You will indeed, Coriander said.

Elise stood up. "I think I'll go upstairs myself," she said.

"I think we all will," Julian said. "But first I have a surprise." He reached behind his chair and pulled out a box, beautifully wrapped in silver paper.

Elise's breath caught in her throat and she felt her eyes grow round like two O's. It had been so long since Julian had given her a gift that she had forgotten how much it meant to her. She almost choked in the face of his love, and her hand flew up to take the box, knocking her water glass over. "Oh, Julian," she gasped. "Thank you."

"It isn't for you," Julian said coldly. "It's for my little dove, Hildy." He handed the box to his daughter.

Elise felt suffocated. The air in the room moved, thick and clothlike, up her nose and into her mouth, blocking her windpipe. She rushed to the window, threw it open, and began to suck in great gulps of oxygen. She was so grateful to be breathing that, blessedly, she did not see the long, silken gown that Hildy took from the box, didn't hear Julian tell her to go upstairs, take a warm bath, and put it on.

30

Hildy left Julian and Elise in the dining room and moved up the stairs like a shadow, attached to feet that were taking her where she did not want to go. Things had frightened her before in her life, things like thunder and black spiders, and once she'd almost been run over by a machine that was sweeping the street in front of her house. But now she realized how simple those fears were compared to what she was feeling now.

She placed her feet one in front of the other and walked down the hall toward the bathroom, not because she wanted to, but because she was afraid not to. She paused outside of Christian's door and listened. She thought about going in to see if he was all right, but changed her mind. If Julian caught her, he would blame Christian, and she didn't want to think what that might mean.

She shuddered and moved on. She was almost to the bathroom when she heard a door open behind her and Christian's voice whisper in a half sob, "Hildy, I'm scared."

She ran back and slipped into his room. He was standing just behind the door, and he looked so small and helpless that Hildy felt sick. But how could she defend him when she didn't even know how to defend herself? So she put her arms around him and hugged him tight. "Ssh, Christian," she whispered. "It's going to be all right."

He looked up at her, his dark eyes swollen and red. "Are you scared, Hildy?" he asked.

"Of course not, silly," she lied. "Why should I be scared?"

"Because we're all alone."

"We aren't all alone. You have me and I have you. Isn't that good enough? For now?"

Christian shook his head violently, closed his eyes and began to cry hard. "I want Mama," he wailed.

Hildy knelt down in front of him and took his hands. "Listen, Christian. You have to be brave." Her mind was racing, trying to think of something that would make him stop crying before Julian heard him. "How can we make plans," she said sternly, "if you keep crying all the time?"

"What plans?" he said, looking at her through his tears.

"You don't think we're going to stay here, do you?" she said, trying to sound convincing.

"We aren't?"

"Of course not," she said, and just hearing the words gave her a spark of hope. "We have to help Mama, so stop crying and give me a few minutes to figure it out. Okay?"

He wiped his nose on his sleeve and nodded.

"Okay," Hildy said. "Now I have to go, before Julian catches me in here with you." She stood up. "Promise me you won't cry anymore." He nodded, and she bent over and kissed him on the cheek. "See you in the morning," she said. "By then I'll have it figured out for sure."

She was almost to the door when she heard him whisper, "Can I sleep with you tonight?"

She shuddered and turned back, trying not to let him see how much his question frightened her. "You can't, Christian," she said. "What if Julian catches you?"

"He won't," Christian said, running to her. "I'll hide under the bed if he comes." He looked up, pleading with his eyes. "Please, Hildy. Just tonight. I promise I won't get caught."

Hildy considered only for a moment then nodded, not just because Christian was too scared to sleep alone, but because she was too.

At the door she turned and blew him a kiss. Then she left the room to take her bath.

It didn't take them long to get to the Westchester County Airport. Kaiser had used the charter service there dozens of times.

"I'm sorry, Mr. Kaiser," the clerk said, "but there's nothing we can do. If you'd been here an hour ago, you might have had a chance, but as it is now, the Nantucket Airport is fogged in. Nothing going in or out right now, and maybe not for quite a while. You know the way it is out there."

Kaiser cursed under his breath. "But we have to get out there tonight," he said. "Do I have any alternative?"

He checked a schedule. "We can fly you to Hyannis. If you leave right now, I think there's a nine-thirty boat."

"Jesus Christ," Kaiser said. "That means we won't be on the island until midnight."

"It's the best we can do, I'm afraid."

Kaiser was glad that Francesca wasn't standing beside him. She was on fire as it was. "All right," he said. "How soon can we take off?"

"Anytime you say."

He could see Francesca coming toward him across the lobby. "We're ready whenever you are," he said to the man.

"When can we leave?" Francesca asked, taking his arm. Her voice was steady, but he could feel the panic in her touch. It was as if she were bristling with electricity, and he knew she was trying not to scream out loud.

"Right away," he said. "Only one problem—we have to go to Hyannis and take the boat. The Nantucket airport is fogged in." He said the words quickly, as if their rapid passing would help get them there sooner.

"Dear God," she whispered.

He put his arm around her. "Maybe the fog will have lifted by the time we get to the coast, and if it has, we'll fly right on to the island. If it hasn't, we'll have to take the nine-thirty boat."

Kaiser saw her clench her teeth. "Let's get started," she said.

She spoke only twice during the flight, once to tell him that she was sure Julian had already destroyed the contents of the box, and once to ask him if he believed in God.

"I do," he said.

"Then pray to Him to keep Julian from hurting my daughter."

Elise heard the footsteps inside and outside of her head. They were Hildy's, going down the hall to the bathroom. Then she heard the sound of running water. Hildy was going to take a bath, and Elise knew with a sinking heart that she would have to wait until Hildy had finished and was settled in for the night. She couldn't risk Hildy seeing what she was about to do. She felt a sudden wave of panic. What should she do while she was waiting? What would become of her? She would grow old and weak and unable to move. She put her arms around herself and began to rock slowly back and forth on the edge of the bed.

What is the matter with you? Coriander roared. *If you are going to behave so badly, then I must go away. Forever.* And he soared off above the high plains.

Elise leaped to her feet, shocked beyond belief. Never before had such a thing happened. Sometimes Coriander had hidden from her, but never had he told her he was leaving forever. She was filled with a deep, penetrating fear, but underneath it there was a terrible, wrenching loneliness. Come back, Coriander, she begged. I didn't mean it. I'll do whatever you say. Just don't leave me.

She rushed to Anna's jewelry box and began to cover herself with bracelets and rings. See? she called to him, now miles distant. I'm getting ready. Please come back, Coriander. You are all I have.

She listened for his voice, but her world was filled with a silence so pervasive that it left no room for anything else. And then through it all her earth ears caught the sounds of footsteps scurrying down the hall. She crawled to the door and put her eye to the crack, just in time to see Christian disappear into Hildy's room.

Elise collapsed in a heap on the floor. "All is lost," she wailed. "How can I destroy him if he is with Hildy? Oh, Coriander, please help me."

One last time, he said, reappearing in a crackling whirlwind of dry, autumn leaves. *But you must hurry. The work must be done now, before Hildy finishes her bath and goes back to her room.*

At the sound of his voice Elise was filled with the strength of ten. She jumped to her feet and grabbed the letter opener from the night table where it had been waiting for her all these months. She turned it over once in her hand, feeling its heat soaking through her skin to her very soul. Then she dropped it into her pocket.

We will be saved, Coriander said. *Without the boy, Francesca will never return. Julian will thank you. He'll probably even buy you a gift.*

Do you really think so? Elise asked.

I'm sure of it, Coriander said.

Elise smiled and walked to the door, opened it and slipped out into the hall. She moved like a whisper past Julian's room—no sound there—but just outside the bathroom door she stopped. Inside she could hear faint sounds of water splashing.

Good, Coriander said. *That means the boy is alone in Hildy's room.*

Elise almost danced the rest of the way down the hall. I

must hurry, she said to Coriander. I am going to finish this business once and for all, and she quickened her pace.

Slow down, Coriander warned. *Make no mistake*.

It is not I who have made the mistake, she answered. The boy thinks he is safe in Hildy's room. He doesn't know that I saw him sneak in there.

She stopped outside the door just long enough to click her heels five times and touch the door frame lightly with her fingertips. Not that she needed to. She knew that at last everything was in order. She simply did it for old times' sake. Then she opened the door a crack and slid into the room. Silently, like oil on water.

Hildy sat on the edge of the tub, fully clothed, and splashed her hand in the water. She had to think, she had to make plans. She'd promised Christian that she would come up with some way to help them.

But she couldn't. She was too afraid. Afraid to get undressed, afraid to take a bath, afraid to put on the gown that Julian had given her. And most of all she was afraid to go to her room. "I'm sorry, Christian. You'll just have to be brave tonight and sleep alone, because I'm going to sit right here until morning," she said, tears running down her cheeks, dripping in a steady stream off the end of her chin. "You can hide from him, but I can't." But you can lock the door, she said to herself. He can't get to you if you're locked in.

Hildy jumped up and almost fell in her frenzy to reach the door, and then with a flash of horror she remembered. There was no lock. Mama had had it removed after Christian locked himself in one night and couldn't get out.

Hildy sank to her knees on the floor, weak with fear, and like any frightened child, began to cry for her mother. "Mama," she whispered. "Please come. Please. Before he does."

* * *

Elise held her breath and listened, but there was no sound. Outside she could hear the waves crashing on the distant shore, and beyond, the warning call of a ship somewhere at sea; but inside the room it was quiet as a tomb. She leaned back against the door and felt every nerve in her body suddenly relax. It seemed as if she'd been on a journey all her life, but now her old world lay far behind. Ahead was a new and glorious existence where there would be no bars on the windows, no icy wet sheets on the beds.

And no more Christian, Coriander said.

No more Christian, Elise echoed, reaching into her pocket, taking out the letter opener. She hesitated only a moment, waiting to see if her old world had truly disappeared, but there was no rushing of wings to weaken her, no melting of ground beneath her feet to slow her forward motion. There was no pit.

She crossed the room with the stealth of a cobra, not seeing the boy in the bed, but sensing him. She struck in one single swoop, attacking with all the fury of her own private hell, raising her arm up then down with such maniacal force that within an instant she had buried the blade up to the hasp in yielding, human flesh.

She heard his voice shriek out in terror, and at the same time the sick gurgling of life draining away, like water down an old, rusty pipe. "You're dead!" she screamed in triumph. "Dead!" She grabbed hold of the letter opener and yanked, but her hand slid off. "You can't have my letter opener," she hissed. "Julian gave it to me." She couldn't see, but she could feel the sticky, wet-warm gush of blood pumping up around her fingers as she tried to pull the blade free. She began to rock the handle back and forth with as much strength as she could muster, and all at once it came loose. She fell back on her heels on the floor beside the bed

"You are dead," she said. "Finally." Coriander soared high above, his hair ablaze, streaming sparks. She called to him. Come see, she cried. I've done it. The boy is dead. We are finally safe, Coriander. Are you pleased?

She listened for his answer, but Coriander was silent, and then she became aware of another sound in the room. An earth sound. A gagging, gasping that came not from her own mind but from under the bed.

"Who is it?" she said, feeling a savage stab of terror at the back of her mind. It was so severe that for a moment it caused her to lose all sense of direction. She didn't know whether to look up or down, whether she was sitting or standing. She drew her knees to her chest and fell over onto the floor. She could still hear the sobbing, but she was unable to comprehend it, even though she knew it was real. Or was it? An echo of doubt blew through her mind and she tried to grab it, hold it tight. She had heard things under her bed before. Maybe this was one of those old demons come to destroy her one moment of triumph.

Turn on the light, Coriander commanded, swooping down. *Look under the bed*.

Elise's mind was paralyzed, but her body pulled itself up and crawled to the nightstand, flicking on the light. The first thing she saw was the blood, thick, dark red pools of it, soaking through the sheets, oozing down the side of the mattress to drip-drip sluggishly onto the carpet. She touched it with her fingers, curious to find that it was still warm. So much blood for one small body, she thought.

Look under the bed, Coriander said.

The sight of the blood had calmed her, reassured her that the boy was indeed dead. And if that were so, then nothing could harm her. What she had heard before had been the gasping of a demon about to be cast out. Nothing more. She lifted the edge of the spread and leaned over, her head almost touching the floor, and she looked.

There is nothing here, she said to Coriander, and at the

same time, she saw him. He was flat on his stomach in the corner, pressed up against the wall, quivering like a captured bird, and at the sight Elise almost bit her tongue in half. "Christian!" she gasped, and slammed her eyes shut, trying desperately to unsee what she had clearly seen. It can't be! she screamed to Coriander. I killed him! She pushed herself up on her knees and looked again at the blood. You see? she said, rubbing her hands in it, and then all at once her fear and confusion turned to white-hot rage. "Trickster!" she roared. "You think to fool me again?"

She grabbed the blood-smeared letter opener that was lying on the floor beside her, and with demonic strength she pushed the bed aside.

Christian let out a shriek of terror and tried to scramble out of the way, but she was on him in a flash.

"Mama!" he screamed.

"Mama can't help you now, you devil!" Elise raised the letter opener high above her head, and at the same moment all reality became a lie. There was the feeling of the blade in her hand, the gagging sound of the child struggling in her grip, but then beyond it, the sudden crashing open of the door.

"Mama!" Christian shrieked again, and to Elise's eternal horror she found herself looking across the abyss at Francesca Ferrare. As her eyes slammed back and forth from Francesca to Christian, the walls began to melt around her. She tried to run but she had lost all contact with her arms and legs, and then the floor split open beneath her and she began to slide toward the pit. Coriander! she screamed. Help me!

For a moment she thought it was too late, but then she heard him. *Come then, precious one*, he said, swooping down, lifting her up on his back. *You have suffered enough. It is time to go home*. And together they flew where Elise had never been before, far away across the high plains.

31

Kaiser stood back and watched as Francesca knelt and gathered her children to her, holding them close, calming them. Then she led them out of the room into the hall.

"I knew you'd come, Mama," Hildy said, drying her eyes. "I just knew it."

"Julian came in and I hid under the bed," Christian said, sobbing and hiccoughing at the same time. Then he burrowed in against his mother like a small animal.

"Hush, my darlings," Francesca said. "It's all right." She pulled them both close. "Everything is going to be just fine. You're safe now. Nothing else matters."

Kaiser watched until they had disappeared down the hall. Then he closed the door and crossed to where Elise sat rigid on the floor, knees drawn up to her chest. Her eyes were wide open, but except for a sporadic blinking of the lids, there was no other movement. Her mouth was ajar, and a trickle of saliva mixed with blood dribbled out of the corner.

Kaiser moved cautiously. Only moments before, when they had thrown the door open, they'd seen a thing possessed, a snarling fiend making sounds that came straight from Hell. Kaiser had rushed forward to keep her from stabbing Christian, but before he could reach her, her whole body had convulsed upon itself like a closing fist and she had slumped to the floor. She hadn't moved since.

He stood looking at her, wondering if he should try to move her, then decided against it. He turned and walked around the foot of Hildy's bed, pushed almost against the wall, and then he saw the body. "Jesus," he whistled.

Julian Ferrare was lying half under the quilt, his left side exposed, and Kaiser knew without going any closer that he was dead. No one could have sustained such a mutilation of his chest and still be alive.

"That's how they kill vampires, isn't it? A stake through the heart?"

Kaiser turned to see a pale but controlled Francesca standing close beside him. "Where are the children?" he asked.

"I took them next door to Mrs. Minstrell. She's going to call the police," Francesca said. "I didn't want them to see any more of this than they already have." She waved her arm around the room. She shuddered. "Why did she kill him, Patrick? She loved him more than anyone else in the world. In fact I think he was the only person she ever loved."

Kaiser put his arm around her. "I don't know," he said, shaking his head. "I doubt that anyone ever will. Have you seen the condition she's in?"

Francesca nodded, and together they walked back to stand in front of Elise, who still sat rigid, unmoving. "What's wrong with her?" Francesca whispered.

"I'm not sure," he said, "but I don't think we should try to move her."

Francesca shivered. "Why do I feel so sorry for her?"

"Because we both know she isn't a criminal. She's a victim."

"Do you think she can hear us?"

Kaiser shrugged. "I don't know."

"She saved me, Patrick. When all is said and done, I owe

her a great deal." She knelt down beside Elise. "I don't know why you did it," she said. "I don't know if you can even hear me. But if you can, thank you. For Hildy. For Christian. And for me." She put her hand out and touched Elise on the shoulder, then drew it back with a jerk. "Something's wrong," she said sharply.

"What is it?"

Francesca pointed toward the floor, and then Kaiser saw it too. A sluggish ooze of blood was inching its way along a crack in the floorboards.

Kaiser frowned. "What the hell . . . ?" he said. He reached down and pulled Elise's legs away from her body.

She didn't fall over. She sat upright, but now Kaiser could see that her hands were clenched around the hasp of her silver letter opener, the letter opener that was buried five inches deep in the soft flesh of her abdomen. The blood that had soaked through the fabric of her dress had formed a thick puddle in her lap and was now spilling over onto the floor.

"Dear God," Francesca whispered, jerking back. "She's dead."

Kaiser pulled Francesca to her feet. "Let's get out of here," he said. "We've both seen enough—more than enough. The police can take charge from here on."

"What are we going to tell them?"

"The truth. That Elise killed Julian," he said. "We don't know why. The rest is none of their business."

"Then what?" She was whispering as if someone could hear.

"We've found the box. We'll take it back to New York. To Judge Denning. He'll handle the rest."

Without looking back, they left the room and started down the stairs, Kaiser holding Francesca by the arm to steady her. "Take it easy," he said gently. "It's almost over."

She stopped short and turned to him with a look of real

surprise. "It is, isn't it?" she said with wonder. "It really is almost over. I can begin to breathe again. To live again."

Kaiser couldn't look at her. "Do you have any plans?" he asked, trying to sound casual. He loved her, but now so much had happened, so much had changed. In all fairness he knew the first move had to be hers.

Francesca said nothing. She stood stone still, then all at once, as if she'd just remembered something critical, she grabbed him by the hand. "Come with me," she said. "Quickly. Before the police get here." She began to pull him back up the stairs to the second floor.

Kaiser could hear the sound of a siren. "They'll be here in a minute," he said.

"Never mind them," she answered over her shoulder.

Kaiser followed after. Francesca was free now, and eager to begin her life again. But would her plans include him? Stop thinking about it, he said to himself. There's nothing you can do.

The sound of the siren was louder now, coming up the road, but Francesca seemed completely unaware of it. She turned a corner on the second floor and took the stairs to the third two at a time. She stopped just outside the last room on the right, breathing hard. "This is where I found the box," she said. She opened the door and went in.

Kaiser followed in silence, wishing this would all end before he said something he would regret.

Francesca knelt on the floor under the eaves and began feeling around for something behind a stack of folding chairs. Kaiser couldn't see her face, but he knew she was frantic, and then all at once she jumped up and came to stand before him, her hands hidden behind her back.

"Once upon a time," she said in her soft accent, "when I was very, very young, I found a magic ring, in a secondhand shop in Copenhagen. It cost more than I had, and it didn't even fit my finger. It was way too big. But I knew it was magic from the moment I touched it, and so my dear step-father bought it for me.

"I hid it away. I knew it wasn't meant to be mine. It was meant for a prince. The man who would come and carry me away someday to live happily forever and ever." She stopped, breathless, and looked up at him.

What Kaiser saw then in her eyes made all his doubts vanish. She loved him.

"I never gave it to Julian," she whispered. "I couldn't. It wasn't meant to be his, you see. So I wore it on a chain around my neck. But when I found that wretched box, I knew my life was over. There was no magic, no handsome prince, and there never would be. I took my ring and threw it as far as I could, over there under the eaves." She sucked in her breath. "But I was wrong. There *is* magic. I found *you*. And I want you to have my magic ring. If you'll have it." '

Kaiser didn't see what she was offering. He didn't have to. He knew. He pulled her to him and kissed her.

Somewhere downstairs he heard a door slam, then Fred Minstrell's voice calling. Kaiser didn't answer. Not right away. He was too busy.

ABOUT THE AUTHOR

DIANE GUEST was born in Winsted, Connecticut, and graduated from the College of New Rochelle. She began writing six years ago. Her first novel, *Twilight's Burning*, was published in 1982. Ms. Guest, who has four children, lives in Canton, Connecticut, with her husband Gerald Biondi. She has a summer house in Nantucket.